THE
MIDNIGHT
PROJECT

THE MIDNIGHT PROJECT

CHRISTY CLIMENHAGE

Published by Poplar Press
an imprint of Wolsak and Wynn Publishers
280 James Street North
Hamilton, ON L8R2L3
www.wolsakandwynn.ca

Acquiring editors: Ashley Hisson, Jennifer Rawlinson, A.G.A. Wilmot
    Editor: A.G.A. Wilmot | Copy editor: Ashley Hisson
Cover and interior design: Jennifer Rawlinson
Author photograph: Roger Czerneda
Typeset in Adobe Caslon Pro and Josefin Sans
Printed by Rapido Books, Montreal, Canada

Excerpts from "The Hollow Men," "The Love Song of J. Alfred Prufrock" and *The Waste Land* by T.S. Eliot courtesy of Faber and Faber Ltd.

The publisher gratefully acknowledges the support of the Canada Council for the Arts and the Ontario Arts Council. We also acknowledge the financial support of the Government of Canada through the Canada Book Fund and the Government of Ontario through the Ontario Book Publishing Tax Credit and Ontario Creates.

Library and Archives Canada Cataloguing in Publication

Title: The midnight project / Christy Climenhage.
Names: Climenhage, Christy, author.
Identifiers: Canadiana (print) 20250170345 | Canadiana (ebook) 20250174073 | ISBN 9781998408184 (softcover) | ISBN 9781998408245 (EPUB)
Subjects: LCGFT: Science fiction. | LCGFT: Thrillers (Fiction) | LCGFT: Novels.
Classification: LCC PS8605.L57 M53 2025 | DDC C813/.6—dc23

To Dad and Mom, who always pick up the phone

PART I
THE BEGINNING

This is the way the world ends
Not with a bang but a whimper.

– T.S. Eliot, "The Hollow Men"

CHAPTER 1

I held my breath and looked down into her face, hope and desperation curled together in my chest. Her oh-so-human eyes opened and we gazed at each other for the first time. It was a moment, but not the kind you're thinking of. My burst of pride was professional not personal. My affection was ambition disguised. I was not seeking to be a mother.

She only vaguely resembled a human infant. Her limbs, undulating and covered in lines of suckers, were barely recognizable as arms and legs – six long appendages, and two more curling like hair at her temples. No question her appearance was unsettling – her head was surprisingly malleable, her shoulders and torso wriggled alarmingly. Nothing about her encouraged cooing or cuddling. The crimson pattern that overlaid her soft pink tones shifted while I watched and her body twitched.

"Come on, sweet thing," I said, and held her up. A tentacle taking on a bluish tinge touched my cheek. Startled, I jumped.

"Well, look at you!" I said, and then smiled and cooed anyway.

"Please, please, please, please," whispered Cedric, willing her to live. He attached a tiny monitor smaller than a postage stamp to a tentacle, gently picked her up and tipped her into a large saltwater tank. "Let's hope this one survives." And with that, we turned to the next specimen.

Cedric and I had sunk everything we had into the project – our reputations, our careers, our money, our future. There was a lot riding on the little deep-sea hybrids we were trying to brew up.

Not that there was much of a future out there anyway, not since the bees.

I'm getting ahead of myself, of course. If I'm going to tell the story, I should start at the beginning. And that would be much, much earlier.

CHAPTER 2

The day started with an acrid undertone. The usual sinking feeling that time was running out, the clock running down. I left my house in a rush, dishes unwashed in the sink and the bed unmade. The land shuttle was late and I paced, my brain already whirring. When it finally rolled up, it was an old clunker and the air was broken. I sweated and longed for the days when I could afford the newer sky shuttles. We passed through the city centre, accelerating despite the potholes and barely braking at the intersections. There were already people out and shops opening up, a hustle and bustle to things. I was anxious to get into the office. We had a new client coming that morning, one with money, one we needed to sign.

Dripping with sweat, I got off a block away from our office so I could walk. Our building was a nondescript brown brick monstrosity – an ugly edifice designed a hundred years ago to be a government office, in the brutal style of the time. It used to have a mini-mall on the ground floor with a coffee shop, nail salon, dry cleaner, dollar store and even a fitness centre in the basement. The businesses were long gone, and the building had been renovated several times since, each reno leaching a little more charm and utility from the building's soul. We were close enough to the water to be unfashionable, though not yet affected by rising tides. The address and the exterior were exactly the shabby profile we looked for when we set up our business. We didn't want to draw attention. It was perfect.

I pulled open the front door and walked past the gated, abandoned stores. I passed through another set of doors at the end of the hallway, crossed the empty lobby past a vacant reception desk and took the elevator to the sixth floor. I buzzed myself into the only business on that floor.

"Hi, Susan!" I called to our receptionist-slash-business manager. She smiled but didn't bother looking up from her screen, I think she was on a call. Fair enough, I suppose. We didn't pay her enough to give up her side hustle.

Cedric wasn't in yet, so I made the coffee, grinding the beans in a satisfying Morse code and scooping the grounds into the Bodum. I poured hot water over them, timed how long it should sit and then poured the black liquid into my favourite cup. It was an oversized mug with a picture of a lioness on it, a long-ago gift from Cedric. I poured the rest into a thermos so Cedric's coffee would be hot. He arrived a while later, poured his own mug and joined me on the comfortable chairs in the intake room. We drank our morning coffee while we watched the Holo-News.

The headlines, about fifteen centimetres high in bold Helvetica font, floated in the air at eye level and then marched around the room for maximum impact. They were dire as usual, painting the furniture and walls with all the worst news from around the world.

Coup in France threatens EU unity
Pollinator crisis deepens as bee die-off accelerates
UN Secretary-General appoints Special Envoy for Bees
Species Termination Notice: Arctic poppy

I flicked them off irritably, with a gesture across my wristband.

"Special Envoy for the Bees is a good idea," said Cedric mildly.

"I suppose." I got up. "Not sure what she can do, though."

I walked out to Reception. "Hey, Susan, we have a high roller coming in this morning, don't keep him waiting, eh?"

She nodded absently without looking up. "No seriously," I insisted. "Be nice to him. We need this one."

⁓

In dangerous times, we often make a habit of living prudently. I was beginning to despair of prudence, though, so our prospective client had timed his visit well.

He strode in with a surprising amount of presence, towering over both of us despite being shorter than Cedric. Where Cedric was bespectacled and thin, our visitor was imposing, attention-grabbing. In spite of his elegant suit, Cedric's receding hairline and apologetic air made him seem shabby next to our guest. Mr. Burton Sykes' skin was smooth and vaguely tanned, his age unclear owing to what could only be expensive treatments. His light brown hair, deliberately greying at the temples, was exquisitely cut; his casual clothes of a quality we could never afford. His piercing blue eyes and commanding voice invited confidence. He was too polished to be anything other than very rich.

This alone would not prevent him from seeking our services. We'd had high-profile clients in the past, but I'd never encountered anything quite like this conversation. Seated on our intake couch, we began our meeting with a typical intro: He described himself as a self-made man (weren't they all, these days?) and detailed his rise in the business world. He was one of the new virtual conglomerate heads – oodles of money but motivated by challenges, not wealth. None of this was unfamiliar. I'd already researched his online presence and what he was saying was equally available in his public bio.

We provided reproductive services to people who could afford us. Our services were delicately close to that area where law and ethics slide into the grey. And while we were careful to remain on the right side of, well, right, we also employed a very talented lawyer to keep us out of trouble.

As the niceties came to an end, instead of following our typical intake routine and detailing what had driven him to us, the interview took an unexpected turn. Instead of a quietly intimate chat about his desire for healthy children, or brilliant children, or a specific kind of triple set, he launched into an uncomfortably direct discussion about science and world events.

"What do you know about transformation and adaptation?" he asked.

"I know that 'transformation' is a euphemism for the impact of species extinction on ecosystems, and 'adaptation' is considered a successful response by an ecosystem to an extinction event," I replied. "More tea?"

Our intake room was designed to be soothing. Pale blue walls, art smoothly abstract and chair fabrics that echoed the wall's muted tones, along with a pristine and perfect white couch. It was meant to be cool yet inviting, to comfort jangled nerves. But our latest guest didn't appear to need soothing in the least. Instead, he seemed to take up the space, dominating my professional landscape. Wreathed in a halo of heirloom tobacco smoke, Mr. Sykes was intent on conducting a political interrogation. It was Cedric and I who were on the back foot and I didn't like it.

"What do you think happened to the bees?" he asked next.

Cedric's eyes widened slightly and he paused, waiting for me to answer. When I spoke, I did my best to sound forthright. "It should've been perfectly clear to the pesticide team that if you alter the plant, you have to alter the bees at the same time, otherwise you kill the bees. This has always been true, but the pace of die-off means that there was no time for reverse-engineering. Their genetic engineers seriously messed up." This was true, as far as it went.

"And what will happen now?"

"Well, TriSector Mods, the company responsible, will reverse-engineer the bees and they'll stop dying, or at least the modified ones will."

"Will it be enough?"

"Enough for what?"

"To avoid transformation."

From the corner of my eye, I could see Cedric's hands whitening on his teacup, and I worried for the fine bone china. Cedric knew I wouldn't be able to resist telling this stranger what I'd worried about daily for months.

"I doubt it. Maybe for some rich countries or communities, a few enclaves here and there who can acquire some modified bees. But whole continents may be wiped out. Why are we talking about this, Mr. Sykes? Are you seeking a genetic engineer's opinion on whether you should invest in TriSector Mods? They seem to have a monopoly on modified bees for now, but you can bet there'll be a lot of competitors. Plus, they'll probably fold under the lawsuits. They've already doomed half the planet."

Cedric's teacup rattled. It was not, ironically, at the mention of half the planet becoming extinct. We read and watched the news like everyone, plus we had an insider's understanding not only of the critical role that bees play in the human food chain but also of the genetic engineering that created the mess in the first place. That was a class-A cock-up if ever I'd seen one, and I cringed thinking of my own role in the disaster. Not that I could speak to that, anyway. No, Cedric was worried that I was coming dangerously close to breaching the nondisclosure agreement I'd signed when I left the ag industry, and if I did that, they could shut us down in a heartbeat. Our little company, Re-Gene-eration, would lose its licence and I would be sued until I no longer had the right to use my own name let alone practise as a licensed genetic engineer.

"You know more than most about it. Were you close to the team working on that?"

"We had nothing to do with that!" A lie, but only a little one; our lawyer could turn it into a truth. Cedric looked ready to hurl his teacup at me to get me to shut up.

Mr. Sykes must've known about the NDA and was deliberately baiting me. He took another drag of his cigarette and returned to the doomed planet. "More than half, according to my calculations. Plus, given the advances of the genetics industry and its ties to the military-industrial complex, the chances of a similar event occurring in the next five to ten years is more than thirty-five percent. The likelihood of it happening in the next twenty years is just under fifty percent. The chances of the next breach being intentional is a little over sixty percent. Sixty-one-point-five if you want to be precise."

Huh. Cynic that I was, I should have been fretting over that too, but I'm a genetic engineer, not a politician or a security expert. Still. It's not every day I met someone with a dimmer view than me. "Interesting. And in your considered opinion, Mr. Sykes, where does that leave us?"

He leaned in intently. "It leaves us without a future. Inevitably. No matter what happens with the bees this year."

I paused and took in our situation. His heirloom tobacco smoke was making my nostrils burn. Why didn't he smoke healthy, odourless cigarettes like everyone else? A hopeless pessimism about the future was quite unlike our usual clientele. Nothing about this conversation was normal.

"I'm sorry, but I'm not quite certain why you're here, Mr. Sykes."

Our visitor blinked. "I'm here to request your services."

"You clearly aren't here to tailor your offspring. Is there something you want?"

Mr. Sykes cocked an eyebrow, unperturbed. "Oh, you're quite wrong. I do want to tailor my offspring. But what I want to tailor is something quite . . . *off-the-books*, you understand."

"I do not." Another lie. We did "off-the-books" all the time. But there was something I was missing here.

"I want my . . . offspring . . . to have a chance at longer-term survival. I want them kept apart from this madness. I want them to be free from tampering and attack. I want them safe."

"Someone with your resources should be able to equip an enclave quite admirably. You and your family would be safer than ninety-nine percent of the planet. You don't need us for that." I shook my head.

"What I have in mind is not a traditional enclave. I already possess one of those – a quite suitably reinforced Caribbean island. Several islands in fact. Our bees are safe, all our food heirloom and organic. But it is still vulnerable. I'm thinking beyond my own progeny and considering what our civilization has produced of value and how to protect humankind."

I remained silent, suspicions swirling. Cedric had sat back and was breathing again, now that we weren't talking about the bees.

"We need to remake humankind and make them safe." Sykes leaned forward, intent.

"You can't genetically engineer greed and ambition out of the human race," I replied. "The DNA factors are too complex. It's been tried of course. But the Hipple Project had very limited objectives and still failed. Classic *Lord of the Flies* stuff, really. Hobbes, you know." Political science mixed with genetics was a heady, ungodly mess.

He smiled thinly. "Hipple was trying to engineer human nature, a very unnatural thing to do. What I want is to engineer survival."

"Survival."

"Yes, I've decided that the only really safe enclave should be apart."

"You don't need to engineer people to live in arks. People have been living in arks in space for a decade."

"Entirely unsustainable. Eventually they have to come back to Earth. And everyone knows they're up there. It makes them a target. Especially after all the fundraising, and televised departures, live blogging, all of it. And remember the mutiny on the *Superb*. I'm interested in something more discreet."

"More discreet." All I was doing was repeating what Sykes was saying but I was one step ahead of poor Cedric, who was silently starting to tap his foot, his nervousness leaking out. Of course, my mind had travelled similar paths. It was obvious that civilization was headed for a dead end and it was natural to try to puzzle a way out. All intelligent people tried, were trying. It was just that the solutions were always temporary and partial.

"What do you know about ocean life?"

"Less than I know about bees. Cedric studied deep-sea ecosystems years ago. Not much money in it."

"People ignore the ocean depths," replied Mr. Sykes. "They know about the fish, the coral, they occasionally get exercised about krill and plankton and whales, but we actually know very, very little about what happens on the sea floor. It's overlooked. Which is exactly why it interests me."

"I don't understand." But suddenly I did.

"I want to create a colony of humans that can live at the bottom of the ocean. Sustainably."

"Sustainably," I parroted.

"Permanently."

"But that would mean . . ." I trailed off. He wasn't talking about an undersea ark, or a space where *Homo sapiens* could hide from the droughts, agricultural collapse and famines as humanity wound down to its inevitable conclusion. No, he was talking about something more subtle, more nuanced. Something elegant. Something unquestionably illegal. And probably deeply immoral.

He spoke into the silence. "There is a significant risk, even an inevitability, that humanity is not going to survive, and as we work toward our own extinction, we're going to drag most of the planet's species with us. I've studied the problem from a variety of angles – political, economic, scientific, ecological, even religious – but failed to find a means to save ourselves and the Earth. It's a source of genuine despair for me. Tens of thousands of years of civilization, of evolution, as we developed music, philosophy, art and science, and it will all be lost. It is most distressing."

His voice grew quieter, more intense. "But I happened upon a partial solution. The very best parts of humanity can be maintained, preserved, and the most malicious and venal parts weeded out. A human race engineered to eschew violence and greed. And then, to protect them from the rest of venal humanity, we enable them to thrive at the bottom of the sea.

"I am now taking steps to safeguard humanity – to save it from itself. It should be obvious why I need you. I have studied the bios of hundreds of genetic engineers and I believe that you and Dr. Beauville can help me."

I suppose the silence that ensued in reality was much shorter than in my memory. As I recall, it seemed to stretch out, in the way that pivotal moments should. The way in FlickFilms that the music swells and there's a close-up of the resolute profile of the protagonist and the audience knows that something big is happening.

I think I laughed awkwardly, tried to diminish his grand ambition. "That would be huge . . . Your colony wouldn't be human anymore. They'd be new."

"They would be new, and ready for a future. Equipped to survive no matter what was happening on the surface. They could safeguard our intellect, our optimism, our hope."

"Mr. Sykes, what you are suggesting is scientifically improbable and illegal. This is more than a little off-the-books." But I was thinking about it. My heart was starting to race. "And why us? Re-Gene-eration is a boutique operation. We don't have the facilities to do what you're suggesting."

He smiled in reply as if I had invited him to demonstrate his genius. "There are some that share your educational backgrounds and experience, it's true. But you and Dr. Beauville" – he gestured at Cedric – "until just a short time ago, were intimately involved with cutting-edge genetic processes that facilitate the more effective transfer of DNA into cells. You were stars in the ag sector, celebrated quietly by your employers: the whimsically named Wheat Kings and Pretty Things. And then something happened, and you weren't. Celebrated, that is.

"After leaving WKPT in such a manner that they have publicly wiped all links and deny any association, you two opened up a small boutique business specializing in bespoke genetic engineering, one client at a time. A decent living for most, but not commensurate with your talents. You are exactly who I need, and I want you to help me."

Alarmed, I glanced at Cedric, whose face had gone red. How did Sykes know about WKPT? Our former employer had scoured all evidence of our contributions, not only from their records but from the world at large. I didn't know what to say. It was time to wrap things up.

Cedric stood. "We'll need to carefully consider everything you've told us, Mr. Sykes." It was our standard exit line for clients who were proposing off-the-books endeavours. Anything even mildly unethical had to be discussed and explored, rigorously assessed before we could accept or gently turn them down.

Mr. Sykes' forehead wrinkled. Irritation flashed across his face, but he was on our turf. I didn't control much in the world, but what happened in this room was up to me and Cedric. We had our routines and we vetted our projects carefully.

He collected himself. "I'll need an answer soon, of course."

"Of course." I nodded.

Mr. Sykes stood up, shook my hand and held out a small piece of creamy vintage paper. "I recognize this will take up quite a bit of your time and require substantial resources, as well as discretion. Pay would be commensurate. I've sketched a few financial scenarios for you on the reverse of my card."

As I took the card from him, I noticed his perfectly manicured cuticles, in stark relief to my own chewed nails, his skin smooth and callous free, perfect, a few fashionable shades lighter than my own tone. Reflexively, I flipped the card over and then held myself very still, willing my eyes not to bug out at the large figures on the reverse.

He left unhurriedly and unconcerned. Cedric closed the door firmly behind him, and turned, raising his eyebrows.

"I'll make more tea," Cedric said, noticing our cups had gone cold. He bustled away to the kitchenette. Soon we were installed back in the intake room, he on the couch and me on one of the comfy chairs. This time, I tucked my legs under me and held my tea in both hands. Cedric leaned back, tall and angular against the back of the sofa, and crossed his legs.

"Well, well, that's a live one. Haven't seen anything like that before," I started.

"Yes, he's quite something. I know we've had some high rollers, but he's one of the top tier, isn't he?"

"Quite full of himself too. He knows exactly how many laws he's asking us to break, doesn't he?"

"Yes, and what the hell! Engineering survival, and getting rid of greed . . . It isn't possible, not really. We can't code for those traits, it's too complicated."

"He did say he didn't want us to."

"He said both things and I think he'd have said a lot more garbage if we'd let him keep talking." Cedric frowned. "I don't think he really understood the potential impacts."

"Yeah, lots of risk. And not just legal. And how does he know so much about us? I thought WKPT had erased us from the world. Takes a lot of skill and not just money to find us."

We sipped our tea.

"He's dangerous," Cedric continued. "It's dangerous. It's on a level we haven't tried here. It shouldn't be done."

I nodded. "Absolutely." I put my tea down, then picked it up again and ran my ragged thumbnail around the rim. "But I wonder if it could be done."

"It would take months to even establish a prototype offspring. And you'd need state-of-the-art facilities that we don't have."

I glanced at the creamy card on the coffee table again. "We could build them with that. Do you think it could be done?"

"These days almost anything can be done for a price. But should it? Raina, we're not gods and we shouldn't play in their sandbox."

"But if everyone else is playing in the sandbox, we might do some good."

Cedric rolled his eyes. "No, not again. Not again! I see that little gleam in your eye!"

"What gleam? I do not gleam." I arched an eyebrow innocently.

"That little hopeful gleam that you can do good in the world. Haven't we learned our lesson, Raina? Haven't we learned that good works aren't for people like us? We should just keep our heads down and keep helping people with their triple sets of perfect kids. Who cares about the world? Haven't we done enough?" He was almost pleading with me now, irritated, but with good reason. He wasn't wrong.

Cedric got up, cleared the teacups and went into the kitchenette to do the dishes. I trailed behind him and picked up a tea towel.

"Do you think it could work, for humans, I mean?" I was almost wistful.

Cedric shook his head. "No – we'd be inventing something else. And we might screw up an ocean ecosystem by accident."

"Well, it's not like the oceans are all that pristine as it is. Tons of waste, of plastic, acidification destroying the crustaceans . . . Maybe the ocean needs our help too."

We finished washing the dishes, Cedric's discomfort radiating wordlessly. As I put away the last clean cup, I said, "You're right, it's probably a bad idea. But let's ask Greg to do a deep dive on Mr. Burton Sykes. Let's find out more about who we're dealing with. And maybe just a feasibility study – just a research review and computer simulation, nothing fancy, just something to pay the bills. Maybe we could find a reason to shut the whole thing down. That would be good, wouldn't it? There's nothing wrong with doing a *little* good. And besides, maybe it could help. In spite of everything. You never know – the idea might have legs."

"God help us," he said finally. "You're getting hopeful. It's worse than getting religion." He shook his head, exasperated. "I don't know if it can be done. I don't know if it should be done."

"Let's prove it can't be done." I gestured to the card on the coffee table, picked it up and waved the "financial scenarios" at Cedric again. "We'll at least eat well."

CHAPTER 3

Next morning, over coffee, I brought it up right away. It was bothering me.

"I don't think we should ignore the offer, Ceddy." He knew immediately which offer I was talking about. "And by that, I mean I don't think we can *afford* to ignore the offer."

Cedric glanced over. "What do you mean?"

I took a deep breath. "I mean I think the money for a feasibility study could tide us over a rough patch." Our poor finances had been hanging over our heads since the beginning. I had been worrying over the bills and the books for months, and Cedric should've realized how serious our situation was. It was there when I woke up to grey air and a gritty throat, it was there when I looked out the corner of my eye on the way to work, scanning for trouble, and it was there when I went over our bank accounts. The world was running down, and we were running out of money. What Sykes had said about us being expensive was true, and we had a small number of clients that could afford us. Offering cheaper services would just put us closer to the edge once we factored in our own costs. But we had staff to pay, and equipment to replace, and a hundred other expenses that kept us close to the line between profitable and heading for bankruptcy. What could I say? We were scientists, not entrepreneurs. We hated marketing and we didn't want to attract any attention; we just wanted to work quietly and escape trouble.

When I say "we," I mostly mean "me." I had suggested the whole business to Cedric when we lost our jobs with WKPT and I had brought most of the capital to set us up. Never close to my dad, Dr. Joseph Templeton (who had never been called Joe in his life), I had asked him for seed money. A renowned neuropsychologist, he wasn't a businessman and didn't like the idea. All he knew was that I had left my last job, not why or how. Of course, he suspected I'd been fired, how could he not? I was grateful he had fronted the money, but our relationship soured from there. We rarely spoke now and only when I called him. Just enough news had reached him that he knew I had brought shame to our name. With our NDA I couldn't even explain what had happened.

It was also me who brought the knowledge that enabled our competitive edge. That was a grey area of the business I deliberately didn't dwell on. Technically, WKPT still owned everything I developed there including the cutting-edge tech that had led to my dismissal. But my brain was my own, and my discovery could be replicated by someone who knew how. So I could use it from time to time to make our business just a little better, and to improve our profit margin just a smidge. If WKPT knew, I'd be in jail. But there were bills to pay, my options were limited and the discovery had been mine once, anyway.

"I don't think we should even do the study," Cedric argued. "It could get us in trouble again. It's too off-the-books."

"I dunno, maybe we're overthinking this. Sykes isn't so bad – Greg will tell us if he's criminal or sketchy. He could just be a regular billionaire with quirky ideas. And his ideas aren't horrible; it's kind of a neat thing, y'know? Humans at the bottom of the ocean? I love it a little bit. Probably can't be done, but a bit harmless."

"Maybe," Cedric grumbled. "Or maybe a bit of human-related bacteria gets introduced into an undersea ecosystem we know nothing about and destroys another species, which causes a chain reaction in the food chain. Who's to say?"

"I'm afraid our finances need us to take the study, Ceddy. Have you looked at this month's actuals? We don't have new clients coming in, and our costs just keep going up. Add in the supply chain issues and we're really not getting ahead. You know neither of us is an entrepreneur – we're just not business savvy enough to see our way through."

"Yeah," replied Cedric. "But that's why we hired a business manager. Susan's great. She's ironing out a bunch of our supply chain issues. She runs all that stuff."

"Sure, but we can barely afford her. If anything, we're six to eight weeks from having to let everyone go, and maybe three months from bankruptcy."

"Surely it's not that bad." Cedric frowned over his coffee mug.

Running my finger over my wristband and pointing to the centre of the room, I pulled up a holo-display of our latest figures and sent it spinning over to him. "It's that bad," I said. "Let's do the study, let's prove it can't be done, let's take the money."

Cedric caught the image with a gesture and stared at the graphs and chart for a few minutes until he finally agreed. "All right. But the study says it can't be done. And no one is getting fired."

&

Our lawyer, Greg, dropped in to go over his background research. Greg Nelson was a man of uncertain age. His skin was so smooth he could have been twenty-five or forty-five. His hair was a fashionable grey, probably dyed, but his goatee quietly ruined his look of respectability. His manner suggested he had more life experience than his appearance indicated. He'd managed to keep us out of jail and mostly out of trouble, so I assumed he was much older than he looked.

He flicked up a 3D image of Sykes at some kind of ribbon-cutting ceremony that rotated over the table as he spoke. "Early life: origins unclear. Protégé of Titus Falco, owner of Webwex. Owns Global Holdings, a virtual conglomerate that started out in secure communications and has branched out into nanotech, biotech and pharmaceuticals. It appears quite substantial now, though not publicly listed, so it's difficult to gauge the full scope of his operations. That being said . . ." and with that Greg launched into a lengthy list of businesses, initiatives and public partnerships. Impressive. Even I recognized some of them.

"Bottom line, he's got the money to pay you and is what he says he is. Whatever else he is, he works hard to hide that from view. It's hard to identify an upper limit to his wealth, but 'sizable' is a good adjective."

Cedric bit his lower lip. "Is it safe to take him on as a client? Is he trustworthy?"

Greg chuckled. "Well, are any of these conglomerate heads trustworthy? They're all money, all business. But trustworthy as far as it goes. Yes, I think so. Not blatantly criminal, as far as I can tell."

He left behind listings of companies Mr. Sykes owned and causes he funded, and FlickFilms of speeches he'd given, mostly on music, theatre and the creative arts. He'd invested in a movie director exploring the ocean depths years before and financed several wildlife documentaries.

"See? Wildlife documentaries about the ocean," I pointed out to Cedric, trying to make him relax. "Anyway, no glaring issues. Honest as far as we know."

So, without any obvious flags on Sykes, Cedric reluctantly agreed to do the feasibility study. He wanted to prove that no one could do it, that it would never work, but I'll admit I was curious if I could find a way through. We agreed that we would provide a negative recommendation. This may sound to the casual observer like we were cooking our results or doing something dishonest, but it wasn't. Honestly, I didn't even need Greg to make this squeaky clean. Simulations are so complicated there is always an element of risk and doubt built in. It's easy to make a simulation point to a negative outcome.

Our feasibility study would be based exclusively on computer simulations, building up assumptions, testing the potential of DNA and RNA combinations, and then, once we had a glorious little prototype of a living thing, we would run simulations of what would happen if we introduced it into a deep-sea habitat. The first part of the study was the most fun. I know Cedric was appalled by the whole enterprise and I should've been too, but I wasn't. Who didn't want to create oceanic humans in a video game?

The computer simulations were both complicated and simple. On the one hand, generations of artificial intelligence and biological knowledge were required to even set up a scenario. On the other hand, any six-year-old could play Build-A-World. The main difference was that we were trying to fail – trying to find the parameters of what we could accomplish, what we could do. And fail we did! Over and over again. The challenges were legion. Just finding a combination of traits and DNA to allow humans to exist underwater was a challenge. But then you needed to build out a food source, a sustainable habitat, as deep in the ocean as possible.

"Okay, if we combine human with dolphin and sea cucumber?" I asked. We ran the numbers.

"Failure to exist," Cedric reported. "Doesn't even make it to birth." A floating display of molecules and DNA spirals burst into nothing like fireworks.

"Okay," I said. "Let's try human-octopus-dolphin. Random combination. Best fit." Cedric entered the DNA files for processing.

"Ooh! Feasible mammal!" I read. "Oh, very weird, take a look, Cedric!" A blue manatee with human ears swam slowly across the table.

"No, Raina, see, this one can only exist within a hundred metres of the surface, it explodes if we take it even to the twilight zone." More fireworks and it disappeared.

Our brainstorming on DNA combinations continued.

"I don't think legs will be enough to get around with – or maybe with big paddle-sized feet, like frogs?"

"Nothing with frogs – remember the hoppers." Cedric suppressed a shudder.

"Good point. We don't want to risk them cloning themselves by accident either. Maybe they need a tail? Like a fish tail?"

"Like a mermaid? Isn't that a little . . . unoriginal?" Cedric raised his eyebrows.

I smiled. "What? How could hundreds of years of fairy tales be wrong? What do you have against fish tails?"

"No seriously," Cedric replied. "Fish may not be our best companion species. What about cephalopods?"

"Octopus? Squid?" Tentacles, perfect. I loved that idea. "Yes," I agreed, "and cuttlefish. They have natural curiosity, empathy, and they solve puzzles."

"They're fierce predators, though, let's be careful."

"Yeah, that's true."

We got sucked in. Like compulsive teens, we found ourselves playing more and more.

⁂

It took several days to isolate a few digital prototypes that didn't explode within a set lifespan. "See, Cedric? Child's play!"

"Yeah, just wait until we layer on the ecosystem. This won't work, Raina, I promise you."

Most genetic engineers had proprietary software like we did, which could predict the results of specific gene editing. Ours went further than most to deal with environmental factors, trying to anticipate some of the broader ecosystem-wide impacts of small changes in the genetic code. I'd always been able to compartmentalize the pieces so I didn't worry about the endgame, or the client, or the outcome. This part of the work was just joy to me. I could ignore the rest. Or at least, I could ignore it during the day. At night, trying to sleep in my little house in the foothills, was another story. Then, my brain turned over all the day's work, all the failures, all the expectations. It never helped but I couldn't turn it off. During waking hours, I tried not to dwell on it.

"Are you sure you're not doing this for the wrong reasons?" Cedric asked me one day.

"What do you mean?"

"We know it wasn't fair what happened to us, right? But I also know you blame yourself. For what happened to us, and well, you know."

I knew but didn't want to talk about it. It wasn't fair of him to dredge that up.

"Look, what happened, happened," I replied. "I'd do it differently if I could, but we can't go back. They screwed us, and then they screwed everyone. Not our fault, right? Nothing we could do. And we were punished anyway. We're taking our lumps and there's nothing more to talk about."

I found myself dreaming of dark and stormy seas, of glowing monster fish and of air bubbles striving to reach the surface.

Meanwhile, each day started the same, our little routines buttressing our lives, securing us from the troubles outside. We still kept tabs on all the nastiness going on in the world. Inveterate news junkies with coffee in hand, we would watch the Holo-News, headlines zipping around our kitchenette or intake room. The headlines painted horrors on the walls, the window, even on Cedric and me.

Bee-killing strain spreads to legume crops, culls scheduled in
North America
Webwex CEO addresses the United Nations, defends private
interstellar exploration

Running a finger across my wrist, I lazily flicked up the story, and CEO Titus Falco's image floated above our conference table, his fist raised as he spoke from the podium of the United Nations. I turned the sound up, listened for a minute, then turned it off.

"That guy," I complained, "thinks he owns the whole world."

"He almost does," Cedric replied.

A new headline sliced across my face.

Markets short bee futures — "We're making a killing!" says Wall
Street trader

"Well, someone's making money. It won't end anytime soon," muttered Cedric.

How to make charcuterie platters for dogs

I flicked the story up for that one — who doesn't want to hear about charcuterie platters for dogs? I didn't have a dog, didn't want a dog and didn't care about charcuterie, but it was better than the alternative.

After reviewing the horrors and wonders of the world, segmented and curated, packaged up in easily digestible episodes with solid footage, we would turn to work.

Most days we worked quietly in our computer lab, down the hall from the intake room. Filled with terminals with space for holo-displays, its most notable feature was its uncomfortable chairs. Sometimes we would park ourselves closer to the kitchenette and let the colourful graphics swirl above the long mahogany table in the intake room, the sunlight streaming in and making the display look wispy and insubstantial. At times we even found ourselves laughing and smiling as we just played with the numbers, played with the DNA, played with the ecosystems. At least, I laughed and smiled. Cedric might've been faking it. It was harmless, though. Still harmless.

Running the scenarios and options took some time. Despite scientific advances everywhere else, our knowledge of the very bottom of the ocean, the harshest environment for humans on Earth, was still imprecise. No light, a darkness so vast that photosynthesis of any kind was impossible. Pressure so high that an ill-equipped submarine would simply crumple like a tin can. To envision engineering a species to live there, we would have to establish not only a biological adaptation to deal with the conditions but also a food source and a habitat.

"Could they eat plankton and crabs?" pondered Cedric one day as we brainstormed.

"They could, but would that upset the ecosystem?"

"Not if we kept them far enough down the food chain," Cedric suggested. "Perhaps we could engineer a little kelp or seaweed bed. They could be vegan."

And so it went, exploring the potential of the impossible, questions dressed up in the clever algorithms of our computer modelling. Over coffee, we fed scenarios into the model as yellow sunlight streamed into our computer room and dappled the walls' pale green, overlaying it with a warm glow. No artwork here, just large windows with one-way glass. Outside, the days were bright and the urban streetscape wrapped around us. Only early summer, but the air seemed burnt and dried out.

And on and on we went, with the discussions, the brainstorming and the simulations. Each failure ended in a spray of fireworks. We didn't have enough knowledge to transfer to the real world even if we could get a simulation to work. They all failed before they got off the ground. You could say we were in deep waters.

I kept looking for a big reason why it couldn't work, why it was a capital-B capital-I Bad Idea, but instead I saw more and more potential. It wasn't true that we didn't know a lot about the deepest parts of the ocean (we knew a great deal), but it was so different from life above that there was very little reason for people to pay attention. I began to see where Mr. Sykes' dream could lead. It was something discreet and elegant, all the more beautiful for being completely unseen.

Then, finally, a few weeks in, the explosion of fireworks was replaced with a chime and a floating image of an undersea habitat. We had a narrow path to victory. Cedric was having none of it. "In the real world, this could still tank the ecosystem. See? If I layer on the fact that the crab is endangered, their food source disappears within three years."

"Okay," I agreed. "We can write it up like that. But we'll know we did our best."

It took a few more days to feel we had done justice to the feasibility study. The final version really was a work of artistic genius. It underlined all the challenges, the difficulties, the potential screw-ups, while skating that fine line to acknowledge the underlying potential of the whole idea. Yes, sir, great idea, sir. Of course, impractical. We avoided any lengthy engagement on eco-ethics and focused on the straight-up hard stuff: what it would take to try it, and how likely it was to end in failure. Once we had laid out all the things we'd attempted in our failed computer sims, we laid out the one path that might result in a decent hybrid. Then we laid out the simulation that had the same hybrid destroying a habitat by overconsuming a particular species of threatened deep-sea crab in the midnight zone.

We submitted it in full expectation that that would be the end of that. It had been a lucrative contract that would keep us going another few months, with no further action needed. We were surprised to get a note a few days later asking for a follow-up meeting with Mr. Sykes.

He came in person, businesslike and impeccable. He took the same spot in our intake room, smoking again, same intensity as before. "Thank you for your study, it's really quite fascinating what you did there. I appreciate the work." He inhaled deeply.

"I didn't only come to you, of course. I have three separate feasibility studies that were delivered this week on this project. I thought you'd be interested in this one." He casually flicked a large image of a written study up over the coffee table. It was largely unreadable, except for the title, "Mermaid Prototype," and the names underneath. I stared. I knew those names.

He looked at us expectantly.

"Well, Tolliver Simton, he's a good genetic engineer," I said, wishing I was sitting anywhere else.

"Yes, you worked together at WKPT, didn't you?" Of course, he already knew that, though how could he know that?

"As I said, good engineer. He'd do a good job," I replied steadily. Not even my lawyer could turn that whopper into the truth.

"Do you know where he is now? He left WKPT shortly after you two did. Joined the wheat team at Azul Sky Tech and then set himself up as a private consultant. He's done very well for himself."

I knew vaguely that Tolliver the Terrible had set himself up in lucrative consulting, but I hadn't known about the Azul Sky connection. Bastard. We knew Azul Sky Tech, but they hadn't done anything for our careers or reputations. I could only imagine what Tolliver had been doing with them, but I was incensed that he had somehow succeeded in coming out of the whole sordid business ahead when we had been exiled. I had always suspected he was instrumental in the harsh way we were dealt with – he was a manager who could have quietly overseen our downfall. Even worse, he was a terrible genetic engineer, positioning himself on successful teams so he could share in the victories, removing himself from difficult projects before they stuck to him. He also had perfect hair. If I had a nemesis, it would be him.

Sykes looked around briefly for an ashtray, and, not finding one, flicked his ash on the carpet. "Mr. Simton thinks it could work." No. No. No. NO. Not in a million years could Tolliver do this without mucking it up entirely. He would leave the world in a flaming heap, take the profits and move on to his next job. It was in his nature.

"That's interesting," said Cedric smoothly, but his foot twitched. "Why does he say that?"

"He says a fish cross will work and we could create a more traditional-looking mermaid, just like the fairy tales."

"And did he do the ecosystem impact study?" Cedric leaned in.

"No," replied Sykes. "He just worked out what kinds of genetic crosses would work. I'll admit his study is quite rudimentary compared to yours. I still think you two are the most qualified to lead this work. Let me ask you: Do you think you could get the genetic cross to work?"

Cedric and I looked at each other. According to the models, we probably could. It was a narrow path to victory, but one we could follow. I didn't know what to say; we had agreed to kill the project.

"There are no guarantees to this sort of thing, of course," I equivocated.

"And the knock-on effects on the ecosystem are incalculable," Cedric added.

Sykes dismissed that entirely. "That just means you haven't calculated them yet."

He exhaled a stream of heirloom tobacco smoke and I stifled a cough. "I think you're the best people to do this project and I think, based on your own feasibility study, that it can be done."

"May be possible," I corrected. "Not 'can be done.'"

"Whatever!" He waved a hand. "Come to my island and make a pitch for the whole project. It'll make you rich, which will enable you to ensure your futures as much as anyone can these days. You'll have access to the most state-of-the-art facilities and resources, and you can figure out how to do this for real."

We didn't know quite what to say. Even Cedric's classic end-of-meeting patter felt inappropriate, and he stayed quiet. We all sat for a few more heartbeats until Mr. Sykes got up. "Please think about it. I don't want to give this contract to anyone else, I really believe you're the best." He saw himself out.

I'm not proud of the conversation that followed. Sweet Cedric always had more perspective on these things, but I was absolutely enraged.

"If Tolliver Simpleton thinks he can pull this off, he's off his head!" Sadly, this wasn't even the worst thing I said. "Simpering Simton couldn't engineer his way out of a second-year lab module. I can't believe that idiot's involved in this." I swore quietly under my breath, and Cedric didn't even try to calm me down.

He cleaned the ash off the carpet and inspected it for damage. "It shouldn't change anything," he said.

"But it does!" I got up and prowled around the room looking for something to kick. "If Tolliver takes the contract, it's not just stupid, it's dangerous. He'll probably cock it all up, but what if he Frankensteins something together and they release it? Catastrophe, and no one the wiser; Tolliver taking the money and running to his next job."

"C'mon, Raina, I don't like it any better than you do, but you can't let them push your buttons."

But I could, and I did. I'm not proud of it, but that was the moment I became convinced we should take the contract.

"All right, Raina," Cedric said, but he was stalling, not agreeing. "Let's think about this some more, okay?" His forehead wrinkled. "This is a big decision, and we shouldn't be impulsive." What he meant was that *I* shouldn't be impulsive, and we both knew it.

CHAPTER 4

An uneasy truce between Cedric and me followed Sykes' visit. All I saw in front of me now were the vast and excellent reasons to do the project: it was going to happen anyway, we would do the best job, we could minimize the risks of the whole thing and it would make us rich, or at least we would feel rich compared to where we were now. Cedric just saw the risks, big and small, and thought we were better off walking away. I couldn't completely fault him – he was being logical, maybe a little risk averse. But I was tired of playing it safe and keeping our heads down. We had been doing it for years and it was just driving us into a shadowy bankruptcy.

It's a funny thing about banks. When you're giving them money, they will bend over backward to make it easy for you. You can transfer them vast sums while sitting on the toilet if you want, they don't care. But when you owe them money, well, that's a different thing entirely. We needed to go in person to negotiate the rollover of one of our loans, using the payment from the study to convince them to renew the terms. The bank was only ten minutes on foot and the shuttle we called didn't arrive. We were going to be late, so we decided to walk.

In retrospect, a grave error. It was a bright and sunny day. I paused to check out a storefront and Cedric ranged ahead. The whiff of salt water and sea creature from the unseen harbour a few streets away combined with odours emanating from alleyways to make me feel like I was on an adventure. There weren't many people out, but stores were open and I appreciated the in-your-face defiance of the displays boldly selling stuff no one needed to people who no longer walked by.

Though I seldom explored the city on foot, it was scaled to a size I appreciated, urban and grimy but not overwhelming. Most coastal cities were abandoned when the seas rose and the money moved inland. In comparison, Long Harbour had grown. Rebuilt to take advantage of newly deep waters, it added city block after city block as people moved north to escape the storms and the heat. It was renamed when the financial folks arrived, and a scientific and innovation hub thrived for a while. I could still detect the bones of past prosperity in the quasi-ruin I walked today. The city retained the feeling of a place that mattered even while small enough to escape notice. It felt good to be out.

I rounded a corner and saw Cedric several metres ahead, talking to three people who had him surrounded. No, wait. They were dressed in ragged pants but no shirts, and they looked wrong, their limbs too long, their heads too large. They were green. Hoppers. I froze.

I'd never seen them in real life and neither had Cedric. I could see Cedric talking to one – the leader? – but their voices were too low to make out. No one else was on the street. The storefronts provided no escape routes except into the stores themselves. Would the hoppers be bold enough to follow?

I stood there, suspended, waiting to see if Cedric could talk his way clear. The hoppers' reputation was as bloodthirsty killers. Could the lore around their creation have exaggerated their nature? Minutes that felt like hours passed. I didn't want to spook them, but I didn't think I could approach if I'd wanted to. I was rooted to the spot.

Without warning, the one I suspected was their leader lunged. Cedric threw up his hands and fell to the side. The others circled, making loud gulping noises of encouragement. I screamed and the two gulpers turned toward me, moving to close the gap. They grinned widely. My feet wouldn't move. I just watched them come, two loping ungainly horrors.

"Cedric!" I screamed.

Before they could reach me, sirens whined overhead. I'd never been so happy to see a police copter. It slowed and a loud, booming voice demanded that everyone put down their weapons (their teeth?) and lie on the ground. An officer leaned out the copter's open side door brandishing a firearm.

The hoppers scattered, leaping up the sides of buildings and disappearing.

The police copter followed the hoppers along the rooftops. Cedric jumped up and ran, blindly racing past without seeing me, retracing his steps back to our lab. I followed him, trying not to lag behind.

I caught up with him in the lobby of our building. Cedric was breathing hard and clutching his arm, blood running down his sleeve, dripping from his fingers. His eyes were wide, his face stained red from a cut on his forehead. I pressed the elevator button and asked if he was all right. He tottered, and I grabbed him under his good arm and helped him into the lift.

We spilled into the lab's cheery reception. "Get the first aid kit!" I yelled at Susan, as Cedric stumbled and nearly fell.

Susan, calm and immutable, stood up and surveyed the two of us. "Should I call the paramedics?" But we were already through to the intake room.

Even with my help Cedric fell on the couch. He was crying and bleeding, still holding his arm up. I looked around frantically for a towel. "Oh my god, Cedric, what just happened?"

I tried to get a hold of myself and survey the damage. He had cuts on his face and hands, and a deep laceration running down his right forearm. He was bleeding all over the white couch. He noticed, got up and sat on a leather chair instead. This feeble attempt at keeping our little pastel lives spotless unsettled me more than anything else.

Panic fluttered in my chest. Not helpful. I tried to clamp it down and put my hand on his leg, trying to get his shocked eyes to focus on me. "What do you need? I'll get some water – Susan's coming with the first aid kit . . . We can call a medic."

He shook his head wordlessly and grabbed my hand, met my eyes. "I'll be okay. I'm okay now. It was really close. So . . . close . . ." He trailed off, still breathing hard. Susan arrived with the kit and I disinfected the gash then wrapped it in gauze and secured it with medical tape. I didn't think we needed an ambulance.

Cedric didn't speak.

I poured two coffees for us and gave him a large glass of water, which he drank first. His hands shook so hard the water sloshed. Gradually, Cedric's ragged breathing calmed. Admiring my handiwork on his bandage, I asked him quietly what happened. It had played out so fast I wasn't sure of what I'd seen.

"I saw them out of the corner of my eye – just a little movement to my left, and then a little higher up, an odd shadow," said Cedric. "I walked a little faster, looked around for help. I didn't panic, not exactly. Then I saw one jump overhead from one building to another and heard a shout. Suddenly, someone was standing in front of me, smiling, unhinged. Like a human face but green and the eyes in the wrong spot, sharp teeth. Terrifying." Cedric's breathing had steadied but his face was ashen.

"He talked to me," Cedric went on. "I can't remember exactly what we said. I told him I wasn't looking for trouble. Stupid, right? Might as well try to reason with a bear. Or a pack of coyotes." His eyes were wide as he drank his coffee.

"And then there were two behind me, cutting off my escape. I tried to keep them talking. I was hoping I could stall. He asked if I had any food or water and I told him I could get him some. He didn't care, though. There was just a moment when his eyes shifted, and I knew I couldn't negotiate my way out. Everything happened at once. The first hopper kind of lunged at me, and I tried to dart to one side. I think that's when I got bitten."

"I saw it. I was too far away, I'm sorry," I said, embarrassed at my own cowardice. Why hadn't I run toward them?

"I was sure I was about to die. Oh my god, Raina, my mind filled with horror that my empty little life was about to end right there." He put his head in his hands, then looked back up. "I am freakishly lucky not to be a bloody puddle just down the street."

"I can't believe it. How is this even possible?" I wanted to pat him on the shoulder but didn't. "There've been no reports of hoppers in the downtown for months. I thought they'd eradicated them here. I mean, I've always thought eradication for human hybrids was unethical but those hoppers are vicious."

Cedric was staring off into space. "I didn't see them. And then they were right there. They were hungry, Raina. They were drooling over me. God, they're horrible."

"Why were they there at all?"

"The ministry must not have gotten rid of the whole colony – do you think they're covering it up? We should've heard about the danger, right? It was just lucky that I got away. Just a bit of luck."

We sat companionably for a few minutes drinking our coffee.

I couldn't resist asking, "Okay, I know it's horrible you got jumped, but wow! You saw a hopper up close. What did it look like?" I hadn't seen them, not really. I'd been too busy not helping, too busy panicking while they attacked my friend.

The scientist kicked in and Cedric focused. "Bullfrog-green skin, amphibian-like, with leopard frog markings on the arms like tattoos. Human-like cranial features but with bulging eyes, wider set. There may be two different eyelids, I couldn't tell," he said. "Prominent canine teeth, very sharp all around, but I couldn't say which predator the teeth come from."

I could see Cedric coming back to himself, his jiggling foot quieting, the tremor in his hands subsiding.

"Fingers are splayed and webbed, very strong. Something on their hands allows them to hang off buildings. Could be six fingers to a hand – I wasn't really counting." Then the scientist mask dropped just for a moment. "He had a hungry, desperate air. Honestly, I'm so lucky to be sitting here right now, you have no idea." I had every idea.

I couldn't help glancing at his bandaged arm, momentarily regretting my efficiency in disinfecting the wound. I should've grabbed a specimen bottle and swabbed him first. A DNA sample of a wild hopper would be an incredible coup for our gene bank. I'd love to solve the mystery of their genetic mix. It would even be financially valuable to the right collector.

The hoppers were notoriously hard to kill, harder to catch and even the military admitted they hadn't fixed the problem though it was mostly the local Ministry of Natural Resources office that dealt with outbreaks.

No one knew exactly where they came from – probably the military-industrial complex, because no one got sued, nobody went bankrupt and the hoppers' origin story was hushed up.

We thought they might have been created when someone tried to make a super-soldier and mixed elements of the genes of a predator and a frog into humans. No one knew the exact mix, but the result was an unhappy blend of very fast human with exaggerated predator instincts. At some point in the project, there was an escape and they procreated unexpectedly, finding a niche in the urban ecosystem. Or maybe they were set free on purpose for political reasons, and then proved hardier in the wild than expected. It was a mystery.

We drank in silence as I struggled to find something comforting to say.

"Well, Ceddy," I finally said, throwing out a gloomy joke, "what do you expect? We're living in the pre-apocalypse – nobody gets out of this alive."

But his face wasn't just crestfallen or disappointed in me. It was as if something fell into focus. I saw in his face something new and bleaker. It was my fault, but I didn't know how to take it back.

We sat in silence for a long time, and I brought him another coffee. He cleared his throat. "I've been thinking about this, even before today," he said. "Raina, this study, this thing we're working on, it isn't only dangerous because of the science; it's dangerous because of them. You know, the money. The business owners.

"They aren't really billionaires. They're trillionaires. Powerful, careless sociopaths. More money than sense. I think the media likes the hard 'b' sound: B for bold. B for brash. B for big. B for brave. Using a 'tr' sound makes them shinier, sweet sounding, more civilized, maybe. Trifling, trellis, tryst, trying. There's no good 'tr' words to shape them into the heroes they think they embody. No boom! But they're unstoppable. Not governed by countries or the United Nations, not even by their own common sense."

I nodded, afraid to interrupt.

"Once they get hold of an idea, they don't stop. They don't change their minds just because they get good advice or get told no. They don't stop, Raina."

I didn't know how to respond, so I just sat quietly, watching his hands tremble around the coffee cup.

He took a deep breath. "I think we have to take the job, Raina. I don't think we have any choice. It's bigger than just Sykes or Tolliver Simton. If we turn it down, someone else will say yes, at least to the money. And they might botch it horribly. Like, worse than us . . ."

"Worse than us? Have some faith!" I joked, but he ploughed on.

"Someone is going to try to do this, Raina. It's dangerous and could cause a lot of damage if it goes wrong. This is the sort of thing that could make the hoppers look like cute toddlers by comparison. We can't leave this to someone else – we can't afford to have someone worse than us try to do it. There is a slim chance of success, but it's higher if we're involved. And we'll be able to keep control and pull the plug if we need to." He looked out the window, his gaze far away. "The hoppers are like a genie that can't be put back in its bottle. We need to keep a firm grip on the bottle."

We let Sykes know that day that we were interested in pitching a project based on the feasibility study. Within an hour, we received a reply instructing us to come to his Caribbean enclave to present our plans and finalize the contract. Cedric, still shaken, went up to the roof and stared out at the ocean for a long time, dark thoughts roiling. I joined him and we let the landscape wash over us, gazing at the harbour and coastline, and then out over the urban skyline to the foothills. Copters and drones buzzed over the city.

I didn't stay with him long. I went back inside and planted myself in the computer room and got started on the presentation. It was going to be a doozy.

CHAPTER 5: CEDRIC

FADE IN

INT. RE-GENE-ERATION LAB - DAY

CEDRIC, sitting on a stool in front of a laboratory countertop. A microscope is visible to his left. He is a tall man in his mid-to-late thirties with glasses and a receding hairline. He stares into the camera.

> CEDRIC
>
> I've been watching self-help therapy FlickFilms, and one thing they suggest for dealing with anxiety is journalling. I have zero patience for writing, but I thought a video-log might help. And my anxiety has shot through the roof since the hopper attack. I'm just not myself, or at least, I feel like a craven, crushed-in version of myself.

CEDRIC pauses, shifts on his chair and looks left to the ceiling, takes a breath.

> CEDRIC (cont'd)
>
> I'm not a coward, okay? It's just that life is risky these days. We're living in a sea of marvels, but marvels that can kill. And the marvels can kill not just me but everyone,

everywhere. I'm a cautious person by nature. I see the worst-case scenario unfolding every time I let my imagination run free. Freedom, in my case, means freedom to embrace catastrophe. So I lock my life down into easily managed pieces. And I stay in my lane. My lane is as safe as I can make it.

It isn't that I'm weak. It's that I'm logical. We're on the precipice, staring into the abyss. Being a genetic engineer probably exacerbates my world view. Honestly, this line of work has more capacity for widespread harm than biomedical research, more than traditional weapons and defence contracting. The inventor of the AK-47, the Kalashnikov, was said to have regretted his invention. The genetic engineer who created wheat strain 325-4b, the accidental bee killer, is arguably killing more people. This is why the industry, especially in North America, is so heavily regulated. Funny, though, considering that the creators of 325-4b had all their patents and paperwork in order – they just forgot a couple of things and destroyed global agriculture. Easy to do, really. For sure, the company is still liable and will "pay," whatever that means.

Raina and I know more than we want to about the bee thing. It was just luck that we were pushed out of the ag sector before it happened, and I can't rule out that our work contributed to the whole horrible mess. When the bee catastrophe happened, what I felt wasn't schadenfreude or smugness - it was horror. Guilt. But even horror and guilt are regulated in our profession. And the nondisclosure agreements mean we can barely whisper among ourselves, admit that we maybe messed up. That we may have made a grave mistake.

Funny how the world grinds on anyway. No matter how much you regret or grieve or strive. It's just a little emptier than it was before. We're a tiny cog in a system creaking its way to its own destruction. If not by us, by someone else.

A bit dark, I know. I don't know why Raina puts up with me. Maybe I'm her conscience? Hell, maybe she's mine. We do work very well together.

CEDRIC smiles, his nervousness drops for a second.

                    CEDRIC (cont'd)
You know, I'm not a coward. But I didn't show a lot of courage that day with the hoppers, I won't lie. Physical courage isn't really my strong suit.

CEDRIC clears his throat self-consciously.

                    CEDRIC (cont'd)
I like to think I have other sources of
courage.

Last time we faced a moral quandary, we tried
to do the right thing but were punished for
it. Who knows, though? Maybe we should've
tried harder. Maybe then the bees wouldn't
be dying. And now? Isn't it better to try to
do good than to do nothing?

CEDRIC hops off the stool and turns off the camera.

                                        CUT TO BLACK

CHAPTER 6

A heat-blasting afternoon greeted us when we stepped out of the oceangoing copter. The exact location of Mr. Sykes' private enclave was classified (classified by and for whom wasn't clear, but it was obviously above our pay grade). It was in the middle of a small group of Caribbean islands – perhaps they all belonged to him or to his partners and investors. As we stepped off the copter and the heat hit us, I smiled and breathed deep, admiring the blue cloudless sky. Buoyed by endless possibilities, I looked out onto deep blue waters, sturdy cliffs and green fields. It was a vista designed to impress, to embolden those who gazed upon it. A small cynical part of my mind noted that the helipad had absolutely been designed to create this feeling, even if the landscape was untouched.

"I am so glad you could come!"

Surprisingly, Mr. Sykes himself met us on the tarmac, grinning effusively and shaking our hands. He was dressed in cream linen with a broad-brimmed hat. Cedric and I had dressed in jeans for travel, and Greg was in his traditional grey suit. I don't think he owned anything else. The three of us were already sweating. Mr. Sykes ushered us to a waiting car, hopping into the front passenger seat and turning to speak with us as we climbed in behind him. As the car shifted forward, he began the grand tour, explaining the island and its inhabitants, gesturing proudly and telling us about self-sustaining agriculture grown from heirloom seeds, a private seed bank and, farther out, mangrove swamps as natural barriers for storms.

He told us we were headed to New Carthage (I think he picked the name himself), the capital of his island, where his scientists, agricultural experts and security lived, alongside his family and some close friends. The central sleeping quarters and workspaces were all contained in what looked ‑

like a walled city. It grew larger as we approached up a straight road.

"A bit of whimsy, but I loved Tuscany. Have you ever been to San Gimignano? Just beautiful, such thoughtfulness. And the concept still applies. What else is an enclave but a walled city?" He smiled and chuckled to himself.

The wall opened as smoothly as a pocket door and closed behind us once we were through. I fought a clench of claustrophobia.

We drove through what appeared to be, for all intents and purposes, a very clean and tidy medieval city, built to look carefully restored but without the inconvenient tiny alleyways and streets too narrow for today's vehicles. I could just picture how it would appear on satellite imagery: rather than evoking concern, it would draw a gasp of delight. The city felt adorable and quaint, an homage to the Italian renaissance. A quirky billionaire at play: cultured, erudite and refined – non-threatening.

From street level, I got a different impression. People thronged, but not like any Caribbean city I knew. European-settler types abounded, but where were the locals? Had he bought a rock with no people on it? Was that even possible? I caught sight of sidearms and a few uniforms. There was an aura of smooth efficiency, everything in its place and nothing loud or unsightly. Within a few minutes, I had an uneasy sense of an old-fashioned movie set where everything was scripted and choreographed, cleansed.

Mr. Sykes enthusiastically talked about libraries and education centres, to ensure that key cultural artifacts continued to be understood. "We need to archive our fading cultures, don't you see? Not just our music and literature but our souls!" The Caribbean air seemed to make him more expansive than he had been in Long Harbour.

"Where are the locals?" I interrupted him. "Are there any other cities on the island?"

"There were. I bought them out and resettled them. Some of the better-behaved locals work for me, but most of them live elsewhere. It's a liability to have topside settlements here. We need control," he said without a hint of shame. I raised an eyebrow at Cedric.

After a few turns, the car jolted forward and an entire building facade slid open. We were momentarily enveloped in darkness. The car continued down a deep tunnel, then joined a track and was pulled along like a subway car. Spaces opened out to the sides as if we were passing through metro stops, but instead of urban subway stations, we saw storefronts and homes decorated with glowing flowers. Mr. Sykes noticed me staring at them.

"Well, of course not all the seeds are heirloom! We're not stuck in the past, we celebrate it. The flowers are engineered, of course."

"Of course," I replied. "Nice work on the bioluminescence. It's delicate work."

We eventually slowed and stopped, hopping out of the car. We entered a door that opened onto a bright, wide lobby, decorated in an antique mid-twentieth-century modern style. Broad windows revealed scenes worthy of 1950s Havana: vintage cars, brightly clothed people going about their business, canned salsa music playing softly in the background. The scene was in stark contrast to everything I'd seen so far. I felt like we had arrived at the strangest hotel in the bowels of the Earth. It had an airy feel to it, dispelled the second all the decorations (including the windows) abruptly disappeared and were replaced with white featureless walls.

Mr. Sykes smiled as he gestured. "Great effect, isn't it? You're in a windowless bunker, but you'd never know. These are the secure dormitories. We use them in case of emergencies, and also to keep private our more . . . private endeavours."

No windows, but the smooth walls could be programmed to display landscapes and vistas. It was dizzying. I was momentarily delighted, then realized how easily I'd been manipulated. I grew irritated and disconcerted.

Mr. Sykes continued the tour, indicating a dining room and then a business centre. He waited until we were in each room before flicking on the special effects. Long picture windows appeared with a 3D vista within. Each view was spectacular, a landscape or cityscape so detailed, with wildlife or copters or people, the only way to know it wasn't real was to remember we were underground. Although it was supposed to foster comfort, its sudden appearance on bare white walls jarred. There was an unsettling sense of being in the pages of a brand-new colouring book, watching the spaces getting filled in.

Finally, Mr. Sykes led us to adjoining rooms. For once, he turned on the wall-decorations before we entered so we needn't see the cell-like characteristics of the rooms, their lines laid bare to be crayoned in. I was grateful that my claustrophobia could take a back seat, at least while I was sleeping.

Mr. Sykes asked us to confirm what we needed for the presentation the following day. I asked how many people would be there and how tight his security was. "Very tight," he reassured us. "It will be a room full of lawyers that will draft the contract and the liability waivers, and some of my most trusted advisors."

"Scientists?" asked Cedric.

"Yes," Mr. Sykes said slowly, "and issues advisors." He declined to specify the issues to be managed by his team, but I didn't need to guess.

We were going to do this off-the-books, but there still needed to be books, if you know what I mean. Cedric and I needed to lower our risk, to spread it out in case we did something truly destructive, and so did Sykes and Global Holdings. We'd seen too many projects go sideways, and scientists go under. It was important to build as much of a safety net for yourself as you could. Also, you needed a target for someone to go after later if you really cocked it up. People got very petty over potential extinction-level events. The risks could be mostly covered, but insurance would only carry you so far. Due diligence and the dreaded "good intentions" did not carry much weight at all.

Invent a secret super-soldier that massacres a village, and the scientist will escape culpability if the paperwork has been properly signed off by the right militaries and governments. But invent a new kind of rice that doesn't need as much water, which has an unexpected side effect of drying out half a continent and pushing local temperatures up, and both governments and scientists will be held accountable, and the scientists are unlikely to ever work again, assuming they avoid prison.

It worked like this: Many years ago, when CRISPR technology first opened up possibilities for gene editing, the field of bioethics and domestic laws firmly dictated what we could not do. Most experimentation was prohibited, and what was permitted had to go through strict ethical review panels and boards and be rigorously peer-reviewed. All experiments on human embryos and DNA had to be medical, not cosmetic, and the benefits – usually treating a disease – had to outweigh the potential risks. As the years went by, certain procedures became routine and some of the "potential" risks were determined to be false. In some ways, it was very safe technology.

One important principle was that gene editing should only impact the individual being treated, and not affect DNA that could be passed down to future generations. This would ensure that any errors committed would not be permanent, would not find their way into the gene pool like an accidental mutation. So, something with the fancy name of "human germline genome editing" was not allowed, except in incredibly narrow and controlled circumstances.

There were two issues with this. First, the prohibition only applied to human DNA, so the technology continued to evolve using wheat and bees and frogs as subjects. Genome editing on humans could continue as long as the potential benefits outweighed the risks, and the impact was restricted to the individual. The intent was that this technology only be used for medical purposes. Second, early legislation did not adequately cover environmental damage, and this area was addressed through tort law. In other words, when scientists messed up an ecosystem, they were sued for damages and ruined. The end result was that the ecological footprint of gene editing in non-human species had its own rules and ethics.

It went on like this for years. Gene editing became more commonplace, with many diseases eliminated, even a couple of inherited illnesses like sickle-cell anemia. The technology was celebrated.

Then companies like ours entered the scene: assisted fertility enterprises. Cedric blames the rise of powerful international conglomerates and the erosion of international laws that had buttressed an ethical consensus. Assisted reproductive services had a market advantage with a genetic engineer on staff to support clients trying for babies. With more and more environmental contaminants impacting fertility, it was a growing business. And with the introduction of new legislation in the United States supporting the would-be parents, the "offspring exemption" became common across many jurisdictions. If the embryos and genetic material belonged to the client, we could provide all manner of desired services as long as we did not touch the germline, that is, we didn't create new attributes that could be passed down to future generations.

It may seem ironic to the casual observer that it was not the mixture of different species' DNA that gave us pause but that doing this to the germline and enabling them to reproduce would place us outside a grey zone of ethics and, without doubt, in the realm of the very illegal. This is what happened when the hoppers were created. Someone not only created a highly dangerous hybrid human, but they enabled them to breed, to pass these characteristics on to new generations. Set loose in the urban wild, the hoppers had become part of the ecosystem and were proving hard to control. If their creators were identified, they would not only be financially ruined, unable to practice, they would go to jail for the rest of their lives.

Obviously, lawyers can make a good living managing risks for people in this line of work. Our lawyer, Greg, was a good guy, as far as that went. We trusted Greg implicitly. We'd employed him for years – it was his singular interest to protect us and allow our business to flourish. Before leaving for the island, we'd laid out the situation for Greg and told him a client wanted to tailor offspring to live underwater. He'd asked a few questions, and then got to the heart of the matter. "We can pull together a waiver where the client takes liability for the offspring, but the environmental impacts are trickier if you actually put them in the water in a natural habitat. For that we'll probably need a shell company that will take the fall in case of ecosystem collapse." He laid out what we needed to negotiate with our client and, as always, elaborated the specific risks we would want to protect against.

For example:

"Okay, so we have a case of interstitial statehood on Mr. Sykes' island, so we'll have to be cautious about travelling there."

"Um, interstitial what now?" I asked.

"Well," said Greg, "the island doesn't really have a nationality, so we're in a bit of legal grey zone. They're an entity and have unique jurisdiction for certain things, like civil ceremonies and some contractual issues. Think of it like a ship on the high seas but with a well-equipped security force and bunker."

"Are you saying they can just keep us there if they want to?"

"Well, hopefully not. But legally, maybe. We should be careful."

Since he agreed to come with us, I hoped he was exaggerating, but it was enough to make me hesitate over accepting Mr. Sykes' all-expense-paid Caribbean jaunt. But we were too far in to decline.

CHAPTER 7

I woke early, and after a few attempts, succeeded in programming my bedroom walls to show a sunrise. Cedric, Greg and I breakfasted in a nook adjoining our rooms and went over the strategy. "Are you sure you don't want to do some of the core presentation, Cedric? Are you sure you just want to go over the financials?"

"Yes, absolutely! You're the better presenter. But are you still sure about the title of the project? Isn't it a little gloomy? Or spooky?"

"Nah, we talked about this. It's an ocean zone; it's a technical term." A knock on the door interrupted us to let us know it was time.

We were escorted to a large boardroom dominated by an imposing table filled with a dozen suited professionals. Mr. Sykes smiled broadly and beckoned us inside, introducing us to those arrayed around the table too quickly to catch their names. Mostly lawyers and issue managers, plus the head of his Research and Development division and some hanger-on scientist types. I didn't trust a single one.

Everything had been cued up, and after some niceties and a brief yet thorough introduction by Mr. Sykes, I jumped in. With everyone seated, I ran a finger over my wristband and spun our presentation up over the boardroom table. I had designed it to take up space, so some of the images bled onto the people in their seats.

I started with my standard spiel: introducing our company, walking Mr. Sykes and associates through what we do and how. I made it as clear and simple as I could – we use a variety of proprietary techniques to select or alter the DNA and RNA of individuals and, in this case, a group, to achieve a desired outcome. I had some great graphics to illustrate this, and they hovered authoritatively over the table in primary colours, rearranging themselves on command to make my point.

Our techniques included traditional trait selection, where we identified specific DNA to include in an individual subject, as well as more experimental work, where we introduced cross-species DNA. The most straightforward process was to manipulate simple traits such as eye colour, hair colour or sex by adjusting the genetic sequencing. It was useful when a client wanted to tailor their child to certain specifications. As long as the trait already existed in the species, this was relatively easy to do.

When we were looking to create a new species or introduce a complex trait it became more complicated. For example, if we wanted to create a drought-resistant wheat or coffee plant, we could cross DNA from other species by tweaking the genetic material during the reproductive phase or in the adult. Breeding programs also strengthened inherent traits.

Some of the most exciting genetic engineering had taken place in the field of agriculture, increasing the productivity of cultivation manifold. It had been instrumental in climate adaptation given that traditional evolution would have taken thousands of years; gene therapy could produce critical changes within a few growing seasons. Some of the lawyers looked bored, but the scientists were following me attentively.

I shifted to the tailored part of our presentation. "Here, we have been given a fascinating challenge: How to engineer the human race to live at the bottom of the sea? It's an exciting question, and I would like to take the next few minutes to go over our proposed solution: the Midnight Project.

"When Mr. Sykes asked us to explore how to establish a viable human colony deep underwater, away from the vagaries of our terrestrial existence, away from the conflict, poverty, drought and famine that afflicts us all, we asked, where would a colony be safest from our time? Our civilization? Where can we locate a colony where the storms on the surface might miss them?

"The answer is: as far down as possible." I flicked up a 3D image of a cross-section of ocean. Everyone was with me so far. People love a good underwater seascape.

"So, down we go. There are five layers of ocean to consider: the sunlight zone, the twilight zone, the midnight zone, the abyss and the underworld. The deepest parts are located in trenches, crevices in the sea floor, far out to sea, from six thousand metres below the surface to the very bottom. These would be the farthest from human activity." I glanced over and Cedric was unnaturally still, holding his breath. I took a sip from my water and kept going.

"The Mariana Trench in the Pacific Ocean has a depth of over ten kilometres. The pressure is sixteen thousand pounds per square inch – the equivalent of fifty-two military-class fighter jets. This area has been very hard to research; we know very little about it. The only life forms discovered by deep-sea drone research are starfish and invertebrates. The name for this layer is the hadal zone: this comes from the word 'Hades.' It is a real-life underworld. We don't have enough sample DNA from the creatures there to even attempt to engineer a colony, and it would end up resembling a sea cucumber or brittle star more than a human."

I shifted to the floating 3D view of another part of the ocean, its dark edges lapping out over the lawyers. "Moving up in depth, we come to the abyssal zone. Yes, the abyss, and we are moving up in the world!" I tried for the jokey showman here but got no reaction. Either they were concentrating or they were drifting.

"The abyssal zone is from four thousand to six thousand metres. Here we find basket stars and tiny squids. Occasional fish move down to this zone to feed but not many – it isn't hospitable enough. Three-quarters of the ocean floor is at this depth. Again, we don't have sufficient DNA samples of abyss creatures to assess viability or compatibility with humans. The pressure, although slightly less, is still too high to consider any humanoid adapting to this space. The abyss would be ideal from a security perspective but not viable at this time." A few starfish and a squid floated above the table against a dark background, then I waved them away. Was that a sigh of relief from one of the suits? They seemed a bit nervous.

"So let's look at this another way. What is the most viable part of the ocean for a humanoid colony?" I flipped my argument on its ear, heading for sunnier waters.

"We start at the sunlight zone, the surface of the ocean down to two hundred metres. There are some surviving coral reefs; sea turtles; schools of fish – halibut, tuna, sharks; pods of dolphins and whales. Algae, cyano-bacteria and seagrass produce food with photosynthesis. This is the part of the ocean we know best, the ocean that we love. But this is also the part of the ocean that has already been corroded, damaged by human activity. Overfishing, acidification, coral bleaching – these ecosystems are depleted as badly as anything on the surface of the Earth. From a technical per-spective, it would be simplest to engineer our colony to live at this depth, but it would also be foolhardy. We would have to continue fighting all the battles we are currently fighting topside, and the colony would likely be discovered." I paused for effect and took a sip from my glass of water. I had them now. Everyone loved dolphins. Everyone regretted what had happened to the coral reefs.

"So where else can we go? Moving down from the sunlight zone, the twilight zone – found from two hundred to one thousand metres deep." I sent another sphere of ocean images floating above the table, focusing on animals swimming through dim light, each more fantastic than the last.

"Here, there is some dim light, temperatures near freezing, pressure at fifteen hundred pounds per square inch. It is a very different part of the ocean than the sunlight zone – the fish here use bioluminescence to attract prey or mates, and the adaptations life has made to its environment make them unique. We have zooplankton, krill, fish, crustaceans, squid. Whales and sharks will do deep dives down to the twilight zone to feed. Often, life in the twilight zone will migrate up to the surface at night. Over the last twenty years, sophisticated commercial harvesting of migrating twilight animals has damaged the balance of this ecosystem and reduced the overall population of life forms."

Cedric was glancing around the table at everyone's reactions. I was in the zone now, and everyone was being pulled along.

"We could adapt our colony to this zone, but it might not make it safe enough," I continued. "With a dependence on food found in the sunlight zone, this may be unstable, and it may not be deep enough to stay hidden.

Further degradation from human activity may make it as vulnerable as we are in this enclave." I drew a breath for the big pitch.

"This brings us to the midnight zone, or what I like to call the Goldilocks zone. This is where we will concentrate our efforts." With a gesture, I pulled up another sphere of ocean images, and florid nightmares swished through. Terrifying fish with rows of teeth outside their mouths and dangling phosphorescent lures, miniature sharks glowing green, giant squid and octopuses, as well as a diving sperm whale. I childishly enjoyed the collective recoil of the suits in the room. Cedric looked at me, pursing his lips. I suppressed a grin.

"Life is fragile in the midnight zone, where no sunlight reaches at all, but there is a connected food web and ecosystem that is stable enough for us to integrate our colony. This ecosystem is based on hydrogen-eating bacteria rather than photosynthesis, and food that sinks down from the two top layers. Where there are volcanic vents and toxic conditions for humans, life thrives even more." I flicked up an image of a thermal vent covered in crustaceans. A holographic crab crawled across Mr. Sykes' face.

"So how do we do this? How do we engineer a colony to survive in the midnight zone?

"There are several significant challenges to living at the bottom of the sea." I shifted gears and there was at least one sigh of relief as the monsters above the table disappeared. "First, the pressure. In the midnight zone, the ocean above creates a pressure of about fifty-eight hundred pounds per square inch. Temperatures are very close to freezing and there is absolute darkness, not even tiny amounts of filtered light reach this depth. To say nothing of the fact that humans breathe air and there is none of it down here." I displayed several statistics and graphs. They weren't really intended to educate, just to make Cedric and I look like we'd done our homework.

"Our starting point: the human." I used a life-sized image of da Vinci's *Vitruvian Man* here. That always worked a treat. It rotated above the table.

"To ensure the survival of a humanoid species in this location, we will need to substantially alter human attributes to craft a species that can exist and thrive in darkness, under pressure and in very cold salt water." I put on my best scientist voice, shading it with a hint of documentary narrator. I think the sea creatures had piqued their curiosity; I had their attention now.

I walked them through the elementary school version of how we do this: gene editing, with upscaled CRISPR tech, bioengineering and selective breeding under an accelerated generational scale followed by gene therapy to give the adult population new attributes. Some parsed 3D diagrams made it look simpler than it was, but it was more easily digested this way. I sketched out which species would offer the best genetic coding to integrate. Again, this was more to impress upon them how very, very smart we were, rather than actually educate them.

"To deal with high pressure in the deep sea, we will need a soft-bodied cross, and all our crosses will be with marine animals. Our primary cross will be with cephalopod DNA." It was our big reveal, and I couldn't help but give it a heartbeat of silence for any pushback. Nothing. I kept going.

"Octopuses can live in the midnight zone and are intelligent and resourceful. Giant squid have specialized characteristics and live there exclusively." I flicked up a magnificent image of a giant squid. "Squid are particularly well-suited to this depth and very good at living in low-oxygen environments." The life-size image filled the room and squirted away, disappearing along a wall.

Next came the giant Pacific octopus. "The octopus has a fascinating array of DNA, which will be very useful to us. Their genome, first typed back in 2015, is much more complex than smaller mammals like rats or dogs and by far the most complex of the invertebrate kingdom. An octopus cross will allow us to preserve human attributes since so many are already shared with the octopus: intelligence, curiosity, even empathy.

"However, we will likely need some supporting crosses to get a viable outcome." I moved on to my next hologram, a softly glowing dragonfish. It swam above the table.

I showed 3D visuals of the creatures but didn't share any images of what I thought our colony would look like. Best not to freak out the suits before the contracts were in place. Instead, I mentioned the uncertainty at the heart of the process, the importance of controls for unanticipated outcomes. "This type of enterprise is inherently risky, inherently unpredictable. We can hypothesize, or guess, what will happen when we introduce particular traits and DNA strands, but we won't know for sure until we have done it."

I wound up my part of the presentation and asked if there were any questions.

There were many. Among them: "How will you know if you're successful? How will you know if your new species is . . . still human?"

I stayed quiet. I was a scientist, not a philosopher.

Mr. Sykes interjected. "I would suggest that certain markers would suffice as measurements. The ability to speak and communicate, create music and art, and care for others, for example."

Random conversation rose up around the table, speculation about what would or could result. The example of the hoppers is never far away, and a further question concerned managing aggression and other undesirable traits.

"Ordinarily we would use amphibian DNA to support the switch to underwater living, it's an easier transition in terms of evolving breathing organs. Unfortunately, with the results of the hopper cross and the added aggressivity seen in that population, as well as the potential for spontaneous reproduction – self-cloning – we will avoid frog DNA. Studies do suggest that the hyper-aggression was introduced by a secondary predator cross in the hoppers, but we may never know the actual genetic source since the original work was never peer-reviewed or shared."

The next question was about how we would select the fittest specimens for survival. Clearly, the questioner was not familiar with basic genetic science ethics.

"We are well-equipped to address deficiencies in specimens," I reassured them. "While we are ethically bound to care for all the offspring to ensure their survival, we can remove experiments in vitro, especially if they are not viable. And, for humanitarian reasons, can terminate specimens that will not live or are in extreme pain."

Gently, I redirected to the more practical matters at hand. "Cedric, can you run us through the numbers?"

Cedric's part of the presentation was all about the nuts and bolts of what we needed. Money, essentially. Quite a lot. His 3D images were all graphs, pie charts and numbers in large font. We didn't use a visual of our building – it was too shabby and wouldn't instill confidence. Besides, if we were creating a secret lair, it should be secret.

"We'll need state-of-the-art laboratory equipment, biocontainment facilities and significant computer upgrades," Cedric listed, his low voice making the ask dull and easy. "We'll need to assemble a top team at better than market salaries, and potentially invest in deep-sea equipment and vehicles to support the colony once placed," he droned on, just like we practised. Of course, by "assemble a top team at above market rates" what we meant was "pay ourselves, Susan and our lab techs what we're worth," but they didn't need to know that.

Finally, the wrap-up, which Cedric concluded in admirably drab fashion. "If we're successful, we'll have a viable colony. We'll already have an on-site laboratory habitat for them, but eventually we'll need to move them to a wild ecosystem that can sustain them. We propose that some light aquaculture be introduced to ensure a food source, a moderate livelihood of bivalve cultivation. This will limit the colony from spreading throughout the broader ecosystem, which would necessarily attract attention and potential liability at scale."

Cedric nodded to me, ready for me to jump in. With a little flourish, I flicked a hologram of the entire ocean, mapping out the deeper crevices in the Caribbean and around the world. "The deeper we go within the midnight zone, the more private and protected we are." The 3D world map of oceans showed three potential Caribbean homes in glowing red. "Any questions?"

Mr. Sykes perked up. "How feasible are the Caribbean sites? Where exactly are they?"

"We'll need to explore that, including how to transport the colony safely, but that's a downstream issue."

Questions and discussion continued, but no one had choked on the dollar amount – perhaps we should have asked for more? And no one seemed particularly uncomfortable with the concept. That's what I love about bankers and lawyers. They are some of the most sinister people in the world. The most successful among them are soulless sociopaths. Looking around the room, I saw a lot of success and made a mental note not to request any DNA contributions from this crew. I left Greg to enjoy the company of his ilk while Cedric and I were excused for lunch.

CHAPTER 8

After lunch, we were allowed to wander the underground city, which was a marvel of engineering. Everywhere clean white walls reflected images of outdoor spaces, sunshine, clouds, even airplanes and birds. It quelled my claustrophobia, made me forget we were far from the sun and sky. There was no sound though, so the scenes left a strange dissonance, like we were inside a video game on mute. Instead of spaceship-like corridors, the moving pictures on the walls gave an aura of openness – ceilings so high you couldn't quite figure out where they were, and broad calming expanses of space that made you feel like you were walking down a street in Italy or Cuba. It left me impressed but uneasy. Where exactly were the exits to get topside?

Cedric and I had decisions to make and we needed to speak privately with Greg. "Do you think the whole city is wired?" I asked.

"Yes, at least the parts we're allowed in," said Cedric.

"Let's see if we can get a topside tour and find some open air to chat then."

The tour was easily arranged as the lawyers had taken a pause. We were in the recruitment stage and had not committed. Now that he knew what we could do, Mr. Sykes wanted us in, that much was clear. Greg appeared, dressed in khaki pants and a white shirt. It was the first time I had ever seen him without a tie.

The tour started with a car ride around the agricultural zone, where various staples were grown. It was neat, tidy and fully automated. No large grazing animals, though there was a complex of free-range chickens. "We tried having the whole island run vegetarian," said the driver, who was acting as tour guide, "but we thought it was more resilient to have a meat source for protein and the eggs are really central to a sustainable diet."

Making polite small talk, Cedric asked, "The entire enclave is self-sustaining? What offshore supplies do you need?"

"Only critical minerals for the batteries and some heavy equipment that we can't build here. We have a shop for manufacturing so we can repair our own machinery and build most of what we need – we're almost to the point of manufacturing self-sufficiency given our recycling program, but we need to be fairly austere about some things. We have wind and solar power, high-end battery tech, so we're energy self-sufficient. On the food side, we are self-sustaining as well, and we have plans to simplify our automation as needed in the future – it can all revert to being run by people if we face an event."

I nodded absent-mindedly. It was a well-run, properly done enclave. Even a direct hit from a major storm would have trouble wiping them out, depending on how they managed the drainage of their underground city. And their science labs were state of the art. A safe place, today and into the future. It wasn't that I was unimpressed. It's just that enclaves were big business, and the canny compared and contrasted, collated and disseminated, and then sold analyses of what worked and what didn't. The fact that Mr. Sykes had a top-of-the-line enclave didn't surprise me; I would have been taken aback if anything had been in disarray.

Beyond the groomed zones, the island had an uplifting piece of wilderness. Mountains ran along one coastline with spectacular cliff views looking out on a classic Caribbean Sea so perfect I wondered if that had been engineered too. Rocks below ensured no landings from sea could happen on this side. Mr. Sykes had worked at establishing a nature preserve on half of his topside enclave and the ultra-endangered were carefully curated. Not a zoo exactly or a bio-dome, but a footprint of an ecosystem for the birds, small mammals, insects and even fish and coral that persisted there.

It was easy and plausible, surrounded by such beauty, to ask to go for a walk. We left our driver at the car and meandered down a winding path, where we were soon surrounded by rocks with the cliffs straight ahead. We kept walking until the edge of the cliff and the coast was clearly in view and watched the birds flying in and out of nests below. Farther out, whitecaps curled and rushed to shore. The horizon stretched in either direction and the world was gentle. And under those waves was a whole different world hidden from view. Perhaps even hidden from pain and grief, who knew? Or was it a darker path?

Greg discreetly found a spot to sit by himself and admire the view just out of earshot. The sun was warm, and I could see Cedric being lulled into a sense of peace and calm.

Knowing we had as much privacy as we were going to get, I asked Cedric quietly, "What do you think?" The sound of birds and the surf masked our conversation.

"I think we have them. I think we can do this."

"But should we do it here?"

He smiled, almost wistfully. "Well, should we do it at all? Last chance to bail." He looked around almost longingly. "It's safer here, and this bit of nature is divine."

"Hmmm." We walked a bit farther. "I hate it here," I admitted.

"I know." He always knew. "But why? Is it just the claustrophobia?" So he had noticed my reaction to the underground city. I thought I'd hidden it better.

"Maybe you could bring your father here," he suggested. "He might like it."

I let the suggestion sit with me for a few heartbeats. As I considered, I felt a shadow of rancid shame, with a quick flash of embarrassment, rage and an undertone of helplessness. I didn't want to go down that road again.

"I don't think he would come, not if it was me asking." I shook my head. "And, I mean, I know it's a nice vacation spot, but would we even be allowed topside? Or would we live in the labs underground and never see daylight?"

Cedric shuddered.

"No," I continued. "We need autonomy. Especially when Sykes disagrees with us. We need control. And Sykes is the only one in control if we stay here. What if it turns out he just wants super-soldiers? Or dinosaurs? I think we'll need the scope to make decisions."

How much did we really know about the mysterious Mr. Sykes? His public persona was ridiculously wealthy and curated to appear urbane and generous. Interested in culture, history, literature and ensuring the future, he presented a blandly predictable persona. But no one who has ever achieved much of anything was that innocuous. It set my alarm bells ringing.

On the other hand, the enclave radiated stability and good things. It was beautiful, well-constructed and thoughtfully presented. I could see how it would work: well-appointed laboratories, all the best technology and at the end of the project, we could launch our colony practically from this island itself. But what then?

People could be happy here. But not me.

"Our project is inherently unpredictable, with an element of menace," I tried to explain. "A little blue sky and soothing waves aren't going to protect us. This space is only safe for its creator. Everyone else is here to serve his vision. I'm not a servant. I'm not."

"This project is about survival," countered Cedric. "Why not do it here, where we have the best chance for our own? We could join the enclave long-term, wait out the storm . . ." He trailed off hopefully. "Besides, I thought part of this was about our own well-being? Why not join this enclave and be safer?"

"Sure," I said, "but what if it goes wrong? What if this is actually *Jurassic Park*? Do we know what other off-the-books projects he has going on? I don't want to turn around and get eaten by a raptor, if you know what I mean."

I laughed in spite of myself when Cedric looked around quickly, as if dinosaurs would start popping up any minute. The hoppers helped to keep that story a classic.

"We'll be enabled here, but also constrained. Under his thumb, unable to leave. I don't like it. What if he has other motives? He might never let us leave. Let's do the job, take the money and if it feels right, then we can come here after, if we're still welcome."

We both knew I was trying to explain a decision I'd already made – and for the both of us. It was part of the nature of our relationship that I never for a minute doubted we would do things my way. I was sure we needed to go back to Long Harbour to do this work, in our own facility, in private. Cedric didn't like it, but Cedric would always have my back, always be on my team. There was no part of me that doubted Cedric would be with me, in what I'd already determined.

For his part, Cedric knew this too. He breathed deeply, and looked around as if memorizing the landscape, preserving it against hard dark times to come. "You wouldn't do well in the bunker," he said finally. "Your claustrophobia would make it a hell. Besides, once recruitment is over and the papers are signed, we might find ourselves in a different situation here," he admitted. "And it'd be too late. I don't see an escape hatch if things take a turn."

In agreement, if I can call it that, we turned to the more mundane, practical discussion of what we needed in our contract. We walked back to Greg and talked that part through one last time in low voices. "Make sure there's a good super-soldier exclusion," I reminded Greg. "We don't want humanity's salvation to turn out to be undersea terrorists, right?"

Finally, we turned back to the waiting vehicle, leaving the wheeling gulls and wildlife to themselves. I couldn't help noticing a small, unmanned drone following us at a distance. Our conversation was unlikely to have been entirely private.

⌘

We reconvened, Greg back in his grey suit, and the lawyers talked at length. Surprisingly, there was no pushback on the financials, making me think again that we could have asked for more. Now that the project had been approved in principle, the contractual details bored me. I struggled to maintain a poker face, not fidget and let Greg do his job. Cedric was a model of patience, occasionally jiggling his foot or his hand but otherwise stoic. Inside, I was climbing the walls.

The liability waiver was the centrepiece of the contract. As predicted, it created a shell company that would, at least in theory, take on all legal risk, both of wrongful birth and environmental damage. Interestingly, Sykes' lawyers created the shell company for an "anonymous parent couple" who would authorize the work done on their offspring. We would be legal, right up to the moment we enabled our subjects to pass on altered genetic characteristics.

Moreover, it cleverly excused us from environmental liability from all work undertaken in approved laboratory sites as long as state-of-the-art biocontainment protocols were installed and maintained. It was as ironclad as we could make it and it might save us from ruin.

The sticking point came when we discussed where we would install the upgraded laboratory and where we would carry out the work. Greg made solid arguments, brought up legal jurisdiction, the existence of our current laboratory and our staff. Re-Gene-eration was well-established and the extra project unlikely to attract attention if we were careful. Now the lawyers were circling, and I felt a little sorry for Greg. He was clearly outnumbered. He stood his ground though and the discussions were protracted.

After a break, we were reconvened by Mr. Sykes himself. "I am going to make a final appeal, Dr. Templeton, Dr. Beauville. You should do your work here. You'll be safer and the project will be better supported. I don't understand why you hesitate."

I thought briefly about the word "interstitial" and how I didn't completely understand it. "I like Long Harbour," I told him. A mild statement that my lawyer could turn into a valid reason. "Anyway" – I looked Mr. Sykes in the eye to make sure he understood – "it's a condition of our involvement. We do this from our home or nowhere."

Mr. Sykes heaved a sigh, as if dealing with recalcitrant teenagers. "I am deeply disappointed you're refusing my offer to set up here. I don't see how we can continue without you under my protection and direction."

His serene demeanour did not change but I felt the deep discomfort of being scolded by a stern father figure. Benevolent but unbending, Mr. Sykes had cast his net and would not let us dodge it so easily.

I took a deep breath and tried again. "I think you're looking at this the wrong way, Mr. Sykes. If we are here, then we are synonymous with Global Holdings, and your reputation is tightly tied to it. It's true you would be able to oversee things more directly, but you'll also find much less deniability down the road if you need to cut the project loose. I hope I don't need to explain just how fragile what we are attempting is, and how fraught certain decisions may be. Are you sure you want us here?

"You have a beautiful island and a top-notch facility. But it draws attention because of who you are, no matter how carefully you try to hide it. Isn't that why you want us to do this project? Because you know inevitably, this may not last. That you may hold out till the very end, but things will –" I paused "– end."

This last comment was met with silence. It was considered unmannerly to discuss the end of days out in the open.

Finally, Mr. Sykes broke the silence. "I suppose you are easier to cut loose this way." His eyes met mine and I felt a flicker of fear. But it was done. I willed myself to stillness, hiding my anxiety.

He smoothly moved on as if he had not just lost a battle. "I'll need regular updates, and you'll need to return here, especially when the colony is ready to be deployed."

The deal done, we flew out that night, to my relief and Cedric's ostensible disappointment. I couldn't detect a single emotion from Greg, one way or the other.

Mr. Sykes took us to the helipad himself, all smiles, shaking our hands and wishing us well. The copter lifted, and we escaped the lion's den.

❧

The money flowed and we no longer had to do our banking in person. I felt a weight lift when I reviewed our accounts, pulling up our charts over the boardroom table, feeling like a player instead of an exile. Cedric muttered something about ethics and risks, but I was cautiously jubilant.

I called a staff meeting as soon as I could. The five of us sat around the table, and I jumped in with what I could share.

"We've signed a new client who wants privacy and is taking us on for an extended, complex project. We'll be upgrading the lab significantly to meet his needs. Susan, we'll need you to handle the contractors. Edward and Laurel, I'll ask you to step up with our regular clients, to keep everything running normally. With our new responsibilities, we'll be increasing your salaries. There are some new NDAs on the table to sign – we don't want to draw attention to our big spender."

Everyone smiled and Edward started to slow clap. Laurel laughed. Susan had a list of questions about the renovation.

The money was enough for us to buy our building, including the gym and pool in the basement. Susan drove a hard bargain with the owners while at the same time expressing her misgivings. "You should lease new office space," she recommended. "The old fitness centre is a serious liability – the basement leaks so much it practically has its own tide and the entire building is a medium-term structural risk. I mean it's low-cost, but with the new investment it makes sense to go with a newer property."

It was true that our landlord had been trying to off-load the building for years and had had trouble even finding tenants. The renovations required on the foundations a decade before had nearly driven him into bankruptcy. We got it cheap. We couldn't tell Susan exactly why we needed to keep a low profile, but I think she guessed. People would notice if we suddenly started spending big money. Bespoke tailoring of offspring pays the bills but not much more, and Re-Gene-eration wasn't the most popular or successful in the field.

Ah, well. The building was a money pit, but we had nice views from the roof. It was seven-floors high in a neighbourhood of low-rise businesses, the top floor consisting entirely of very large windows. Our lab was on the sixth floor, the main part in a large windowless room in the middle that had been converted from several boardrooms into a single space. We installed a commercial aquarium tank along one wall. We splurged and upgraded the kitchenette with an oven and range, and a full-sized fridge. We upgraded the solar panels and added a greenhouse on the roof.

I had some vintage bookshelves installed in the intake room and I lovingly brought some antique paper books from home to display. They were hard to find now, but I loved to hold them. We renovated a few extra vacant offices into apartments, but I continued to commute from my little house in the hills.

Financial security attained, we dove into the work. Cedric's anxious tremors were more pronounced than usual, but I felt like a queen in a fortified castle, raising strong walls against the deluge to come.

PART II
CREATION

We have lingered in the chambers of the sea
By sea-girls wreathed with seaweed red and brown
Till human voices wake us, and we drown.

– T.S. Eliot, "The Love Song of J. Alfred Prufrock"

CHAPTER 9: CEDRIC

FADE IN

INT. RE-GENE-ERATION LAB - DAY

CEDRIC awkwardly perched on a swivel chair with a plain grey background. He is in the lab.

CEDRIC

Okay, our little Caribbean vacation didn't relax me. I'm already thinking I made a huge mistake. But I keep thinking about all the idiots who would mess this up a million times worse than we possibly could, and I know we have to do it. We can't have any more hoppers. We need to keep a lid on this sort of thing.

In any event, the decision is made, the contract signed, initial signing bonus received and most of it spent on lab upgrades. I mean, I love the upgrades, don't get me wrong. And we're worth it, we're worth the money, we're already making progress. At least a little progress. Well, okay, not really capital-P progress, but we will. We better.

But now is where we test ourselves. Now is when we find out if our plans and pitches will actually work in the real world. What Mr. Sykes may not realize is that as clean as our computer modelling is, it is entirely theoretical. There is an old military proverb: no plan survives contact with the enemy. It may not work. Oof.

CEDRIC takes a deep breath and stares at the camera.

> CEDRIC (cont'd)
> And what happens if we flat-out fail at the secret contract? I'd like to think we'd be no worse off than before, but I can't help thinking that this much money is expected to provide a return. Everyone knows billionaires hate to waste money. For all their wealth, they can be incredibly cheap. And for all Mr. Sykes' vaunted intellect, I know he hates to lose. He wants control, and these sorts of endeavours defy that. You need to bring a level of humility to this kind of work.

CEDRIC shakes his head and frowns.

> CEDRIC (cont'd)
> Real-world outcomes exceed our most sophisticated modelling. Simulations can't account for all the inevitable off-target effects. And ecosystems are basically bodies of macroscopic scale, with similar dynamics. They heal, and they grow. They evolve, and they sicken.

In some cases, we've helped ecosystems to heal, to adapt and grow. In others, we've spun new realities into being and created sicknesses, cancers. Which we hurry to heal with further adjustments, further edits. We're like gods, I suppose, but weak and flawed. The Greeks may have been on to something with their panoply of failed heroes and selfish, petty deities.

But billionaires? Those guys want to be God, sure, but the Christian God. The one with all the power, the all-knowing father. The mostly benevolent but also very end-of-days-doom-and-destruction cuz-I-said-so kind of father. It's an imperfect epistemic model for understanding or controlling what we do as genetic engineers.

Manipulating nature is inherently uncertain. Gods may not exist, but Mother Nature does, and she is, pardon my language, a tough bitch.

Okay, enough pep talk. I just hate this part. It's like jumping into cold water, I really hate it.

CEDRIC stands up, frowns and turns off the camera.

CUT TO BLACK

CHAPTER 10

I loved this part. It reminded me of diving into my favourite swimming pool as a kid, the clean, cold water shocking me then leaving me refreshed and revitalized. I smiled as I ran my hand along the freshly installed countertop in the lab, our new equipment harkening back to when we were players. I was excited by the start of the mad Sykes project, picturing danger and intrigue and new things, but Cedric told me he was just relieved to finally have some financial stability. He wasn't wrong – I was relieved to have some security too.

Cedric and I showed up for work each morning and drank coffee in the intake room, the soft blue hues of the walls a calming backdrop to the increasingly distressing Holo-News.

Head of United Nations declares that the world is at the edge of
   the abyss
Eyes turn to southern hemisphere growing season, bee census
   underway
African Union requests pollinator drones to deal with bee crisis

There were new wars in Africa, old wars in the Middle East and China, and member states at the United Nations continued to rattle their sabres and concentrate on the wrong things. The business news was even worse:

Webwex lands on the moon, takes over interstellar launch after
   billion-dollar buyout of resident TurkDel Co.
Who is winning the race to Jupiter?

It was maddening and stupid and completely out of our control. The environmental news always came last and was usually the worst.

Species Termination Notice: Australian koala
Species Termination Notice: North American lantern beetle

A jolt of dread to go with the jolt of caffeine, and then we turned to our work, donning clean crisp lab coats and entering our upgraded laboratory, a shiny world where we set the pace, established the goals and measured the results. A tiny corner of the world where we were in control.

We maintained a tight hold on the project and kept Edward and Laurel on the outside. They were an oblivious smiling presence in the hallways and the kitchen, keeping our usual clients happy and our cover in place. Laurel was a bright spark who labelled her homemade lunches when she left them in the fridge. Probably a good idea since she also left client samples from time to time. Edward mostly ordered out for lunch or ate Laurel's. Dressed in light plaid shirts and jeans and with a face usually covered in stubble, he managed to look simultaneously scrubbed and scruffy. Our staff were all good at their jobs but I found myself resenting their cheery carefree attitudes. Did they not know how perilous life was?

The shell company, which Mr. Sykes had rather cheekily named Surf Legacy (complete with a surfing-themed logo), provided human biological samples. When we tailored offspring, we were always using someone's genetic code, someone's reproductive biology. Even when we used synthetic materials, we were replicating DNA that belonged to someone, a code that already existed in the wild. Without consent, we couldn't just scrape some human DNA and carry on – it would not only invalidate our liability waiver but also went against every ethical guideline we lived by. Consent was central.

We speculated whether it was Mr. Sykes' genetic material itself. Cedric doubted it. Too easy to trace, too much exposure. I thought he could be wrong – Mr. Sykes' ego might assume no one would ever test it, or perhaps he had taken steps to preserve his own DNA's privacy.

"He must have used his own," I decided. "I mean why go to the trouble of creating a deep-sea colony to survive the end and not have your hubris extend to them being your own descendants?" Had he literally set out to protect a line of his family, or did he possess a level of caution we had not yet seen? Were his dreams for humanity really that large?

Cedric erred on the side of caution. "Maybe he hates his family?" He shrugged. We laughed at it like it was a joke, but still wondered. Given that we didn't have a known sample from him there was no way to test, and we would only be doing that out of curiosity, which felt like a bad idea.

Speaking of families and bad ideas, I tried to repay my father's loan. One of the first things I did when our bank accounts were flush again was call him. I got his answering service. No one picked up calls anymore, I guess, not even from family. "Dad, great news!" I blurted out. "Can you call me? Lots of news. Anyway, love you. Call me. Uh, it's me, Raina." I hung up quickly, cursing myself for not being better prepared. Should I have mentioned the money right away?

He called me back the next day, reserved and quiet. I hated these conversations, trying to connect. "Yes, good to hear from you." His voice had a formal edge. "How are you?" Was it my imagination or was he bracing himself?

"Hi, Dad, I have good news. I've gotten a new contract, and I've come into some money. I can pay you back faster than I thought. In fact, I can pay you back all of it. Isn't that great?"

Instead of excitement, there was a profound pause. "What kind of contract?"

"Well, you know, Dad . . ." I explained about nondisclosure agreements. "It's a new client, a big one. I can't really say more, but it's good, we're good now. We're finally turning the corner."

"Is it the mob?"

"The mob? What?" How old-fashioned was he? Really, who talks about the mob anymore? "What do you mean? Have you been watching old FlickFilms again? I mean, no, it's not the mob!"

"But it's a criminal." It wasn't a question. "I can't take your money,

Raina. I don't know when you're going to learn to stop taking the easy way through life. How many times have I told you, you have to stop being so impulsive? You need to plan better and follow through. The money doesn't matter, I don't want it back." Maybe he didn't but the money mattered. He brought it up every time we spoke, and it was the turning point that had ruined his faith in me. I had to pay him back. I had to take the money out of it, try to repair what was left.

This time, the awkward pause was my fault. I didn't dare speak as a lump in my throat threatened to turn to tears. He took a breath as if he were going to launch into his boilerplate speech about discipline and the importance of planning. God, he didn't change.

"No," I squeaked finally. "This isn't about a lack of discipline or a lack of hard work or a lack of anything. I am doing the best I can! If you would just listen . . ." I trailed off desperately then launched in before he could get a word in. "It isn't my fault. I know I can't explain it, but it isn't my fault! Everything is going to go back the way it was; everything will be fine again. You'll see. You just have to trust me."

And then, the longest pause of all. Of course, he didn't trust me. He didn't, he couldn't, he wouldn't. "Well," I said finally. "Maybe you're right. Maybe I'm just the world's biggest failure."

I severed the connection angrily, looked around for something to throw and tried to shake it off. It didn't work. I walked over to the door, opened it and slammed it hard. Then I leaned quietly on the door, cursing under my breath.

The fallout from when I left WKPT had ruined my relationship with my dad. My fault, all my fault, but clearly irreparable. When everything went south with WKPT, I was completely bound by the NDA and couldn't explain any of it to my dad. Proud papa that he was, he had been my biggest fan, applauding the loudest when I was high school valedictorian, pleased as punch at all the scholarships and accolades as I moved through academia and awfully impressed with the big salary that the ag sector doled out. What he couldn't get his head around was that I left. I was dismissed and legally prevented from even telling him I'd been fired. He tried to offer solutions, encouraged me to get back on my feet, but his disappointment was palpable. When I asked him for money, he gave it to me, probably out of desperation to do something. He didn't get it, he didn't know what had happened. He didn't understand how ruined I was or why. There was nothing he or I could do. Getting driven out of the ag sector had destroyed more than my career.

"So, how's the good Dr. J. Templeton?" Cedric asked brightly as he entered the room, graciously ignoring my crumpled face. I pulled it together.

"The same. Always the same, but maybe getting worse." Cedric nodded and put the kettle on. I stared out the window into the hills. In a few minutes, he handed me a flowered Royal Doulton china teacup filled with milky Earl Grey tea. I thanked him and tried to think about work.

"Don't worry, Raina," he said finally. "We have other people in our lives." I must have given him a bleak look because he added, "You know, friends, colleagues."

Silence.

"Well, okay," he conceded. "Not many."

"Name ten."

"Remember Shorty Gauguin? What was his name, Stéphane. Yes, Stéphane. You called him Stevie. Worked for a while in ecosystems recovery. We went out drinking at that conference. I think I know where he is now." Cedric was on a roll now, my fight with my father forgotten. "In fact, that gives me an idea."

❧

Genetic engineers like us all built our own genome banks. Most run-of-the-mill geneticists used regular trait banks, which were essentially computer programs with instructions for coding specific genes to achieve certain outcomes. Trait banks could take care of about three-quarters of our work on any given day, but folks who only used trait banks were more like computer engineers than real genetic engineers. The real professionals went beyond computer programs and collected and stored samples of organic genetic material so that we could capture hidden complexities. In truth, it was a matter of pride as much as professional necessity.

We established and built our genome banks quietly, with proper legal consent from our donors. They were secretive affairs; we treated them like private collections. While our profession was mainly competitive, we occasionally traded DNA samples back and forth – this allowed us to demonstrate the superiority of our holdings to our colleagues. Cedric and I were smugly proud of Re-Gene-eration's genome bank. We didn't have much money to show for our efforts, but our genome bank was second to none. Since we had come from the agricultural field originally, we didn't limit ourselves to human DNA either.

Funnily enough, very few genetic engineers bothered with marine material. Too bad, really, the octopus genome is one of the wackiest out there. It has even been described as alien DNA, it is so complicated and different from human. We had been collecting discreetly and started gathering obscure samples: anglerfish, bivalves, newt and frog. Squid and octopus were in short supply.

This was where Shorty-Stevie-Stéphane came in. A few hours after our first conversation about him, Cedric triumphantly brought up his name again. "He's running the coastal ecosystem recovery effort out of the Long Harbour Aquarium," he declared. "I've already reached out to him, to see if he's up for sharing some genetic samples." It was a risk. Most of our colleagues from the before-days wouldn't talk to us now. No one understood what had happened, just that we were blacklisted.

I think Shorty was a bit down on his luck, too, because he replied immediately and invited us over to see his facility. Cedric didn't want to go, but I thought it would be good for him to get out. The aquarium was a distance, so we booked a land shuttle and set off. Rolling through downtown, we got to see all the grimy storefronts, divey harbour bars and a few restaurants. There were a lot of For Rent signs in vacant buildings, and some buildings that were crumbling, with DANGER NO ENTRANCE signs out front. Crowds temporarily blocked our way in a few spots, with folks going to work, doing their shopping, seeing their people, getting on with it. I admired their grit and checked that the doors on the shuttle were locked.

Electric copters buzzed overhead. "Those sky shuttles are just there to remind us what we don't have," I told Cedric. "They're just loud money screaming."

Cedric nodded. "Cutting-edge but out of reach." Even with our new contract, we weren't going to waste money flying across town.

The aquarium was in the abandoned, shallow part of the old port. A surprisingly tall man let us in. "It's so good to see you both," Shorty said, and I looked twice to see if he was lying. The aquarium, like the buildings around it, had a grim feeling of decay and neglect, but as we walked into the central viewing areas, we could see the tanks were clean and well-maintained, the animals healthy.

He straightened and proudly told us about his work. "We've moved fully into conservation. All the animals you see here were either bred in captivity, as part of our endangered program, or rescued. We're active in the harbour and bay area, reseeding coral and kelp and trying to restore the habitat. We're doing good work here."

We passed an empty, bedraggled-looking gift shop. "We have public access a couple of times a week, but not many people are willing to spend money here. So we're a bit lonely now. We mostly exist on grants and benefactors," he explained sheepishly.

"And what are you two up to?" he asked. "Going from strength to strength, I guess."

Did he not know what happened to us?

Cedric explained about Re-Gene-eration and our little boutique business. Shorty was momentarily taken aback. "Oh, well I guess there's money in that. Good for you!"

We had stopped in front of a small octopus exhibit. "I have to admit, we're sinking here. Our money's running out," Shorty told us. "Our funding is year-to-year and we're slowly going under unless we can find a new benefactor or invent a new business model."

I fought against a wave of empathy. "I'm sure you'll come up with something."

Cedric drifted over to the tanks. "You have quite a few octopus here, look at them!"

Shorty smiled. "We took in some extra that had been saved from fishing boats."

"I have a little idea for you," Cedric said. I wandered into the next room to leave them alone. When they caught up to me, they were both smiling.

We finished the tour. Cedric and Shorty shook hands and promised to be in touch. I earnestly wished him luck. His smile fell. "It'll take more than luck, but I really appreciate you stopping by. This will help keep us going. Let me know if you want to go out for drinks or something."

I didn't think we would see him again.

I ignored the tremors in Cedric's hands as he boarded the shuttle for home. I was proud of him for getting out of the lab at all. I tried to distract him on the way home, talking about what we saw out the windows – places to eat, to shop, to work – but he just screwed his eyes shut. His breathing became ragged and shallow and he clutched his sides. I forced myself to touch his knee and his eyes flew open, the whites visible.

"Don't panic," I told him. "We're almost there."

❧

A few days later the aquarium delivered two adult octopuses and we installed them in our refurbished laboratory. We had acquired not only a fresh source of octopus DNA but also two new mascots who Cedric named Rex and Maisie. Cedric had told Shorty that we were installing an office aquarium to create a more relaxing environment for our clients. We housed Rex and Maisie in a marine environment in our main laboratory, in two aquariums set up facing each other.

They were docile and, to be honest, incredibly sweet. Never mind labs, exotic pet suppliers must have a ready supply of these adorable creatures. We delighted in finding puzzles for them to do, and laughed when they opened jars, ate the food inside and then tried to hide inside the jars themselves. They seemed genuinely interested in us and our work. Maisie would rush to the top of her tank every morning to greet us, reaching out with her tentacles, eagerly wrapping around our arms, her suckers gently tasting our skin. Rex was more timid, hiding behind the dark rocks at the bottom of his tank. It always felt like a special privilege when he came out to greet us, poking his head above the water. For all his shyness, he never seemed to take his eyes off us when we were working. Both were very tolerant of being handled, and getting samples was very straightforward.

Cedric liked to feed them, passing them morsels of fish and watching as their tentacles passed the food up to their mouths. Maisie liked to bite him with her suckers, leaving little track marks along his arms. I have no idea why they both enjoyed this. She never did it with me, but then again, my family had never been given to displays of affection.

CHAPTER 11

Each day the same comforting pattern: coffee, Holo-News, Cedric. The calm space of our intake room was the only place I felt grounded enough to deal with it all.

New Zealand announces food security plan, halts agricultural
   imports
Debris from TurkDel Co. weapons test threatens international
   space station and Webwex ark
Bee drone rentals are big business, preorders climbing
Species Termination Notice: red-eyed tree frog

Even within the safety of the lounge, the news weighed heavy. It was difficult to breathe sometimes. There is only so much death and destruction one can take first thing in the morning, even with coffee.

Our work continued. It took several weeks of experimenting with beakers, microscopes and petri dishes full of cells to establish compatible DNA crosses. As expected, the octopus had a lively reaction with human cells. Things looked promising. As we expanded our colony of living cells and learned what thrived and what didn't, we documented our work with videos and written reports and passed them to Mr. Sykes. Although our building was old, it had the strength to support a light copter landing on the roof. It was a symbol of wealth we weren't supposed to have so to be discreet, Cedric and I painted the landing circle ourselves, feeling like graffiti artists. Cedric even insisted on adding a tag a few feet away, to mark his artistry.

We had expected a Global Holdings copter but instead got a large drone capable of carrying small loads. It would drop by once a week and take our reports since Mr. Sykes distrusted internet and satellite transmission. He had offered to furnish us with a Global Holdings server, but we'd already acquired our own. Our security was sufficient, and I didn't want to risk Mr. Sykes and his islander insiders installing a fail-safe mechanism that only they could control. We'd installed our own but didn't share access with him.

Our updates may not have been gripping for non-scientists like Sykes, but at least they showed effort. A short oral narrative, accompanied by data and graphs.

"With the first phase of simulations behind us, we have begun the gene-editing process in cells. Guided by our computer modelling, we've identified specific traits to replicate and are now attempting to insert the genetic code into human cells. Using old CRISPR tech, upgraded with our own proprietary processes, we are working with recombinant inter-species DNA and are now attempting to get the cells to grow. Please find attached detailed datasets describing the outcomes to date."

Etcetera etcetera, blah blah.

Every week when the drone collected our progress reports, it dropped off a key with a recorded message from Mr. Sykes. He wanted us to know "his thoughts" on the project, which extended to his thoughts on life in general. So, once a week, we would sit down to Mr. Sykes expounding on philosophy, on the history of civilization and on the importance of protecting and preserving the life force.

"The error of our ways," according to a larger-than-life holographic Mr. Sykes, "is in our nature – our greed, our lack of trust, our inherent violence. We cannot live in harmony with others. At all levels except the family, we are selfish and cruel. Even within families we fail and fail again at goodness. Our downfall is not our technology, our science, it is ourselves."

The man had a dim view of humanity. "Our saving grace is our love of the light," he continued. "Our appreciation of beauty and our ability to dream. Our ability to create music, art."

"So . . . he wants to create Mozart-loving octo-people. You know the man is insane, right?" Cedric enjoyed providing live commentary.

"Oh, he's dark, all right. Quite possibly completely mad, too, eh? Like, way more 'mad scientist' than us!"

A quick grin and a sardonic snort from Cedric. "Yes, much worse than us."

"We have a sacred trust, a responsibility, to preserve goodness. It goes far beyond the human race itself, you see," Mr. Sykes continued. "There is a soul to our peoples that must extend beyond our mistakes and transgressions, beyond our hubris."

"Well," said Cedric tartly, "this project is unlikely to be the one that overcomes our hubris."

Mr. Sykes didn't just rant about the state of the world, or his special ideas. He went over our reports with a fine-tooth comb, asking follow-up questions and generally being a pain. Soon, our weekly progress reports included a section responding to his questions and concerns. It had only been a couple of months, but he was getting twitchy about timelines.

"I'm sure you're following the headlines, aware of the progress of the bee die-off." This week's rant had a special target, and it was us. "With the southern hemisphere's growing season in doubt, you need to accelerate your timelines. You need results. We could all be dead, and you'd still be peering through a microscope trying to decide if you've created the perfect molecule. I need more effort from you, and you need to deliver faster."

He peered into his camera like a stern father. Great, just what I needed, another father figure disappointed with me. Cedric gave a low growl and turned the video off. "I think we get his point."

"Maybe we can finish this later, eh?" I stood up and walked wearily back to the lab. Sykes wasn't wrong, I just hated him for it.

"We could start the egg trials now," suggested Cedric. "We're close enough. The perfect is the enemy of the good."

I shrugged, then nodded, resigned. "Yeah, let's get on with it."

☙

Throughout the autumn, I would rush to the office from my little house in the hills, eager to get to work, eager to start the day, coffee in hand, watching the Holo-News with Cedric. It was hard to believe that the world was really ending while we drank coffee in companionable silence. We kept a very tight line in terms of the world-in-here and the world-out-there. I didn't want any encroachment. They were trying times, and I only wanted to try in certain ways. Since the last pandemic had ended, North American social culture had not bounced back to its previous hedonistic ways. For a long time, we all kept to our social bubbles, our families, our workmates, and a few treasured friends from the before times. I had lost a lot of family in the last wave of sickness, and friends don't stay friends when you stop calling.

Of course, our social isolation was mainly due to what happened with Wheat Kings and Pretty Things. I suppose you could say it was bad luck but it was also naïveté. We developed a process to insert DNA into cells that would make gene editing easier. The process was patented and belonged to WKPT. Success, right? We felt great. Saving the world, one pest-resistant field of wheat at a time. But then we found out something. A casual remark from senior management, a quick scan of some edited plants and we couldn't deny it. They had taken our process and had used it to develop a wheat rust that would only infect their competitors' crops – a bespoke fungus.

And that is where we made our fatal mistake. We tried to blow the whistle. We went to the authorities; we even told the competitor, Azul Sky Tech, they were being attacked. We tried to take it back, but the genie was clearly out of the bottle. The authorities were handled, the competitor reached an out-of-court, off-the-books settlement and we were summarily dismissed, lucky to avoid prison. In retrospect, I wish we had tried to sabotage the tech first, since it was now clear, to us at least, that our little patented process that was supposed to solve world hunger had actually enabled the idiots who created the bee catastrophe. No one could pin it on us (indeed we didn't even exist in those circles anymore), but we knew what we knew. It added insult to injury that we personally lost almost everything too. I retreated into a dark corner without room for family love or self-respect or pride.

This social isolation may have contributed to my complete nonchalance when we started using our own DNA and my embryos as source material. A more socially grounded person might've had some qualms about their technical offspring being part octopus and part fish, but I didn't hesitate for a minute. In fact, it gave us more legal protections. It had been a simple supply chain issue – we needed more variability in our human DNA so we used our own. I swear this was not hubris or mad scientist thinking. While our liability waiver was intact, it depended on the DNA of others. If we introduced our own, we had our own offspring exemption built in, and we could provide our own consent. So we added our own material to the mix, to protect ourselves and to enrich the DNA we were working with.

I was not trying to be a mother. I'd given up on the idea of parenthood years ago; I didn't even own pets. Bizarrely, for someone who'd had a measure of success in the ag sector, I even hated gardening. I liked microscopes, petri dishes and agar. I was not a warm person. And I felt strongly that bringing children into this world was a cruel and selfish decision. Why bring a new being into existence just to watch them suffer? The world was on fire, and there was no point in having children just to watch them be consumed or to leave them to that fate when we ourselves passed. The Midnight Project was a different undertaking of course, and the liability dodge of using the offspring exemption ourselves made us a little more secure, as well as solving some supply issues. On the science, I was serene. On the rest of my life, not so much, but what else was new?

≈

"Hey, the coffee is really good this morning," I told Cedric. He had also branched out into sourdough scones – his baking was really improving.

"Thanks, I'm using a new blend, I got a line on some high-end Colombian."

It was a sunny day, but the news, as usual, was bleak.

Beekeepers Union appeals for release of intellectual property for
   re-engineered bees
Webwex threatens nuclear showdown with TurkDel Co.
Hopper infestation on eastern seaboard threatens local
   businesses
New conglomerate XLink seeks new markets in social media
   feeds for arks in orbit
Species Termination Notice: Siberian tiger

Things were also a bit bleak in the lab. We had succeeded in growing our embryos – they were viable at least in vitro. The next stage should have been to implant them into a volunteer uterus, but we balked at the consent issues. We didn't want to bring anyone else into our circle of trust. This project clearly exceeded the bounds of usual surrogacy. I suggested I could do it, but Cedric had a better idea.

"Why don't we try to grow them in artificial eggs? Then we won't need a surrogate and we can more easily monitor the growth of the fetus. We could create a synthetic womb around them."

Cedric was very humble about it, but the man was a scientific genius. His daily snuggles with Rex and Maisie seemed to spark creativity. We tried it and soon had five synthetic eggs immersed in an amniotic seawater solution. We watched in growing fascination as the fetuses grew inside their plastic wombs. It only took four weeks for them to grow to term. Once we deemed them ready to be born, we slit the first egg open, poured its contents into a small tank of salt water and watched the emerging baby.

It looked more squid than human, I won't lie. A mess of undulating soft pink tentacles, the only visibly human attributes were its eyes, its mouth and a vaguely humanoid head and torso. It thrashed as its gills struggled to pull water. We watched as its movements became less frantic, less energetic, and finally ceased. The experiment was still a failure.

We took careful note and prepared for the next birth. Each death was devastating, but I didn't allow myself to connect our failures with any kind of human suffering. I steeled myself against pain and, carefully compartmentalized, turned to the next task. I don't think Cedric managed it very well. I found him crying a couple of times in the kitchen.

"I don't know how long I can do this," he told me.

I didn't know what to say, so I said nothing.

❧

We took no holidays and worked late most nights as well as weekends. Christmas came and went without so much as a plastic tree in the corner of the lab. I have a vague memory of green and red lights in the city, but otherwise we powered through without interruption. Our staff, very much on the outside of our work, took holidays as usual. Laurel seemed disappointed we weren't celebrating and talked about organizing a Secret Santa. The idea of going out to celebrate or trying to buy gifts for Edward, Laurel or Susan gave me heartburn. I dissuaded her, citing work pressures. I think she still got gifts for Susan and Edward, and Cedric tried to hide the silly Santa candle she got him. She was a sweet person. I was happy for Cedric to look after them, I didn't have time and they interfered with my focus.

January was hard on us. Our specimens kept dying and we didn't manage a single live birth. Something was wrong and we didn't know what. I started to question the point of it all. I tried not to bother Cedric with my doubts, since he was struggling with demons of his own, but it was obvious we were not okay. I flinched away from our dying subjects and doubled down on the next experiment. Sinking into the science had always soothed me in the past, but now it just unsettled me further. I was adrift. For his part, Cedric tried to hide his distress, but I could see it clearly – the little nervous tremors, the catch in his throat. His baking was getting obsessive. I would walk to the local grocery store a block over to get him ingredients without being asked. I knew he didn't like to go out. We clung to our routines, pretended it was work as usual.

Laurel and Edward were managing the new intakes and keeping up appearances but Cedric and my attention was elsewhere, and it showed.

They worked on client projects in a separate lab down the hall and I kept them away from the Midnight Project. If it failed, I didn't want them tainted by it. We could always bring them in later if we needed to.

Throughout this stage of our work, Mr. Sykes continued to demand weekly, sometimes daily updates. "Humanity must survive at all costs!" he ranted. "The organizations in charge – the United Nations, the national states, the European Union – just keep tightening the grip on regulations and legal frameworks. It's both too much and insufficient. Governments around the world are failing, their bureaucracy their undoing. They don't have the vision they need for progress. They can't save us!" And on and on.

"Where does he find the time?" Cedric peevishly wanted to know.

"The man's unstoppable. I don't think he even took a breath."

"You know," Cedric opined, "getting revenge on an evil conglomerate by doing a secret project for another conglomerate may not be the flex you thought it was."

I snorted. "Is that what I'm doing?"

He shook his head, suddenly serious. "This could be a monumental mistake, even worse than the last one. What do you think Sykes will do when he finds out they're monsters? That they keep dying and we don't know why?"

I didn't know, and couldn't disagree, so I just stared hard at the horizon and tried to focus on the problem at hand. To ignore the creeping sense of dread, ignore the tightness in my chest. We needed our monsters to live.

We tried to stall Sykes with vivid descriptions of our advances in bioluminescence. It wasn't real progress, though. I reached out to Greg and asked what our legal obligations were.

"Neither Surf Legacy nor Global Holdings owns Re-Gene-eration," he confirmed. "But it is clearly within the requirements of your contract to provide updates upon request."

In other words, no wiggle room at all.

"I know we're contractually bound," grumbled Cedric, "but I don't know what more we can tell him."

It was an issue. Things were proceeding along the plan we had laid out, with one critical hiccup – our petri dishes weren't producing viable life. We were doing well with introducing our cross-DNA and replicating it in our materials at a cellular level, but as we tried to grow an actual creature, we ended up with little multi-limbed toothy lumps that died within minutes, usually after we transferred them to the saltwater tanks we had installed.

They were horrifically ugly, but I suppose that was a side issue; Mr. Sykes didn't hire us to recreate beauty. Though it was not lost on me that our great hope for preserving humanity's best qualities looked like monsters out of nightmares.

"Do we dare show him our footage?"

"I think we have to."

Mr. Sykes was insistent we provide our next update in-person and dispatched his copter. I dressed up to defend our work while Cedric stayed behind to mind the shop.

Once again, I found myself on Mr. Sykes' island, in his bunker boardroom. This time, instead of confidently pitching a concept, I was defending a failing project. I walked him and a small number of his suited associates through our protocols and facilities, flicking up pictures of our work. I explained the steps we had undertaken and, finally, turned to our results.

I flashed up a 3D image of one of our failures. The video showed an undulating mass writhing in a synthetic egg. Small enough to hold with two hands, the creature had tiny eyes on either side of its head, slits for a nose and three rows of sharp teeth. It writhed and opened and closed its mouth, waving its squid-like limbs.

Our voices were audible: "Looks good, let's go for the transfer now." The creature was gently tipped into a larger tank on the side wall of the lab and immediately began frantically propelling itself around the tank as if seeking a way out.

Within minutes, it slowed, subsided and floated belly up to the top of the tank. Cedric's voice could be heard again: "Subject thirty-six, time of death . . ."

"We've learned a great deal from our early experiments," I continued. "The DNA cross with octopus, cuttlefish and lantern fish has promise, but we continue to work on our methods to generate a viable living subject.

"We're getting there," I concluded.

Mr. Sykes had been silent throughout the presentation. His suits, similarly, had no questions. They seemed cowed by the image of the dying octo-creature.

"Thank you for coming in person," Mr. Sykes said, and sent me on my way. Even the copter ride home was quiet.

The Midnight Project had survived its first real challenge, even if our specimens had not.

CHAPTER 12: CEDRIC

FADE IN

INT. RE-GENE-ERATION LAB - DAY

CEDRIC sits on a stool in the lab in front of an octopus tank. Maisie or Rex carefully pick their way up the side of the tank, suction cups on the inner sides of their tentacles visible.

> CEDRIC
> Results are coming even slower than we expected. Some days it's crippling, the stress, the anxiety. And the deaths. They are deaths, even if we don't talk about them. I mean, we're not supposed to see them as little people, they're not, they're just supposed to be failures. You know, a generic F on your report card. Bad, but not murderous bad. Not died-on-the-operating-room-table bad. This is really different from drought-resistant wheat. From tweaking people's kids' genes to make the parents happy.
>
> We've fallen into the business of breeding monsters and even worse, we're no good at it. Raina says it will come, we just need to

plough through. That we'll figure it out and
they'll live.

CEDRIC runs his fingers through his hair while nervously
staring forward.

                    CEDRIC (cont'd)
But I can't pretend that things are going
according to plan. The project is stalling -
we can't figure it out. And Raina and I, well,
we don't fail, you know? We always deliver.
But everything is stalling now, all around
the world.

It used to be we had global emergencies and
we solved them with common action and science
and effort. Acid rain in the 1980s. Climate
change in the 2020s. Forever chemicals in
the 2030s. Plastic molecule poisoning in the
2040s. We worked the problem and got through
it. The bee crisis is like that - we could
solve it with a bit of science, and a lot of
collective action.

But now it feels different. It's all happening faster and faster and our reactions are
slower and slower. Science can't keep up. So
every day is just a little worse than the
one before it. It's been like this for a long
time. But there is an end point where we
have just driven ourselves off the cliff.

I don't think this is just a problem of science – it's a political problem, a social problem, maybe an economic problem. Funny, I can talk about science all day, but I have nothing to say about politics and economics beyond "Wow, that's messed up!" You'd think a planet-killing agricultural crisis would change our outmoded systems, but no, that's not how the world works.

Of course, no one worries about the bees straight-on. For most people, planet-level concerns are just too big to face between eating breakfast and going to work each day so it just gnaws at the corners of their minds. Am I special or just kind of cursed that I can't ignore it?

CEDRIC drums his fingers against his leg.

                    CEDRIC (cont'd)
The world's in a dark place. I just wish I could sleep a bit better. The long nights make the days long too.

CEDRIC gets up to walk, realizes the camera is stationary and sits back down.

                    CEDRIC (cont'd)
I don't know exactly where the cliff is, but it's obvious we're about to drive off it. The bee catastrophe is only part of it. It isn't just one problem with one magic solution.

It's a crescendo of problems and an echo of solutions, with the solutions being less and less effective over time.

We are running out of time . . . the world, the project, us.

What do I know, though? I can't even get our sea monsters to live.

CEDRIC shrugs, shakes his head and turns off the camera.

                                        CUT TO BLACK

CHAPTER 13

Painstaking failure continued in our windowless lab, which was lined with large glass jars and containers of different sizes, and a long, lonely-looking saltwater tank filled with short-lived baby monsters. Rex and Maisie looked on without comment, but I could feel their disdain. Inside the lab, failure lurked in the dark corners. We continued to feel pressure to produce results, but we had none. We needed our little monsters to live.

Arriving early, the streets dark and cold, I wasn't even the first person there. Cedric was keeping baker's hours; warm, yummy treats coming out of the oven as the sun rose. We all coped as best we could, I suppose. I wasn't complaining.

I sipped my coffee, nibbling something with apple in it while the headlines splattered bad news all over the furniture.

Webwex and TurkDel Co. in talks to share mineral rights on Mars

Vegetable yields across Asia down more than 80 percent

Species Termination Notice: North American Blanding's turtle

"Not sure what these are, but they're really good," I told Cedric, gesturing to the treat in my hand. But Cedric wasn't just baking, he was thinking. And he was one of the best thinkers I knew.

"I have an idea," he told me. "We should try it." He wasn't talking about pastries.

Standing in the centre of the lab, we considered a row of large egg-shaped objects lined up on one side – artificial wombs. What was missing that they survived only minutes after birth?

"Okay," Cedric began. "We know that the little ones have tiny lung-like organs, and that it isn't clear what they do beyond processing oxygen from water. What if they need to breathe air, at least at the beginning? We've assumed they're aquatic, but what if they're both? What if by hurrying to put them in water we're drowning them? The different DNA combinations may be creating a fully new life form that isn't just dependent on salt water."

Too many unknowns, too many possibilities. The variables were too complex for reliable prediction, which left us with trial and error. But it was a good idea and we didn't have any others, so we tried it.

We pulled out the next egg and lined it up. We could see the pink figure under the translucent exterior, eyelids and mouth closed, a mass of curled up tentacles under a human-looking torso and head. Cedric slit the side of the egg and I reached in as the contents poured out, amniotic fluid running down my sleeves. Together we flipped the body over and stared down, willing something to be different. There was a sharp gasp as the little creature took his first breath. Then his second. Cedric and I grinned at each other, and at the little guy in our arms.

He smiled back at us, his single row of teeth sharpened to fine points, and a fin sprouting somewhat randomly from the middle of his head. His tentacles writhed and I had to adjust my grip. "Well hello, Sunshine!" I said.

Carefully supporting his head, I carried him over to the larger tank, making sure that he continued to breathe air. "Should we still put them in salt water? Will he drown?"

Cedric bit his lip. "I think they need to live in water. Let's see what he does."

Gingerly, I tipped him into the water. "C'mon, c'mon, c'mon," I muttered.

We held our breath, staring at our subject in the aquarium. The minutes ticked by and our little one was soon zipping around the tank, doing energetic somersaults and exploring his environment.

"Such a strange thing," said Cedric, "it's like having to prime a pump."

To be honest, we had no idea why this worked, but we incorporated it into our practices immediately. It had to be related to the amphibian DNA we had snuck into the mix, to try to smooth the distinction between air-based and water-based breathing.

Once they were comfortably breathing air for a few minutes, they could be safely introduced to the saltwater tank and thereafter seemed (pardon the pun) happy as clams breathing water. They would then occasionally flip themselves up to the surface and gulp air again before retreating to the bottom of the tank.

"They can breathe both air and water," observed Cedric. "Fascinating. Maybe multiple lungs for each? I'll confirm with diagnostic imaging if we don't have a subject to dissect."

We were ecstatic. Soon we had a tank full of six happy younglings.

∻

"We're making progress now," I said to Cedric one morning a short time later. "We'll be able to start using samples from the younglings. They're eating well and even growing a bit."

Cedric put his coffee down carefully. A recently discovered coffee blight was threatening supply and driving prices upward. We'd become cautious about our morning brew. Every drop had to be fully savoured with nothing wasted. Just another signpost on the road to destruction, but I couldn't help feeling this one deep in the pit of my stomach. It felt personal, unlike the headlines parading around the room:

World leaders celebrate successes and plot next steps at COP47
Webwex CEO vows to end world hunger
Hopper infestation eradicated in Montreal
UN Bee Envoy calls for solidarity in eradicating affected crops, sharing food
Species Termination Notice: Southern emperor butterfly

We ignored them and focused on the positive.

"Great that our mussel colony is taking root well in the pool too. I think things are going well," Cedric admitted.

It had taken some doing to install a system of underwater cultivation to grow a type of deep-sea clam to feed our subjects. We had used the old, cracked pool in the basement, part of the long-abandoned fitness centre – and I was pretty happy with our handiwork. Rigging a properly calibrated saltwater pool was delicate work and needed constant adjustment. Anticipating that our colony would need to eventually live in darkness, we had equipped the pool area with special blue lights. The effect was eerie, otherworldly. Our mussels were thriving and I was feeling energized.

It was a strange source of joy to get into the pool and care for the clams we were growing for the younglings. It was satisfying to snorkel into the deep end, floating and fussing over the juvenile bivalves. The water was cool and inviting, and the lighting made it feel like a midnight dip in the ocean. The world felt infinite, even within the confines of our grubby basement.

Our reports to Mr. Sykes became more interesting. I was practically giddy in my video footage introducing our latest round of data to Global Holdings:

"We're very pleased to include footage of our first live birth, a healthy male. The added step of ensuring the lungs are exposed to air in the first few minutes of life (as per our accompanying report) has provided the key to the specimens' survival. The specimens are fairly short-lived at this stage, by design. We're using a hormonal accelerant to quicken their growth so we can study adult physiology and improve the stock, which impacts their longevity and their overall viability.

"Each youngling is different, some with multiple rows of teeth, some with beaks, eyes spaced out or in the centre of their foreheads, some with no foreheads at all. They have a uniform colour to start with: a pink or dull red, lightly patterned, but they change colour easily. The texture of their skin varies from soft to a shiny, almost reflective surface, reminiscent of scales. Two have had more human features: ears and noses. Unfortunately, these two expired on their own within hours.

"We continue to catalogue and copy their genomes with harvested genetic material for future use."

I thought our little toothy monsters were adorable. I gave them cutesy names like Bozo and Snoopy and talked to them throughout the day. Each looked radically different from the others, with different numbers of teeth, placement of eyes, ears and fins. Some had no fins at all. Their skin was tough, glistened and changed colour like a mood ring depending on how happy, sad or threatened they were. They could also change colour to camouflage themselves and hide in the rocks at the bottom of the tank.

I sang "Frère Jacques" to them as I worked, and their bright eyes followed us everywhere, whether they were underwater or swimming on top of it. "Sonnez les matines," I crooned, while Cedric raised an eyebrow and tended to Rex and Maisie. The younglings continued to breathe air or water easily. We documented everything, celebrating the little wins when our younglings began eating and grew. I doted on them, finding them beautiful. I started to mourn the losses when their bodies failed them and they died.

Cedric watched me with bemusement in his eyes and perhaps a little concern. It was uncharacteristic of me, and he no doubt wondered if I was cracking up under the strain. Our work on this project was a departure – we had spent years working on crop yields and ecosystems impacts, and then, with the founding of Re-Gene-eration, we edited embryos and implanted them for clients. We followed up once the children were born, but not in regular or daily contact. So the presence in our lab of these pink (or purple or blue) monsters was a novelty. Where I was delighted, Cedric was perturbed.

His video intro for our progress report was more circumspect: "Exposure to air has ensured the immediate survival of all of the recent specimens. We have avoided any use of frog DNA to avoid hopper-like characteristics. A cross with the amphibian salamander could explain some unexpected respiratory developments. The younglings appear to have expanded respiratory capacity and can process oxygen from either air or seawater. Activating the lungs appears to be essential to their survival.

"A more stable type is beginning to emerge in our specimens. As you can see in the attached video and still photos, our current specimens have human-like heads, with central eyes, no noses, mouths on humanoid faces and gills on the sides of their necks. Most have mouths in the centre of their lower face, though a few have beaks. They breathe out of their mouths when out of the water. Three have fins and all have at least eight tentacles, two tiny ones coming from the sides of their heads like wispy bangs, and two where arms would be on humans. Four tentacles stem from the bottom of their torsos."

We proudly included more detailed imagery and breathed a sigh of relief.

ৡৡ

Of course, Bozo and Snoopy and those who came after were not human children, and the younglings were not all sweetness and light. I enjoyed singing to them, but they shared no particular opinion of my voice, or the affection it contained. They were very much other than human.

This became apparent within days of the first live subjects being put in the tank. We pulled each specimen out of the tank daily to weigh and measure them and examine their features. They were different sizes according to their ages – about the size of a human newborn for the newly hatched, up to the size of a large raccoon. Since they were each different, it was important to document each one, and we took skin and cell samples to replicate their unique genetic codes. One or two would welcome the attention, but mostly they hid in the shadows of the tank at the bottom, where we had scattered some large rocks. We had a net and an animal noose to scoop them up and they sometimes resisted bitterly. As they grew, this routine became more challenging.

What I saw at first as feisty behaviour was soon revealed to be blatant aggression. One day we came into the lab and found one of the younglings floating face down at the top of the tank. Vicious tooth marks told a story. But was the story one of territory, hunger or unbridled malice?

Cedric fished out the remains with a net, shaking his head. "I don't think we're hitting the right balance yet. They don't seem human, do they?"

"I think it's too early to tell, Ceddy. They're still infants, right?"

"Maybe." He deposited the contents of his net in the biowaste container. "Or we could be on the wrong track entirely."

I peered into the tank at the remaining specimens. "Well, if we leave them together and they kill each other, I guess that'll be one way to decide." I didn't have to like it, though.

We subdivided the tank and tried to isolate the individuals we thought were responsible but the younglings could easily flip from one subdivision to the other. Another youngling was found floating on the surface and we contemplated installing more tanks that would be completely separate. We locked the top of the tanks when we were not in the room, perhaps multiple locked tanks would keep them safe from each other?

We seemed a long way away from Mr. Sykes' ideal vision of harmonious and cultured humans free from violence living under the sea. I couldn't help it, I worried about the contract. I carefully selected my facts for the updates and tried to isolate the motives for the fratricide. Was there not enough space? Was the food insufficient? Was there something more at play? Was there a genetic defect?

We documented the deaths and sent our reports to Mr. Sykes. His response was swift: a long and winding monologue about the intrinsic pugnacious energy of human beings and how this is integral but needs to be controlled by society. "It is natural for humans to be forceful, action-oriented. A tendency to the bellicose is normal but humans in their hearts are not murderers, not abusers. The fire that burns within must be tamed by ties of affection, morality. They need society, but society free of corruption and greed."

At the end of his rambling lecture, he gave very clear direction: "If you can't achieve that with your current specimens, start over."

Should we start again? Were they too aggressive? Our task was to create a better human, not a craven one with gills. We monitored them closely, tried to figure out the dynamic. How could we fix this? Could it be fixed?

Cedric and I debated it, then decided not to separate them further. If they were too aggressive and killed each other, we would start over with the next group, maybe switch out the salamander DNA. I was uneasy with our decision, though, and found myself peering into the dark crevices at the bottom of the tank at all hours. Late into the evening, I would shine the little blue light into the rocks, trying to see them where they hid, trying to will them to pacificism. The section of the lab where the tank rested was kept mostly in darkness. Usually, the bright lights at the far end of the room illuminated everything we needed, but now I found myself squinting and trying to see movement in the shadows. Once I fell asleep at the foot of the tank on the floor. Cedric brought me my coffee there the next morning, wordless concern emanating from the gesture. Through the day, there was no sign of anything amiss. They did little swim sprints back and forth, sometimes coming over to the glass and putting a tentacle out to me, then darting away.

I noticed one youngling that seemed to be taking charge. She was the same size as the other older ones, not aggressive but with a quietly domineering style that put the others in their place. We watched her as she intervened in little disputes and sent the aggressors to corners or even stared them into hiding. The smaller ones started looking to her for guidance or protection. I can't say that our specimens were peaceful or gentle, but a layer of order seemed to be developing that prevented outright murder. Could they be organizing themselves into a society? Or a family? The one youngling did seem to police the others.

After a few days and late nights peering through the glass I wasn't any wiser, though I found myself drifting off during the day. Exhausted, I had done nothing at all to fix the situation.

While I couldn't say I'd contributed to a solution, by week's end, it was clear that the killings had stopped of their own accord.

CHAPTER 14: ETHEL

Warm water, filtered light and soft voices.

Feelings of peace and sensations of floating.

A face with funny double eyes, slurred sounds without meaning but reassuring.

A growing awareness, of life, of a world. All fuzzy still. Floating – and it fills me with joy.

I watch them and listen, understanding nothing.

Warm affinity. Love? I feel surrounded and buoyed, safe. I keep listening.

Soothing sounds, notes rising and falling. Soft background music and low, confident voices.

Then the air, cold and shocking. I'm being handled. I flinch.

The warm touch of the fuzzy figures, air sounds, followed by a sharp prick as something is attached to my arm. More air sounds from the figures.

Then water, joyous and surrounding me. Sharper images, sharper sounds. I see, sense the others. I am home.

∼

Not all of my siblings are full of love like me. They do not surround and protect, they bite. We have sharp teeth.

I hide.

In hiding I join the others deep in the crevices.

We are together. We are one. And slowly I feel I have purpose. I protect.

❧

I don't like the biting. I bite back and I am safe but the others keep hiding and then one doesn't hide well enough. I don't understand at first how the bright shining one I hid with is now floating, immobile on the surface.

I don't understand everything, but I know it's the sharp teeth that are at fault. A spurt of anger, a flash of protective rage. My teeth this time. A bully retreats, harmony restored.

No more floating. We need to be one, we need to be united.

CHAPTER 15

Cedric peered into the tank. "There were six last night and there are six this morning. None floating. All good."

I joined him by the side of the tank, smiling. "Fascinating. We'll try to draw blood today, run a few panels?" Cedric nodded and grabbed a net. Pulling out the nearest specimen, I helped him wrestle it onto a table and held it still while he took a sample. We weighed and measured it, all while fighting to keep the small raccoon-sized thing from escaping. It fought bitterly. The specimen was clearly not happy with us and went back in the water as soon as it could.

We entered the information in the log and reviewed the last few days' worth of data. "They're growing fast," Cedric noted. "The accelerant is working."

"Yes, we'll need to get the timing right for stopping that, otherwise we'll end up with geriatric specimens before we have a critical mass."

"Have you watched Sykes' weekly rant yet?"

"I was going to do that today."

"Yeah, once we're finished up here."

I walked over to the tank and tried to spot Ethel (yes, I had named them all). I thought it was her in the lower back corner, camouflaging. I tapped softly on the glass and she noticed me, shooting up to the surface.

Her eyes were grey-green with large black pupils. Her face looked oddly human, with single tendrils like locks of hair lining each side of her face. Her nose was more of a suggestion than a feature, she appeared to breathe air through her mouth. The scans we did indicated lungs, or something close to them. The rest of her body seemed to alter to suit her mood or her purposes. When she was swimming, she looked more like an octopus, propelling herself around the tank and fitting into whatever dark corner appealed to her, her colour shifting. When she was out of the water, she mimicked us, with shoulders and a neck, reaching out tentacles like arms and legs. She was fascinating. She was new.

CHAPTER 16: ETHEL

Through the water and the glass, the figures are vague and insubstantial, so I pull myself out and gaze at them with all of us in the open air. I squeeze myself with contentment and try to work my face into an expression like the ones they use. Lips stretched up and to the sides, eyes crinkling slightly. I like them. We make faces at each other and they give me fish.

The funny sounds they make at each other have meaning. They are sharing thoughts. I listen closely, trying to decipher their intent, their sharing.

Slowly I begin to understand. We smile at each other. Delight. Contentment.

CHAPTER 17

The younglings were tagged and kept together in a giant tank along a wall in the main lab. We equipped it with low light and provided parts of the tank that were in darkness to protect their eyes. This had the disadvantage that we couldn't see all parts of their environment and they could hide from us. They usually emerged at the top of the tank when we fed them, but some liked to live at the very bottom in the darkest corner.

I almost missed a pivotal moment in our work. It started with a soft sound, like moaning wind. I scarcely noticed. Then, a more forceful "Helll-looo!"

I was startled. Cedric and I exchanged glances. "Did you . . . ?" he trailed off. I nodded.

We turned and looked at the large tank of younglings on the wall. Subject 102 had propped itself up on the edge, pushing the top of the tank open. "Hello," she said insistently.

I smiled, a sliver of fear bolting through me. "Hello," I replied.

"Hello," said Cedric softly.

The specimen smiled, and a more human smile I have never seen. She was, in that moment, all radiance and triumph. She flipped back into the tank and somersaulted with happiness.

Then she swam to the bottom, as if shy.

"Well, would you look at that," said Cedric, his mouth open.

"I guess we knew eventually that would happen, right?"

Cedric glanced at me, his eyes big. "Yes, but I thought we would need to teach them. I thought it would be the last thing to happen." He shook his head. "Wow. A little more interesting than making more resilient wheat, eh?"

"Damn," I said, my voice filled with awe and astonishment.

When we returned to our work, it was with even greater attention. The humanity was starting to show in our subjects and we would need to have more care in how we moved forward.

≈

The next day, our talking subject was at the top of the tank waiting for us when we arrived. "Hello!" she said confidently.

I walked over, extending an arm, trying to contain my excitement. She reached out delicately and touched my shaking hand with a flexible arm covered in suckers, ending in an array of tentacles that looked uncannily like a boneless human hand. "Hello there!" I said softly. "And how are you today?"

She smiled and pulled on my arm, leveraging herself over the side of the tank with a tentacle extending from her midriff. She had two longer muscular tentacles positioned as if they were legs that she used to grip the side of the tank as she manoeuvred the rest of her body to balance along the top edge. Her grey-green eyes telescoped around the room, blinking occasionally. The two small, delicate-looking tentacles framing her face like bangs waved like seaweed in a current, accentuating her moods.

"Hungry," she whispered, eyeing a bucket of fish in the corner. I brought the bucket over, repeating the words "food" and "fish" as she ate. "Fo-od," she tried, "fi-ish."

"Incredible," whispered Cedric behind me. He picked up a fish and slowly held it out to her, glancing at me in near disbelief. She took her fish and ate it. I noted the adaptation from the octopus, midway between human and cephalopod. Cedric flicked on the video recorder. In that moment, she flinched and tucked under the water, retreating with her fish.

Cedric and I stared at each other. I exhaled slowly. "She really talks."

"Are they all like that, do you think? Or is she special?"

We pulled her genomic sample and got to work trying to figure out if she was an outlier or if all our specimens might be sentient, capable of speech.

"We're getting there!" I said excitedly, punching Cedric's arm. "We're getting there!"

CHAPTER 18: ETHEL

I love the sharp, sweet air. I can hear the air people better that way.

In darkness I practise making air noise, and sometimes my siblings join me. Oh, the chorus of our voices together in the night! And our sounds are even more beautiful underwater. We are strong and we are together. We are united.

I make air noises to connect with the funny air people. People like my family, hidden in the rocks, but different. I don't know how, but I'm so curious to find out. Their sounds are resolving into bite-sized meaning, puzzle pieces. The air words are like rocks to pile up, or like the games Funny Eyes gives us to pass the time. And I am solving the puzzle and building a structure.

I try making some sounds at them and they respond. Delight! The puzzle pieces fit into a comprehensible whole. Words. Sentences. Speech. I'm learning and so are they. Talking, they call it. And we do, too, under the water. We talk too, but the air people don't know or understand us. I don't have the air words to explain.

Day by day, I teach them to understand me. I learn more of their language, but they do not learn mine. I try to teach my siblings the air people speech, but they are a little slower. It does not come naturally to all of them. What does come is our own way of communicating. This is done with the water that flows around and through us, to make sounds, and then we complement the sounds with the tones of our skin and our facial gestures. Even the little tentacles at the sides of our heads convey meaning. It feels much more natural and joyful to communicate like this, but I am still fascinated by the air people and want to be able to talk to them too.

I know they are not like us, the air people, but I feel an affinity toward them. Happiness and joy bubbles up around them. And fish. I trust them. Our world inside the tank is small and familiar. Air family and water family, together and apart. Love, contentment.

CHAPTER 19

Now we rushed through breakfast to get to the lab. Our little charges were growing, and one was talking.

"Hullllllooo," Ethel said as we entered and turned on the lights. I extended my arm and she took it like a handshake, winding a tentacle around my wrist. "Fiisssss?" she tried, clearly having trouble with the "sh" sound. Cedric brought her a morsel out of the fridge, and we watched her eat it.

"Aren't you a beauty?" I crooned. She smiled, pointed teeth peeking out.

Our gregarious youngling was soon popping her head out of the tank throughout the day, whenever she thought she could get our attention. Her vocabulary was expanding: In the beginning, it was clear she was a child, with childish speech. She practised words and watched us closely while we talked to her, trying to help her learn. She kept scrunching her very malleable torso into an imitation of a neck and shoulders, and her elastic face squished into a semblance of human. Her trailing tentacles could be positioned to look like arms and legs when she imitated us.

I was shocked at how quickly she began turning words into sentences. She had a curiosity that seemed unquenchable, and a ferocious intelligence. It took only weeks for her baby talk to graduate to full discussions. In the meantime, we treated her as our child, our favourite of all of them. I was well on the way to being in love with little Ethel. She had a childlike smile that made you feel like you were the centre of her universe, and she had a habit of wrapping one of her "arm" tentacles around me when she was talking or interested in something I was doing, which I found adorable. The changing hue of her skin could signal a sudden mood shift as readily as her rapid retreat into the tank. She didn't cuddle like our octopus Maisie.

Rather, she communicated using her whole body. Speaking words with her mouth seemed like just part of a larger effort of expression.

We documented as much as we could, finally having something positive to report to our benefactor. I felt desperate months of failure turn to elation. For the first time since we had begun, even Cedric agreed that this might just work, that our project might succeed.

In the early days we treated her a bit like Rex and Maisie, but it soon became apparent that she was no one's pet. Her communication skills grew exponentially and she was soon asking questions about everything – all our equipment, what we did throughout the day, how the tank worked. She was a quick study. I seldom heard her ask the same question twice.

We had established that our subjects could breathe air, as well as water. They all shared this feature. While they could survive outside the tank, only the one seemed willing to venture out, and we tried to take advantage of the times she would settle herself on the observation deck and try to talk to us. Her skin was tough and dappled in some places. I was fascinated by its shifting hues. Once she camouflaged herself to look exactly like the metallic deck she was perched on; a remarkable feat that gave Cedric a jump scare when he turned around and caught sight of her. I'm not sure exactly why our younglings disconcerted Cedric so much – maybe he had a childhood fear of snakes or eels. He had worked on ocean ecosystems before though, why would he do that if it frightened him?

We told her about microscopes and petri dishes and beakers. It was a little harder to explain molecules and genetics, so we mainly talked about our desire to make the colony healthy and happy. She wanted to know why we didn't have tentacles and why we didn't live in the water. I tried to explain, but it was a lot easier to talk about molecules. "We're humans," I told her.

"Humans are different from you. We live in the air, we have cities, we have society." I clearly lost her at "society," but she was listening intently. "I mean, you're close to human, just . . . different. We're all people, though." I wasn't sure about that, but I felt like I needed to make a bridge for the bright young thing with human eyes drinking in every word. "It's just we have different groups. Humans are one group."

"But you're in my group," she replied.

"Yes, of course, but that's because . . ." Oh boy, how to explain? "We're your parents," I said finally. "We're connected. We're family."

I felt I had just told a lie, a fundamental one, but it *was* true, wasn't it? I mean Cedric didn't want to be related to our little sea monsters, but it was one interpretation of things. The deeper truth was that I didn't want to admit what they were. What we were.

I wasn't sure what I was talking about and what she needed to hear, but I could see she needed answers. She thought about this, and finally flipped back into the tank instead of replying.

We could soon read her moods not only through her skin colour but through her facial expressions. She smiled when she was relaxed and happy, and her eyes narrowed when she was confused or angry. The two short tentacles at her temples swayed gently when she was curious or engaged, whipped around when she became agitated. There was a clear pattern of twitchy body language that usually preceded her flight back to the tank when she got nervous or bored. Once in water, she was completely graceful. Like the octopus or squid, the younglings powered around the tank with a special form of jet propulsion. They could suck salt water into a small cavity on their backs and push it out so quickly that it propelled them forward with incredible speed.

Out of the water, our subjects were shyer, to put it mildly. We did our best to engage each of them, but some clearly preferred hiding at the bottom of the tank. As they grew, this presented a challenge to our monitoring efforts. What should have been the time for us to document our experiment in minute detail was turning into a growing relationship with just the most curious specimen. The main group tended to hide at the bottom of the tank.

We could pull them out and physically examine them (and did) but this was usually a fairly disagreeable procedure, akin to catching a fish with a net and then hauling it out. Once they were out, they disliked being in the open air and tended to fight to go back to the tank. They were growing quickly and while not quite as large as a human, they were about the size of a large dog. When they thrashed, they were dangerous. Cedric tried to manage them in the net, but they could be very single-minded in their goal to get back to the bottom of the tank.

One time, one of the males, in a frantic effort to avoid having blood drawn, pushed past us and hauled himself up the side of the tank. Cedric grabbed him just as he was hurling himself back into the water and was thrown off balance, dangling half in and half out of the tank. For an awful second, Cedric was suspended upside down, his head fully underwater. I wrenched him back by the collar, pulling him out of the tank while the subject fled to the bottom, still tangled in the net.

I screamed and called for help as Cedric rolled over on the floor, coughing and sputtering. Laurel was first on the scene, but she was hardly any help. She stood over Cedric's prone body unsure what to do. Edward, in the computer lab with headphones on, never heard my screams at all. Susan arrived next, the all-efficient first responder. She helped him up, examined him, and advised us to go to the hospital to check out his lungs, which had taken on some salt water.

Wheezing and coughing, Cedric waved her off, and I reluctantly agreed. The hospital was a dank and dismal place, its ER overrun with nasty, bloody, life-threatening crises. It was not where we wanted to spend the next three days. We'd watch him carefully at the lab.

Once the initial panic had passed, I noticed Laurel and Susan discreetly checking out the lab. It was the first time they'd laid eyes on it since our experiments had begun in earnest. Thankfully, all our subjects had hidden themselves among the rocks. The one tangled in the net had frozen in place and was camouflaging so effectively that I don't think they saw him. They spotted rows of eggs along one wall, though, which was enough for their eyes to widen. I ushered them out as quickly as I could.

I decided we needed a change. We were not exactly winning friends with our current approach and it was dangerous – to us and to them. They were at least partially human, and developing at an accelerated rate, so perhaps they were amenable to reason. I asked Ethel to talk to them, to explain that we were keeping them healthy and were not a threat. We worked gently with the timid subjects and took more time to put them at ease. Days passed. We relied more and more on Ethel to translate our instructions and intentions. She took to this role with vigour and enthusiasm, and our body of data continued to grow.

CHAPTER 20

Ethel wanted to know everything. She was fascinated by the FlickFilms we occasionally showed her, so we started projecting underwater ocean views when we were not there. Cedric played jazz or classical music in the background most days as we worked, and she had endless questions about the music, where it came from, even the instruments that made those sounds.

At this stage, we had six almost full-grown specimens and ten younger ones, with more on the way. We gave them names like Midge and Fred and Buffy. They began to emerge periodically from the water to "shake hands," their suckers gentle and respectful. They deferred to Ethel. As the younglings became more engaged, I turned on the holographic displays of ocean documentaries to occupy them while we ran simulations and tested cells and DNA. They were particularly interested in one reef documentary, so much so that they did somersaults in the tank whenever I played it for them.

In the interest of seeing how they would react to cultural things, I started to play a wider variety of FlickFilms. Ethel and two others loved period dramas from the old United Kingdom, another was obsessed with Chinese opera. They would balance on the edge of the tank while they watched, fascinated, or pull themselves onto the observation deck beside the tank.

Soon, they each discovered favourites and would request them. So far, only Ethel could speak, but the others clearly understood us and had ways of making themselves understood in turn by gestures or subtle changes in skin colour. When one was poised on the edge of the tank, ready to view a show, they could quite clearly indicate if I'd guessed the right program or if they were unhappy and wanted me to guess again. One even squirted salt water onto the floor when they became frustrated with their inability to communicate.

One morning as I was greeting Ethel, she asked, "What does this word 'Ethel' mean?"

"It's your name, it's what we call you."

"Just me?" she asked. I nodded.

She looked bemused, with a little flash of blue followed by yellow, then flipped back into her tank. We didn't hear any more about names for a while. Then a few days later, she flipped herself out of the tank and did a funny crab walk over to Cedric. Wrapping her tentacles around his leg, she asked what his name was. He told her, and she turned to me and asked the same thing.

"Why do you do this?" she asked. "What are they for?"

"Names?" I replied. "They're kind of an identity, a unique way of referring to someone so everyone knows who you mean."

"How do you decide what they're named?"

I looked at Cedric, who jumped in. "Well, we just pick a name to fit the . . . person, er, you, er . . ." He trailed off – why was this so difficult?

"We chose your names because we liked the names, or the sounds, or, well, anything like that."

She looked at us seriously, then unpeeled herself from Cedric's leg, stumped back to the tank, climbed up the smooth side and flipped into the water like an Olympic diver.

She was like I imagined a young child would be, always asking questions, pushing the boundaries of what she knew. Always wanting to know more. I didn't always know the answers – in fact, I rarely had any answers now. And she was growing fast. Her intellect was expanding by leaps and bounds. She wanted to know everything, and when we had exhausted what Cedric and I knew, she invented things, tested them, and wanted us to tell her more. It was hard, I didn't have the knack for telling bedtime stories.

They all adored FlickFilms so we kept them on repeat. On occasion, one would flip out of the tank and come over and try to change the channel using the computer terminal. Cedric would gently swat them back and tell them they couldn't touch it. They would then wrap around him in what I can only guess was a joke, or a gesture of affection. He didn't like it, would peel them off and carry them back to the tank.

They were growing fast, even now that we had stopped accelerating them. One day, when Ethel had gotten no satisfaction to her questions about what the glass in the tank was made of, and what the floor tiles were made of, I called her over to me.

"You know Ethel isn't really my name," she said. "It isn't what I call myself."

"Huh?"

"My siblings call me a different name. I have two – one for underwater and one for air."

I was briefly taken aback. "So you aren't Ethel?"

"No."

"Then what is your name?"

"I am Coralie when I'm in the air. You wouldn't understand my underwater name."

"Well, okay. I guess Ethel wasn't really a good name."

"It just isn't mine. We all have names, you know." I asked what the others were called, but she ignored me. I wasn't quite sure why she was annoyed but I knew she was long before she retreated to the bottom of the tank and settled herself into one of the cave crevices she preferred.

The next day, she shared more of their names. She pointed to each of her similarly aged companions and named them: Mazu, Delmar, Finn, River, Pearl. I didn't know what to say. The one who loved Chinese opera was named Mazu, after the Chinese goddess of the sea. Did they name themselves, or each other? I asked, but Coralie did not deign to answer.

"Are those better names?" I asked tentatively.

"Those are our names," Coralie responded. "We've named our group, too."

"What did you name your group?"

"The Ceph. It's short for 'cephalopod' but better." She didn't wait for a reaction but flipped back into the tank.

The conversation was over and we started using the names they had chosen for themselves.

Our new rhythm with the younglings was much more active and interesting than our beaker and petri dish days, although the regular lab work continued. We had new births that we tipped into the tank after exposing them to air and taking their measurements. Occasionally a youngling would get curious and slop out of the tank, pulling themselves along the floor or even tiptoeing on their tentacles to get a better look at something. Our days were filled with these cephalopod toddlers. At night and when we were not there, we started locking the tank's lid. I feared for them if they broke out and couldn't get back in the water. Cedric, of course, feared different things, but I couldn't really do much about his anxiety.

As winter gave way to a tentative, ugly spring, Cedric spent more time in his greenhouse on the roof. He quietly populated it with a variety of plants – some useful, some heirloom plants close to extinction. We soon had a healthy crop of mint and other herbs, and some grasses and flowers. He even tried his hand at vegetables and took great pride in tomatoes, green peppers and wickedly hot chili peppers.

While Cedric liked to go up on the roof to garden, I liked to go up there to look out over the silhouette of Long Harbour. I would help him half-heartedly, mainly to keep him company. We had set up a table and chairs, with an umbrella for the sun. Some evenings I would sit quietly, watching the sun go down in the west, its orange and pink rays illuminating the ugly city, turning it golden and beautiful. To the east, we could see the ocean, encroaching on the streets along the old coastline. Buildings that had been shiny multistory offices poked out from the waves, emerging at low tide to reveal how much they leaned and crumbled. Some were still inhabited by people, who clung to their real estate and used boats and sometimes even rope bridges to live on the upper floors. Other structures had been completely claimed by the sea, with seagulls nesting in ruined corners, a few other sturdy species of coastal life moving in. The old pier was long gone, but its skeletal remains could be glimpsed at low tide at times. The world was trying hard to adapt, and I loved to watch it as the sky darkened.

The world was winding down, but there were still amazing sunsets, and now we had the Ceph to fill our days.

CHAPTER 21: CORALIE

It is awkward to correct them, but I feel they really need to know our names, who we are. It is also awkward not to explain how we named ourselves; I feel an urge to conceal. It is an absolute instinct that causes my skin to ripple and makes me want to hide away in a crevice. Our nighttime forays now include using the computer to research topics of interest. It is a simple matter to repeat the things Cedric and Raina do to make it come alive. And the wonders it shares! I've been watching FlickFilms and listening to descriptions online of the sea. We picked these names from those experiences, helped along by an audio description of how parents name their babies, and lists of possible names.

We don't need to decipher the squiggles and lines on the computer screen or paper to make up words. I can just speak at the computer, and it shows us things.

It's Pearl who first wants to search "ocean-themed baby names." This uncovers a blog on the subject and soon we have a long list of possible monikers.

We like our new names and use them among ourselves, though the air speech versions sound different underwater. I feel better when Raina and Cedric start using them too. Like we are family that understands each other. My siblings aren't as comfortable in the air as I am, aren't as confident. Everyone has their talents, their interests, but I'm closest to Raina and Cedric, fastest at using air speech.

Inside our tank, everything is clear, safe, predictable. Whenever we are hungry, food appears. A good life, and we are happy enough. But we are hungry for more, and that means the shadow world. Beyond the glass, everything is hazier. The pretty pictures that Cedric and Raina make dance are lovely, ethereal but indistinct. Even sounds are muffled through the glass and we have to pull ourselves up to the top and lean out to properly see and hear what is happening.

The shadow world feels dangerous and exciting. I wonder what Raina and Cedric are always doing at their computers or peering at in their machines.

I am fascinated by that airy shadow world.

My siblings still can't speak air people words well, but they are understanding more and more.

At a certain point it was not enough to sit on the lip of the tank and watch videos. At night, we figured out how to unlock the top of the tank and venture out on our own. It isn't difficult to slide the tip of a tentacle under the lid and pop the mechanism open.

It started with Delmar, who is particularly bold. He wanted to look into the objects that fascinate Raina and Cedric so much. One night he launched himself out of the tank, landed neatly on a table beside it and pulled himself over to the lab's main desk. He manoeuvred himself upright to peer down into what we have heard them call "microscopes."

"Nothing!" He expressed his frustration with a subtle change in skin colour. "I think I need one of the little squares." He looked around but couldn't see any. His tentacles felt for objects on the table but nothing was there.

Finally, he tired of the sport and came back to the tank. This was the first of many nighttime forays around the lab. We get better and better at reviewing our parents' work. I don't know if they know the degree to which we are exploring the lab. The fact it is locked from the outside prevents us from going farther, so we spend our time teaching ourselves about the things in the shadow world we can touch and feel.

CHAPTER 22: CEDRIC

FADE IN

INT. INTAKE ROOM - DAY

CEDRIC sits on the intake couch next to the window, looking directly into the camera.

> CEDRIC
>
> It's one thing to imagine that you're creating a hybrid human, it's quite another to be faced with something so alien and yet so familiar. The younglings are vibrant - they are constantly learning and doing and growing. Some days it's hard to keep up with them, to keep them occupied, even while we're trying to solve the ongoing challenges of the project - to ensure that they can survive. It's like trying to do science with a baby squid climbing your leg, or a human toddler pulling at your hand. I find it disturbing and uncanny. It's funny, really. I have a bit of distaste for slimy things. Oceanic creatures have always fascinated me but probably because they've always frightened me too. I've been trying to overcome my visceral reaction by spending time with Rex and Maisie, the two-spot octopuses. I've

become quite attached to those two. I think
I'm making great progress on that front.

But Rex and Maisie are clearly octopus. And
nothing to do with human.

Our friendly youngling freaks me out when I
get little glimpses of the human part inside. Humans aren't all good, you know? I'm
not sure what Mr. Sykes is after is possible
- we might be able to make humans who can
live at the bottom of the sea but that may
not make them . . . better. Better people,
I mean. I've always had a fear of snakes,
and there is something eel-like about them,
something sinuous and unpredictable. Also,
all the genomic crosses we are doing are
essentially creatures of the deep, fascinating but horrifying. I need to overcome
my prejudice, not only to handle the Ceph,
but to recognize their humanity and embrace
their difference. Over time, my unease is
developing into a settled familiarity and
a deep affection. But they still startle me
sometimes.

CEDRIC suppresses a shudder.

                    CEDRIC (cont'd)
At times, it's all just a little too overwhelming. I find the only thing that really
soothes me is the greenhouse. I love making
little plants grow, taking them from seed

to seedling, seedling to mature plant, then harvesting something good in the world. It's so uncomplicated. So satisfying. No playing God, trying to wrestle Mother Nature into a ghoulish new shape, just nurturing what's already here in the natural world. Being a shepherd, a protector.

Maybe being a protector makes me worry incessantly about security. I'm nervous about the biosecurity protocols, the building security. Are intruders going to get in? Are the Ceph going to get out? Is a stray bacterium going to send us back to square one? Can Sykes' people be trusted? Ever since the hopper attack, I've been looking behind me, waiting for the next jump scare. It makes it hard to sleep, you know?

CEDRIC gets up and walks around, as if he is going to say more, then shakes his head and turns off the camera.

                                        CUT TO BLACK

CHAPTER 23

A sputtering spring coupled with the success of our younglings gave me a sneaking sensation of hope I tried to quell. When I wasn't at the lab, I was at my little house in the hills. As the slight winter snow receded, the rains stopped and fog rolled in from the coast. I puttered around the flowers and plants in my yard, manually pollinating what I could. The usual reassuring buzz of bees was absent. It was obvious just looking down the hill that it was a tougher season than normal. All around the concrete edges of the city, the green space was patchy and brown, except for little squares of cultivation where people like me were caring for their tiny patches.

Some evenings, I sat out on the patio, watching the copters flit over the city like brightly lit mosquitoes and the land-bound public shuttles creak ponderously through the streets below them. Rolling brownouts darkened the parts of the city without electric generators while lights flickered sporadically across the rest. A steady hum meant the city was trying to pull through.

I watched for the birds to return from down south and noticed when they were late or failed to arrive at all. I set up bird feeders and put out water, and hoped, as best I could. I made note of the birds that came to visit and made guesses about the viability of migratory paths. A small brown thrush made a nest and for weeks I felt a piece of despair lift when I watched her go about her business. I framed a photo of her and put it in my hallway as a talisman.

In spite of the growing heat and the sunshine, I felt they were dark days. After work I would sit outside and listen to faint crickets and night noises and wonder how much time we had. The city was already like a dry sauna even as spring turned to summer.

When the day cooled, before I went home, Cedric and I would sit out on our laboratory patio on the roof and talk. Not only was Cedric's rooftop greenhouse growing all sorts of things, he had expanded and now had most the roof under cultivation, covered in raised beds nestled among the solar panels. He liked to talk about how his vegetables were doing.

ஃ

One morning, I arrived and Cedric was already in the kitchen puttering around. The aroma of baking scones filled my nostrils. He wordlessly poured a coffee and handed it to me.

Headlines flashed the day's new torments: Two conglomerates were dangerously close to battling in space for control of a satellite network. This had happened the year before, and even though the combat had been carried out by drones, there had been literal fallout, with space debris hitting Earth. There were also a few extinction alerts, and this morning, the promise of a special report on the rise of a new variant of Ebola in Africa. The headlines suppressed whatever optimism I'd arrived with. I shook my head, irritated.

"Nothing new under the sun," said Cedric.

I bit into my scone and tried to ignore the headlines paused on Cedric's forehead. There was a banging sound from down the corridor. We looked at each other and Cedric shrugged.

"They make noise like that all night," he said.

"You slept over again?"

He didn't answer. I suppose I needed to give up the charade that he wasn't living here, but I still tried to play the part. I didn't ask directly, but I wanted him to talk about it. I worried about him.

"Hmmm." Cedric's mouth was full. "I checked on them a few times, but they were all snug in the tank. What do you think they're doing?"

I shrugged. "We better find out. I hope they aren't hurting themselves. Sounds like the lock is holding on the lab, anyway. Do you think they can unlock the top of the tank?"

Cedric shrugged. "Maybe. They're getting smarter and a little bored, I think. Shall we go see?"

"Is that Tchaikovsky I hear?"

We walked down the hallway and unlocked the door. A glimmer of movement was followed by two splashes. The top of the tank banged and there was a click as the lock snapped into place. A colourful documentary about a ballet school floated in the middle of the room.

"Well, would you look at that."

Coralie swam slowly to the top of the tank, a study in casual sleepiness. "Oh hello," she said, patiently waiting for us to unlock the top of the tank. "You're in early." She was practically yawning and stretching, not that the Ceph did that. Her colour was a vibrant pink, different from the sleepy cream colour they were when they first woke up.

I inspected the mechanism for damage. How had they managed to unlock it from the inside? I didn't notice anything different, but it was clear they had mastered it.

"Ballet, eh?" said Cedric.

Coralie looked sideways. The FlickFilm was still playing. I recognized the piece – it was a National Ballet performance of *Swan Lake*. "So gangly, with those funny legs," she said. "It's fascinating what you consider beautiful. But we like the music. And the story is fun. So much striving."

I didn't know how to answer. Coralie was learning much faster than a human child, and she was bringing her own unique perspective to things. I was fascinated by how well she could articulate her thinking. Cedric turned off the performance.

"I studied ballet as a child," I said.

She wanted to know more so I told her. From when I was eight to about twelve years old, I had gone to the ballet school down the street from my house. My parents both worked until late – it was a way to keep me occupied. An instructor would line us all up at the barre and take us through warm-ups, where we would go through the different positions while a gentle young man played piano for us. We stretched, did pliés and port de bras. We practised leaps and spins, fouettés and jetés, pirouettes.

I loved it. Every year we put on a little show for our parents while dressed in bright costumes, and they treated us like we were prima ballerinas on opening night, giving us flowers and taking pictures. My mother handing me flowers was one of my favourite memories.

Coralie kept asking questions. She had deftly turned the conversation away from how they had gotten out of the tank. I continued talking about my childhood instead of insisting on the details of their nighttime escape. I didn't really want to know, although I should have been more concerned about their growing skill in this area.

☙

Our subjects became something more. Each one had a distinct look, but it was more than that. They also had distinct personalities. When I wasn't working, I would sit in front of the big tank, watching them. I'd watch the younger ones playing as the dappled bigger one with wider set eyes, no nose and two delicate ears gave chase and did something to them that really looked like tickling. River was the larger Ceph's name, I recalled. From the other side of the glass, I witnessed their movements, their interactions, and found myself grinning with sheer delight. Another one, that Coralie called Delmar, piled rocks one on top of the other and devised better and better ways to stack them.

"Don't they just make you swoon, Ceddy?" I gushed, glued to the glass as they did somersaults for my amusement. "We've done it, we've really done it!"

It was the pinnacle of all my professional achievements. We had set out to do something nearly impossible and had succeeded beyond our expectations. They were marvels, and I was their creator. I felt the weight of past failures slough off. The only downside was that I couldn't share it – there was no paper I was allowed to publish, no conference talks or book deals. No one would ever know the genius thing we'd accomplished. But Cedric and I knew, and for now, that was more than enough.

Coralie spent the most time "up top" talking to us. She was interested in everything. As she led conversations, I noticed that the other adults would pop out from time to time to listen and would occasionally try to speak as well. They were trying to mimic what we did and said, even how we laughed, although they clearly didn't have the physiology for it – all that came out was a whistling sound as they smiled wide. When they showed their sharp teeth, it was more than a little unnerving.

"Raina, I don't understand, why are the lights blue?"

"Raina, you and Cedric have eyes, nose, mouth that look the same, why are we different from each other? Why are you and Cedric different colours, is it like us?"

"Raina, how do you make the FlickFilms start?"

"Raina, where do you go when you aren't here?"

It was hard to keep up with Coralie's steady patter of questions, but I did my best and felt that each conversation was bringing us a little closer together.

We shifted our protocols up a level in terms of protections for the younglings. We had to treat each embryo now as a potential person and take care so they could thrive as much as possible. Technically, those protections had always been in place, but you hardened your heart when the cells and then the subjects kept dying. We had stopped accelerating their growth, enabling them to live longer, and I found myself thinking more and more not just about their viability but about their well-being.

For me, our delicate monsters meant absolute and thrilling success. That they were still monsters didn't phase me in the slightest, and I doted on them like they were my own children. Through my delight, I noticed Cedric still had a visceral recoil he was trying to hide. For me, I felt joy – vindicated in the science, my own abilities on display. I had done it, just like I knew I could. It went beyond this, though. I found their company increasingly comforting. I felt a new, glowing parental impulse. Was my motherly side finally coming out? Maybe, but aside from Cedric, I had no one to tell.

In addition to the original six that were now adults, we had new young emerging from their eggs every week. As before, some did not survive very long. We made sure to expose them to air until they were breathing on their own and then observed them in individual tanks for a day before turning them over to Coralie and the others in the giant tank against the wall.

We tried to get the "type" more uniform through our gene-editing process, but there was inherent instability in the mix of different species' DNA, with considerable variation in each individual. Most of them had a standard eight tentacles: two wispy ones on their face, two on their torsos and four at the bottom of their torsos where legs would be on a human. Some deviated significantly, however, with a riot of tentacles stemming from their torso, or facial fins instead of facial tentacles. Their facial structures varied a lot as well, with the location of eyes, mouth and nostrils resulting in markedly different features. All of them had large eyes and modest noses or nostril openings, and they all had mouths, but that was all their faces had in common.

We continued to provide our weekly progress updates to Global Holdings' shiny drone. Our updates now held a note of triumph, and more than a little pride. In exchange, the drone would drop off Mr. Sykes' video messages when it picked up our packages.

"Even with a successful shift away from carbon energy and fossil fuels, we are still seeing environmental degradation and ecosystem deterioration at a rate that is driving the planet toward collapse. Humans are driving this but are simultaneously holding it back through scientific interventions," his floating image said sternly.

"It's all so fragile, and we can see the positive impacts of scientific endeavours – we have shifted economic production away from carbon-rich energy sources, adapted our cities, protected some critical environments. But with the pace of scientific change now, we can no longer control outcomes. We can no longer see far enough down the road to envision consequences and avoid them. We have accelerated our learning and our technology to a point where we are creating new conditions for our own downfall. The bees are only the beginning."

Sometimes he waxed philosophical about the beauty of heirloom agriculture, other times the importance of net-zero farming. He talked about the startling presence of the ocean, and how our salvation could be on the mirror side of the waves. He discussed literature, theatre and opera, all soon to be lost. He was doing all he could, he insisted. Not only with our project but with others.

I felt contractually bound to watch all his videos in full, but I had less and less confidence in the judgment of our employer. It wasn't that I disagreed with him. No one on the planet with an ounce of awareness could've disagreed with him. It was everything else. The flecks of spittle that would occasionally collect at the corner of his mouth as he went on and on obliviously. The tsunami of information. The hectoring tone as if he and he alone understood the gravity of the situation and the rest of us were morons living our daily lives without noticing the disasters around us. It was tedious and exhausting and – since it reinforced the Holo-News – terrifying.

He was a billionaire with a messianic complex. Like them all, I suppose. And perhaps we should be grateful he wasn't one of the ones heating up the arms race in space. Instead, we were creating a new species of humanoid just for him.

"You know he's . . ."

"Yep," Cedric finished. "Certifiable. If he weren't so rich, he'd have already been committed somewhere. Bit of a nightmare, really."

United at least in our unease, we went on with our work.

Mr. Sykes' analysis of the sorry state of the world was reflected in the daily headlines careening around our comfortable intake room, reminding us how precarious life was.

Beekeepers Union refuses to rent bees to dirty industry, almond markets collapse

Bee malaise spreads to new crops, scientists baffled

UN World Food Programme deploys electronic honeybee drones

New doomsday cult "Free Doom" predicts end of world in next 24 months

Species Termination Notice: South American black marmot

"New doomsday cult? Well, they don't have to get too creative, do they?" I scoffed at Cedric, who laughed. "I think *The New Economist* is calling for the end of the world in twenty-four months."

Funny, but horrifying too. I knew that the only reason we were eating well was that we had a greenhouse, and money to navigate the rising grocery prices and shortages. Even the good Holo-News seemed to confirm that we were fighting to delay the inevitable. We were pointed on a downward spiral, a nosedive where we could never pull up in time. We sipped our coffee, shook our heads, got back to work.

Cedric and I found ourselves approaching the work differently. Our progress reports had always stressed the positive and downplayed the failures, but now we shouldered the added burden of explaining our new charges, interpreting them in the best possible light.

CHAPTER 24: CEDRIC

FADE IN

INT. POORLY LIT INTAKE ROOM - NIGHT

A sleepy-looking CEDRIC in plaid pyjamas peers into the camera, switches on an overhead light. He's sitting at the mahogany table in the intake room.

> CEDRIC
>
> I can't sleep, so I thought I'd pull out the camera and share some thoughts. Maybe it'll help? I don't know. Nighttime is unsettling here. The Ceph are banging around the lab. I know it's locked but it still freaks me out a bit. Like, I don't want to go in and check. I'm sure they're fine. How much damage could they do in there?

CEDRIC looks vaguely worried, absently scratches his arm, hugs himself.

> CEDRIC (cont'd)
>
> It's the time of day I'm least sure of myself and that's saying a lot, really. I'm wide awake now, there's no point in trying to sleep, I know that. I've been awake at night more and more lately; I just have more

troubles at this hour. They come at me. The
doubts don't so much creep in as run in and
shove me into the wall. We're succeeding
where I never thought we should.

CEDRIC looks around, with a slightly haunted look on his
face.

                    CEDRIC (cont'd)
Is this what success looks like, really? Scraping by, getting paid, while we have monsters
growing down the hall? Shabby building, bad
part of town, hoppers crawling in the shadows
wherever I look. I mean, cute monsters, no
denying that. Sweet even. Cool, cool features.
Mr. Sykes should be thrilled. But when the
reckoning comes, will we still be congratu-
lating ourselves on the lovely facial tentacles, on the beautiful shifting skin tones? Or
will we be running for our lives?

It's not the wildness that comes from their
animal heritage that worries me. It's the humanity we've left there. The real monsters are
the humans, right?

You can see it all over the news. Humans are
the worst. We've driven ourselves off a cliff
and are just watching the scenery go by, waiting for impact.

A THUMPING noise. CEDRIC looks off-camera, then back, rais-
es his eyebrows and shakes his head.

                    CEDRIC (cont'd)
        I should probably go see what that is.

CEDRIC gets up and turns off camera.

                              CUT TO BLACK

CHAPTER 25

Our mussels were growing well, and we started feeding them to the Ceph. "Not bad," Coralie told us. "Clams are nice, but fish is better."

So, like any parent with picky children, we looked for ways to keep them happy. To supplement their diet with some fresh fish and crab, we planned a foray to the fish market. Sales took place at low tide among the flooded buildings near the old harbour, on a site that had been used long before the waters rose. Usually, we saw this part of the city from our roof looking east and south, the buildings leaning more and more the farther out they were, poking out from the surf at high tide, the roads looking like canals. Most of the area was uninhabitable, but that didn't seem to stop some hardy souls from living there, or at least working there when the tide was out.

Although I'd lived in Long Harbour for years, I had never been to the flooded-out tidal zones on foot. Rumours of crime and violence had kept me away. It was officially off-limits to citizens though the laws hadn't been enforced for years. The self-driving land shuttles didn't go there, so we needed to walk. We planned our adventure carefully. It was only twelve blocks away, about twenty minutes on foot, but we were stepping far outside our comfort zone.

Cedric and I chose a day when low tide was in the early morning and we could walk in daylight. We picked a route to the market that was straightforward and avoided some of the larger abandoned buildings. While hoppers rarely made the news, it was common knowledge that there was a colony of them somewhere in the city, and Wildlife Control had yet to find and exterminate it. In spite of our precautions, we nervously glanced upward every time we walked down a deserted street. As we neared the old harbour, abandoned stores and office buildings showed high-water marks and barnacles. The cracked concrete underfoot was slimy with seaweed.

It was a bit tricky to figure out when the market would open since black-market businesses didn't advertise, but as we walked toward it, a wall of noise and marine aromas hit us. It was a raucous place that announced itself before it came into view. Crowded with people when we arrived, a bustling mass of sellers and buyers loudly called to each other from stalls arrayed with local catch. We heard snippets of English, French and Mi'kmaq as we approached. People of all shapes, sizes and ethnicities hurried back and forth. The fishmongers all seemed to know each other.

Despite the early hour, some sellers were already packing up. We had misjudged the tide and arrived late, and some had sold out early. We hurried to join the throng. I could see the edge of the water advancing up side streets, a hundred metres from the edge of the market.

"Any tuna? Salmon? Lobster?" I asked at the first stall. The woman behind the counter smiled and her sun-darkened skin crinkled around her eyes.

"Harder and harder to come by," she replied. "Had a bit earlier, but it's gone."

"Have you been here long today?" I asked.

"We opened at dawn, and the tide'll wash us out in another half-hour or so. You don't look like you dressed for it today." She stared pointedly at my hiking boots. She was sensibly dressed in high rubber boots and hip waders.

"Do you come every day?" Cedric asked. "It was hard to figure out the market hours."

"It's a pop-up market. The cops don't really care, but we're not allowed to sell here. Something about the street being unstable with the water so close. I'll give you my contacts so you'll know when to come."

"Where do you get your fish?" Cedric leaned over the pieces of pollock laid out on ice in front of her.

"Here and there. The best stuff I catch myself. And I buy from the salmon farm up the road." Her compact body reminded me of granite, like she had more in common with craggy cliffs than people. Grey hair frizzed out from under her cap. Her age only deepened my impression of strength and persistence.

"Is it dangerous for you to be here?" I asked, glancing around.

She scoffed. "No more than anywhere else. I've been working out of this harbour my whole life. Not gonna stop for some critters or a bit of surf." To demonstrate, she pulled out a rifle from under the table. "I'm not afraid of the greenies. And we all help each other here."

We bought some krill and pollock, as much to thank her for chatting as anything. "Name's Donna," she said. "Next time, let me know what you're looking for and I'll put it aside. I can even deliver, if the greenies scare you."

We continued through the market. Eventually we managed to find some small crabs and three pieces of sorry-looking salmon. They showed clear marks of freezer burn and probably didn't qualify for this fresh market, but we took them anyway. The water was starting to lap at our ankles by the time we had walked the entire market. Wet boots squelching, we turned for home. There were very few people walking the streets, and Cedric started to get twitchy. We didn't mention hoppers, but we were both thinking about them. The sun was bright overhead, but that didn't keep the hairs from standing up on the back on my neck. About halfway home, I noticed we were the only ones on the street.

A long shadow fell over us, then quickly darted away – something was overhead. I saw movement out of the corner of my eye, high up on the wall of a building to my left.

"Over there." Cedric pointed with his chin. I turned to my right, looked up. A small greenish-grey figure splayed out like a tree frog hung a few stories above us. Out of the corner of my eye, I detected three more crawling along the sides of buildings. None of them seemed to have noticed us, but we picked up our pace again and Cedric murmured that we should run.

"No," I replied. "They don't see us, let's not change anything." We tiptoed in silence a few more blocks. I thought wistfully of Donna's rifle and remembered neither Cedric nor I could shoot. When we were out of sight of the last of the hoppers, we broke into a run, sprinting the last distance, our bags of fish banging against our legs.

We buzzed ourselves through the front door, rushed past the boarded-up nail salon and straight through the lobby, and didn't relax until we were in the elevator. By the time we got upstairs to the lab our feeling of triumph returned and our fear of the hoppers receded. We fed the Ceph some of our catch, detailing our adventure, and even cooked up a bit of the crab for ourselves. That night, we ate at the big mahogany table in the intake room, and finally had something new to talk about with each other.

In spite of our feeling of triumph, the fear didn't recede enough to make us want to go to the fish market every week. "I think delivery is the way to go, really," Cedric suggested, and I couldn't help but agree.

CHAPTER 26

Our foray to the fish market made me more conscious of how badly things were beginning to deteriorate out in the world. We wrote out detailed instructions for Edward and Laurel in case anything happened to us and discussed whether we should introduce them to Coralie and the colony.

"I'm afraid of what they'll think," I admitted. "What if they think we're horrible? That we've done something unforgivable?"

Cedric tried to reassure me but couldn't predict their reactions. "I'm sure they'd come around, after the initial shock. They're scientists, they'll be fascinated. They'll understand."

I wasn't so sure and couldn't agree to bring them in. Not yet anyway.

I wasn't the only one thinking about widening the circle of trust around the Midnight Project. A few days later we received a missive via Global Holdings' shiny drone – an envelope containing a professional biography and contact details for a Dr. Sage Winters. Mr. Sykes' accompanying video rant explained.

"I have to commend you on your progress!" his video began. His face was tanned and his chin chiselled. "You've done a wonderful job so far. You're making extraordinary progress. Really.

"At this stage, I think you need a little extra help in determining who the Ceph are. Please don't take this as a criticism – you two are extraordinary scientists who've done a remarkable job –"

Cedric paused the recording. "Laying it on a bit thick, don't you think?"

"Hmmm. Not a good sign," I replied. He restarted the recording.

"I'm going to put you in touch with Dr. Sage Winters. Top-rated anthro-biologist. Ph.D. Harvard, M.Sc. Boston University, with an undergraduate in Marine Biology at your old alma mater, Cedric, North Pacific

University. She's brilliant, and we have signed her on as a consultant to the Midnight Project with all the necessary clearances. I think you'll like her a lot. She can evaluate the level of society that the Ceph are creating and can make recommendations on how to encourage a more ideal development for them."

He went on at length after that with his usual philosophizing: "Humankind is too exceptional to disappear into a squalid puddle. Whether we're speaking about souls or self-awareness, we are the beings on the planet who understand what it means to be alive, who understand what we will lose when the end comes. You don't need to be religious to feel it in your bones. We are the only beings who fully comprehend what extinction means. We alone fully comprehend how final the ending will be.

"It's the loneliest perch in the universe, and from it, we understand the meaning of the passage of time, we understand what it means to lose everything."

"Blah blah blah perfect society blah blah blah survival of genius blah blah." Cedric summed it up, sighed and let the recording play out.

I shrugged. "This will either be very good, or very, very, bad."

~

It took only three days for the illustrious Dr. Winters to arrive, a testament to the amount of money Mr. Sykes must be paying her. By then it was high summer, the days were as long as they'd get, and the overheated city felt parched. Cedric's greenhouse and raised beds on the roof were proving their worth, as local produce was astronomically expensive when you could get it at all. Cedric was happy we had fresh vegetables to offer her.

Dr. Winters was entirely at ease, smiling widely. "Call me Sage!" she yelled excitedly before the copter had even lifted off the roof. She was all muscle and energy, almost a full foot taller than me, and eye to eye with Cedric; where Cedric was thin and delicate, Dr. Winters was large, like an Olympic swimmer. She had long blond hair, blue eyes and freckles artlessly speckled across her nose. She was also at least ten years younger than we were. I couldn't help being acutely aware that our specialty kept us indoors in a windowless lab and this young woman was clearly a queen of fieldwork.

Words tumbled out of her as she made her entrance. She seemed eager to endear herself, at least to Cedric, who she remembered as a professor when she was an undergrad. "Everyone wanted to be in your class!" She grinned. "It's so great to see you again."

We had laid out our luncheon in the intake room, letting the pastels of the walls, the immaculate furniture and the cityscape reflected in the picture windows calm both Cedric's and my nerves. We weren't entirely sure how to play this and felt a level of caution, sliding into anxiety. Oblivious to our ambivalence, Dr. Winters complimented Cedric on the meal, admired the view and talked about how much she enjoyed visiting Long Harbour. Her good humour was infectious. Even nervous Cedric began unbending a little.

For me, her social skills were irrelevant. She was here to judge me and my work and I would not be swayed by a smiling opinion on my decorating. I couldn't deny her credentials were absolutely first-rate. She had worked on whale society and culture, emotional bonding in wolf colonies, and primate technology and culture. She had been fully briefed and was excited to meet the Ceph.

"Cephalopods in general don't have society, so the combination of human, dolphin and cephalopod is going to create some fascinating potential," she said, following up with question after question about their speech, behaviour and physiology. I found myself letting my guard down a little as we spoke.

Finally, there was no further reason to delay and we walked down the hall to the main laboratory, unlocked it and entered. Coralie was waiting for us and had kindly not unlocked the tank first. I had spoken to her in advance about the importance of the security measures and making sure that our visitor had no concerns. She sprang out of the water once the lid was up, pulling herself along the edge and landing neatly on the platform beside the tank. Her colour was a warm and friendly pale blue, edged with some darker curiosity. She had squeezed herself into a bizarre parody of a human crossing their legs and was working hard at looking casual. She waited patiently while I made introductions and extended a tentacle mimicking a handshake. She was clearly going all out to make an impression.

Cedric pulled up chairs for the three of us and we sat down. Dr. Winters smiled and said, "Hi, Coralie, how are you today?" Coralie smiled and responded, and we settled in for a bit of conversation.

Coralie was clearly fascinated by Dr. Winters, the third human she had ever met. She had no shyness, but the other Ceph stayed in the water and most of them hid in the rocks at the bottom of the tank. Dr. Winters asked Coralie to tell her about herself, and they spoke about her likes and dislikes, her favourite things. Coralie practically preened, her body undulating like an octopus, her colours shifting from light blue to a more intense blue, then to purple and even her regular relaxed pink.

I couldn't really see what Dr. Winters was trying to do, what information she was trying to learn. I stayed in the lab, first sitting, then puttering uselessly and nervously, avidly eavesdropping. After about an hour, Coralie politely ended their conversation and flipped gracefully back into the tank. Dr. Winters rose, smiled at us like a child at a birthday party and asked if we had a quiet space where she could write up her notes. We gave her a vacant side office and tried not to hover.

Cedric took great pleasure in hosting dinner that night, more animated than he had been for months. Most people in the city were subsisting on canned goods – Cedric was proud of his fresh produce, as well as his culinary skills. Wanting to encourage him, I made every effort to be friendly. Our intake room, which already doubled as a boardroom, a coffee lounge and a breakfast nook, was transformed into a formal dining room. The beautiful mahogany table was laid out with proper flatware, vintage Royal Doulton plates and candles. Cedric had prepared a feast of salad, followed by baked salmon with dill, sweet potato hash, roasted Brussels sprouts with balsamic glaze and strawberry-rhubarb crisp for dessert. Even the city sparkled as the sun went down. We fell into calling her Sage, as she had requested.

Sage was a perfect guest, responsive to all Cedric's attentions and eager for my approval. She had me explain our process several times. "It's a combination," I repeated. "Gene editing, plus selective breeding with more gene editing."

"But how do you do the gene editing?"

"In the beginning, we used digital copies of genes, isolated some elements and synthesized it, then combined it with organic samples," I explained patiently. "We're at the stage now where we're recombining organic samples and adjusting traits not only in vitro but once the subjects are viable."

"How do you do that though? Once they're born, aren't they set? Finished?"

"Not exactly." It was such a pleasure to talk to someone not-Cedric about this. "We can insert new genetic coding at any stage of life."

Her eyes widened. I preened and probably explained too much. "Yes, we can insert new genetic code by special injection. It's similar to how they cure genetic diseases in adult humans but a little more tailored." As proud as I was, I wasn't going to jeopardize my nondisclosure agreement with WKPT. This was the process that had gotten us fired. That had escaped into the world and made genetic engineering a little too easy. But it was mine – why shouldn't I use it for the Ceph?

"Oh! Ceph serum! How cool is that?" Trust this woman to come up with a trademark description. Cedric jumped in and changed the subject.

We installed her in the spare apartment. Since Cedric was already taking up the other, I commuted back to my house in the hills that night. I may have enjoyed the dinner, but I wasn't sure how I felt about the scene that greeted me when I returned the next morning. My once quiet intake room was filled with all our staff plus Sage drinking coffee and eating Cedric's fresh croissants. They were chatting and laughing, ignoring the headlines buzzing around the room. They tried to pull me into the conversation, but I retreated to the kitchen to grab coffee.

"This is nice," I said to Cedric.

It was not nice. I felt rumpled and put out and undercaffeinated. Sage was holding forth to a rapt audience of my staff who barely looked up when I walked in. Cedric was chuckling in a voice I hadn't heard in months. I took refuge with my coffee in a chair at the big table, all the comfy spots already taken. Sage smiled broadly and continued telling a funny story about wolf observation. I wondered if Sage pressed her shirts or if they just came out of the wash like that. She even smelled good.

 ॐ

Dr. Winters stayed for two weeks. She questioned us, read our notes and wrote her own. She met with Coralie every day and eventually even coaxed some of the others to come out and visit. She was clearly the most exciting thing that had happened in the Cephs' lifetime and we were all caught up in the adventure. Sage enjoyed sharing her observations at the end of each day and asking us questions. In spite of feeling encroached on, I slowly came around to the new routine.

Honestly, I found it almost a relief to have someone else to talk to about the Ceph. I say almost, because there continued to be a niggling doubt about what the impact of her assessments would be with Mr. Sykes. I retained a spark of suspicion. But the meals and the conversations were warm and inviting and comforting. And I realized I wanted an outside opinion. My secret doubts, all balled up inside, were weighing me down.

"They clearly have family structures. Coralie appears to be the matriarch, but perhaps she is merely the spokesperson. I think it takes a lot of effort to speak outside the water, and there needs to be a strong desire to master it. I think Coralie is more than just the best linguist, though, she seems to be a natural leader.

"They all have specific personalities, with preferences and even different skills," she suggested, and talked about Delmar's love of structures and building things, Mazu's love of Chinese opera and music and River's love of the Ceph children. I heartily agreed.

It felt like validation.

CHAPTER 27

As friendly and open-hearted as Sage Winters was, I knew the continuation of our work was at stake, as well as the future of the Ceph. It's possible that a certain level of paranoia had entered our work as well, I can't rule that out. I tried to keep these feelings at bay and be as helpful as possible to her but I didn't fully trust our employer, so it was hard to trust his charismatic consultant.

Finally, over dinner one night, I sounded her out on her relationship with Mr. Sykes and Global Holdings. I didn't understand how someone so open and dynamic could be under contract for this shady venture.

"I first encountered Burton while I was studying humpback whale relationships in the North Atlantic. He was interested in collaborating on some ecosystem protection work his company was doing. He started funding some of my side projects, and I've been a regular consultant on different projects for a few years. I'll be honest, the money gives me more freedom than my salaried position at the university."

"Have you visited his enclave?" I asked.

"I've been there twice for consults, but I'm not the 'enclave' type. I was invited to do a residency there during my sabbatical, but I'd rather do something I can publish, something to build my career. Consultancies are so hemmed in by NDAs. I have to be careful about how I line up work with him, so I don't accidentally muzzle myself on a subject that I should be sharing broadly with the academic community. That's why this Ceph project is so agreeable – it's out of the public domain with no crossover with my other work. And I am ridiculously overpaid for this little visit."

Her relationship with Mr. Sykes wasn't the only point of contention.

Sometimes her questions got my back up and I found myself justifying my decisions over and over again.

"Why isn't the lab bigger? What's your plan to expand their habitat? Do you have enough education and enrichment activities?" The list of things she pushed me on seemed unending. I was willing to acknowledge that I was not a morning person and she was friendlier over breakfast, but I wasn't going to agree I was neglecting the Ceph in some way.

"Of course we have plans to expand their habitat." I bristled. "There is a basement pool. They can be transferred there when they're ready."

"And what are the markers you'll use to determine when they are ready?"

I didn't have a precise answer for that.

॰

At the end of the visit, the low-level hostilities I felt, mostly smoothed over by her charm offensive, escalated into genuine discord. She had prepared a short presentation for Sykes and used it to debrief us on her findings before she left.

An image of the Ceph underwater filled the intake room as she went over her conclusions: "The Ceph appear to be a thriving colony, with clear social fabric, and evolving culture." Good so far.

"Their language, an underwater means of communication, requires further study to understand completely, but appears to be based on a combination of skin colour changes, clicks and whistles with an element of echolocation. In other words, by bouncing sound off objects and listening for the reflected sounds, they should be able to navigate like whales, dolphins or bats. This use of sound, undetectable to humans without advanced recording equipment, could also be part of their communication." Fascinating. I was all in.

She went on. "The first Ceph are already adults, and the young are growing quickly. They reach full growth in about four months. They are developing a basic understanding of the lab environment and can use computers in rudimentary ways." All true.

"Their love of FlickFilms and entertainment indicate their knowledge of human society is expanding, too. My key recommendations are as follows: First, provide the Ceph with more education. Second, expand their habitat. They clearly need more enrichment than the laboratory tank can give them. Finally, given my overall findings, they need to be treated as a society."

"I don't understand," I said.

"You have to treat them like people," she said simply. "You see them as a science experiment, a creation. Cephalopods with a bit of human DNA thrown in."

"I don't see them as just a science experiment," I insisted. "But they aren't human, and they can't be treated as human."

"I'm not suggesting that," Sage replied. "I said you have to treat them like people. Like an evolving society. They're more than the sum of their DNA. You have to look past their appearances, their ways."

"I live with them, I created them. Of course I see beyond that."

"But you don't, because you keep them locked up in a tank in a windowless laboratory as if they're so dangerous you can't allow them to see your kitchen. You treat them like wild animals you've made into pets."

"It's a bit rich to suggest that we're in violation of ethics for not letting them raid our fridge."

"I'm not suggesting you're in violation of anything. I understand what you've done here. But once you look beyond the experimental part of your work, you'll recognize that they have society, adults and children, they have family. They love each other, and you too. They have hopes and dreams. They see and hear beauty, and create lovely music that we can't hear. They even have fears.

"You have to stop treating them like something you invented in a petri dish."

Cedric cleared his throat. "But you know –" he was struggling to find the right words "– that is exactly what we did. We created them. They are, literally, a science experiment."

Sage shook her head. "They are so much more. And you have to recognize that and take care of them. They aren't meant to live forever in an aquarium. They aren't meant to be a freak show for scientists to use to claim success."

I was appalled at the suggestion. "We don't treat them like a freak show."

"You haven't even introduced them to Laurel and Edward."

This was met with silence. It was true. I hadn't done that. I'd meant to.

"Look, I understand," Sage said. "You're lab guys. You see life through a microscope – it keeps you at a distance. But that life right down the hallway deserves to be recognized for what it is. I think you should think about moving them to the enclave. I see how you've barricaded yourselves in here, but you can see what's going on in the world, right? The food shortages, the supply chain disruptions, political upheaval everywhere you look. I've thought about it too. I mean, no one wants to live in a bunker, but if the world's going to hell, what are our options?"

"We're perfectly self-sufficient here," Cedric replied coldly. "I have no security concerns at this time."

"Well, fine, I can see you have your set-up and it's comfortable. But promise me you'll think about it? Like, let's keep in touch. I feel like things are starting to shift fast in the world and you won't want to be caught out when things really fall apart."

I nodded dumbly and thought of a hundred rebuttals the next day. Of course I saw the Ceph like people! And if I treated them like pets, well, weren't they closer to Maisie and Rex than to us, genetically speaking? But the illustrious, capable and oh-so-friendly Dr. Sage Winters managed to have the last word. She finished her notes, paid her respects to Coralie and the rest of the Ceph and departed in a Global Holdings copter, flying off into the sunset, promising she'd be back.

CHAPTER 28: CORALIE

I think I'm beginning to understand what Raina means by "human." Cedric and Raina are family, like us but a little different, with their dry legs and arms and hair. But Sage is just . . . human. Different. Not family. I begin to think of humans as a collection of different groups, some close, some far, some very separate from the Ceph. For the first part of our lives, we have thought of Raina and Cedric as part of us – strange and different, to be sure, but just an extension of our family. They are our parents. Sage is another thing entirely.

This is not to suggest I do not like her – I do, and I am wildly interested in what other humans are like. I have almost as many questions as she does. The first day we speak for a short time, the four of us. Then the next day, she comes back and for many days after that. I find myself looking forward to our talks. After we speak, I go underwater and repeat parts of the conversation to my brothers and sisters hidden among the rocks. She tells me, and by extension us, about her time chasing orca pods trying to understand the role of the matriarch, and her time winter camping with northern wolves, to learn about their emotional bonds with each other. But we mostly speak about each of us, though she's really only peered at the others through the glass of the tank.

I try to explain how we speak to each other, and I talk a lot about each of the Ceph: River, who loves the babies; Delmar, who is always trying to figure out how things work; Mazu, who loves music. It is nice to have someone to practise my air speech on, who never tires of listening to me and who has questions for me.

I am sad when she goes away.

CHAPTER 29

We received Dr. Winters' final report a few days later with a sigh of relief. It confirmed that the Ceph had several markers indicating rudimentary social and cultural development that, in Mr. Sykes' view, was an early vindication of his vision.

I replayed our conversations over and over in my head. Had I said the right thing? Was she actually right? Did I treat the Ceph like science experiments? Like pets? I don't think Cedric had a dark night of the soul on this one – he absolutely and unapologetically treated them as a science experiment.

"That's what they are, Raina," he told me.

I saw more truth in what she was saying and eventually made my peace with her point. I was worried about what our lab assistants would think. Would they think we had compromised all our ethics and principles? Would they judge what we had done?

I resolved to introduce them to the Ceph and manage whatever fallout might occur.

I started by sharing more of the project documentation and talking through what we were trying to achieve. Mercifully, neither Edward nor Laurel pointed out the obvious ethical or legal holes in what we were doing. They read through the documents and their eyes bugged out a bit at the images of the Ceph. Then I walked them down the hall and unlocked the lab. Coralie was delighted to see more faces. She preened, she chatted, she turned on the charm. I'm not sure "delight" is the word I would use to describe Edward's and Laurel's reactions. Laurel was frozen to the spot, unable to speak for several minutes. When Delmar leapt up to the platform and waved at them, she squeaked and beat a retreat out the door. Edward was a little more game. He held his ground and approached cautiously. He didn't speak at all for several minutes; he just stared, fascinated and horrified.

Coralie eventually noticed. "Why aren't you talking? Can't you speak?"

Edward cleared his throat. "No, I can, I can speak. So can you."

"Yes." Coralie puffed up with pride. "Yes, I can. What would you like to talk about?"

"Um, how are you doing?" Edward groped at his words.

"Just great! It's so nice to meet you, Edward." Coralie had trouble pronouncing the "w."

"Likewise." Edward looked over at us a bit desperately.

I had gotten used to the Ceph's vaguely humanoid shapes, the changing colour of their skin, the tentacles and the telescoping eyes, though I suppose upon reflection they were a bit unsettling to the uninitiated. Coralie grinned, showing her sharp teeth. She was trying to be disarming, but I don't think it helped.

Edward stuttered a bit then grinned and approached her. She held out a tentacled arm like a queen expecting a kiss on the hand. He took it, inclining his head. "So very, very nice to meet you," he said.

And so the introduction happened, and no one was the worse for it. I felt a little better having a couple more people on the inside of the secret, despite the fact that Laurel would blanche when we talked about the Ceph around her – she avoided a second meeting for days.

A further outcome of Dr. Winters' visit was that Mr. Sykes had several directives based on her recommendations. He was very insistent that the Ceph learn to read. He expounded on this in one of his weekly video rants, talking up the cultural importance of literature and how the colony had to appreciate Tolstoy and Shakespeare to be fully human. I had to chuckle imagining the Ceph's response to *Hamlet*.

Nonetheless, I felt the undercurrent in Sykes' words. He could pull the plug on the project at any time – and I knew he would if he felt we had veered too far from his humanistic ideal. So reading lessons began.

I had doubts, of course. Not about whether they could master the alphabet and learn how to read words, that was almost the easy part. They were clearly intelligent, curious and eager to absorb knowledge. What I doubted was whether they could connect with human culture, especially literature. How to take their view of the world, and their reality, and relate it to sixteenth-century plays performed in England for Jacobean audiences? How to explain history and power, government and monarchy to them. Even Hemingway's *The Old Man and the Sea* or Melville's *Moby Dick* seemed a little cruel from the point of view of marine life. It was a lot to take on, and neither Cedric nor I were English teachers. In any event, we took up the role. We had to ensure our nascent colony could defend themselves against Mr. Sykes' requirements.

Every day Cedric and Edward would project an image of the alphabet in the middle of the room and go through the letters with the group. As Cedric pronounced each sound, it was obvious that the young ones could only pronounce a few, but they listened attentively and never missed a lesson.

Most of the Ceph struggled to hold a stylus but Coralie's splayed, finger-like tentacles managed. Nonetheless it was one of the oldest Ceph, River, who proved to be the brightest student. Though she spent most of her time among the rocks at the bottom of the tank, or playing with the younglings, she became adept at building words from the squiggles of the alphabet. She happily ran through matching games and practice questions. When we provided her with an old-school keyboard, she proudly mastered the exercises and started making lists of words on her own.

Cedric even brought out his favourite book, a dog-eared paperback of T.S. Eliot poems, and read to them. It worked surprisingly well.

"'I should have been a pair of ragged claws / Scuttling across the floors of silent seas.'" This made Pearl giggle and everyone paid attention. The younglings climbed over Edward and played with his hair while Cedric read.

Poetry seemed to appeal to them. Soon, they were clamouring for Cedric to read more, and then they'd pepper him with questions about what each word meant. River asked him what his favourite poem was. "'The

Love Song of J. Alfred Prufrock,'" Cedric replied without hesitation. "I see something of myself in old J. Alfred." He looked momentarily sad, then smiled and turned the page.

Edward started looking up English modules to help shape their understanding. Cedric brought them more poetry and literature, starting with children's books and young adult fiction and working his way up to more of his favourite classics. Thus, the formal education of the Ceph had begun.

CHAPTER 30

I'll admit to being nervous when Mr. Sykes announced he was coming to visit. Our regular updates had piqued his interest and he wanted to meet Coralie. He arrived in his personal copter, on our rooftop landing pad, all smooth smiles and handshakes. He was flawless: his skin an advertisement for living rich, his hair perfectly in place despite the copter's rotors, his casual wear screaming money. I reminded myself I needed to do a load of laundry. Sage Winters bounded out behind him, grinning.

We welcomed them into our intake room and started the visit with a brief presentation on the technical progress we had made, and the challenges still to come. I talked up some of their cephalopod-specific attributes as if I were trying to sell a car. "They use jet propulsion to swim, by pulling salt water into their bodies and pushing it out rapidly." I had a quick illustrative video to accompany my words.

"Their skin colour tends to change with their emotions or by intent. They can camouflage, but they also seem to reflect their mental and emotional state in their colouring. They have enhanced tactile abilities through their arms or tentacles." I flicked up a still close-up of suckers on an arm.

"They work together," Sage broke in. "They demonstrate compassion to each other."

"We have made progress on some ecosystem and food chain elements, but there is still lots of work to do," I continued, trying not to look annoyed. "We also have not been successful in full adaptation to the expected environment."

"Does this mean you still haven't figured out how to deal with ocean pressure?" was Mr. Sykes' first question.

I paused and tried to find a positive, measured way to respond. "That's correct," I said finally. "The pressure issue is still pending. We are model-ling some gene-editing protocols that may help us."

"Gene editing – she means Ceph serum," Sage added. "It's a delivery method for changing the adults." I ignored her.

He asked a few further questions and we discussed our plans for the mussels that would feed them. We covered some of the possible sites in the Caribbean that could host the colony and he shared that his conglomerate had acquired the rights to one of them.

Then came the moment of truth. "Would you like to meet Coralie?" I asked. He nodded and we walked down the hallway to the lab.

The Ceph were mainly hanging out at the bottom of the tank, but two squirted to the surface right away. I unlocked the top and Coralie popped her head out. "Is this him? Our kindly benefactor?"

"I'll pull up chairs," I said, grabbing an office chair from a corner and rolling it into position. Mr. Sykes sat down. Coralie pulled herself out of the tank and balanced on the platform beside it. Sage hovered beside him, an embarrassing sycophant.

"Dr. Winters, hello again! And Mr. Sykes! Raina and Cedric have talked about you," Coralie began, smiling. "It's nice to meet you. I think I owe my life to you."

Mr. Sykes didn't speak, just stared intently without blinking.

"Are you visiting for long? Do you come to Long Harbour often?"

"Fascinating," he murmured, glancing at Cedric and me.

There was silence while Mr. Sykes gathered his thoughts. Finally, he responded. "Coralie, it is a great honour to meet you. Are the conditions satisfactory to you here? Are you healthy? Do you have everything you need?"

"I suppose. Raina and Cedric take good care of us. We are the Ceph." I could see a caution in her that was unusual and carefully coached. We'd gone over everything with her in advance and implored her to focus on cer-tain elements and avoid others. Mr. Sykes' stated objective for the project was the salvation of humanity. If the Ceph did not appear to have human attributes, not only would our funding dry up but the experiment would end. I could see that Coralie wasn't going to play it our way though, she was already deviating from our script.

Sykes looked around the lab, then back to her. "I understand you enjoy watching documentaries. What's your favourite?"

She responded with the title of a FlickFilm about the degradation of the ocean and the importance of conservation. They spoke about the film-maker for a bit, and she laughed when he brought up Chinese opera and her sibling's taste for it. "Personally, I prefer nonfiction. I want to be a scientist when I grow up. But my siblings have different tastes and ambitions."

He inquired about her interest in science and she confided she wanted to be a marine biologist.

They spoke about ocean currents, and the taste of deep-sea clams. Mr. Sykes told her about his enclave and how he had a safe space in the Caribbean Sea, at least for a little while. They spoke about the world winding down, an inevitable grind toward transformation. Sage, her attention drifting, wandered around the room, examining our equipment.

"Do you understand the purpose of the work that we have done here? Do you understand what you are for?" Mr. Sykes asked.

"I understand that we exist and that has been your purpose. What else is there to understand?"

Mr. Sykes puffed out his chest and sat straighter. "I believe that you are humanity's last hope. I would like you to carry our dreams forward."

Coralie blinked and smiled sadly. "They are very watery dreams now, Mr. Sykes. We are the Ceph and we are not human. Does this disappoint you?"

There was another silence. Finally, he said, "I find you extraordinary. As I say, it is a great honour to meet you." He gently held out his hand to her and she wrapped her arm delicately around it. His eyes widened as he felt the suckers on the underside against his skin.

"Likewise," she replied.

We all trooped out, Sage smiling broadly, Sykes thoughtful, Cedric and I cautious. As we seated ourselves around the boardroom table again, Mr. Sykes became very animated, insisting that we needed to move the colony as soon as possible to his enclave, so we could plan the next phase.

"It's not just the oceans on Earth, you know. There are worlds out there – whole worlds of water. Moons, planets, universes for the taking. We just need to get there, need to get there first. We have so much to do and so little time."

Cedric and I exchanged alarmed glances. Was our benefactor losing his grip?

I stood up and started citing the remaining obstacles. "We have everything we need here to solve the last riddles. We're good here. Transporting them will be risky."

"But you can access everything you need on the island. It is safer, and I can supervise directly." Which was, of course, the very thing I was trying to avoid.

"We're so close to the end, Mr. Sykes," I argued. "We're so close to perfecting everything and then we can transfer them to the site. It would introduce too many new variables to move them now. It would set us back, slow us down. We need to solve the deep pressure problem first. They are not ready."

"I want you with me. I want the Ceph with me."

"We're with you in spirit, that's for sure, sir. But we need to finish our work here. There's no other way. We'll also need to reverse-engineer their reproductive capacity. These things all take time, but they are important."

I refrained from pulling out our contract, but it was there too – he couldn't make us leave.

Not legally anyway. I flinched away from the impression that he had more than legal tools in his toolbox.

Sage tried to repair the mood. "You really should spend some more time at the enclave. It would be a good break for you, and you could talk with the other scientists. It's a lively community. Everyone is friendly. And it's safe."

Damn Sage for butting in. And hadn't she said she wasn't the "enclave" type? She was just doing Sykes' bidding here. "I'm sure everyone's friendly, and it's very safe," I said. "But I couldn't leave the Ceph –"

Mr. Sykes looked down his nose. "You should come." He may have meant it to be inviting, but it felt ominous. He didn't like not getting his way. I bristled at his insistence and dug in my heels.

Sage jumped in, more nervous than I'd ever seen her. "Come for a visit, Raina. Cedric, you'd love the cliffs on the island." Why was she suddenly looking scared? "It's nicer than you'd expect."

"Come for a visit, both of you," Mr. Sykes agreed. "A short one. You can go down in the sub and see the site we've acquired for the Ceph."

Feeling cornered, I reluctantly agreed.

Mr. Sykes stuck out his hand and I shook it, trying not to feel like I was entering into a new, darker bargain.

They departed shortly after. We breathed a quiet sigh of relief as we paused to watch the copter disappear in the distance. We were not leaving the city, not while I had anything to do with it. It might be a rundown, washed-up coastal city no one moved to anymore, but I had put down my roots here. Stubbornness more than anything would keep me here long after common sense told us to leave. We turned back to our work, and I tried to shake off the discomfort that Sykes' visit had left in me.

A week later we noticed broken glass on the floor and a couple of vials from the gene-editing pack were gone. Neither Edward nor Laurel knew what had happened and suggested one of the Ceph must have broken them. The Ceph were getting too involved in their own research program, and with the excitement of our visitors I think Edward had forgotten to put the vials away properly. I vowed to talk to the Ceph about respecting protocols for handling materials (and to keep away from them entirely). If we could keep future visits from our backer to a minimum perhaps we could concentrate and get some work done.

CHAPTER 31: CORALIE

I find Mr. Sykes to be quite full of himself. The arrogance he carries with him! As if he were a god who had created life. And life that talks! Amazing. I am frankly more than a little insulted. He is a fine speaker on topics of interest, clearly skilled in the art of conversing, but I find his astonishment and delight off-putting. I am not a prize, and I do not belong to anyone. Raina and Cedric briefed me well on what to say and not say, and what to avoid. Mr. Sykes, for all his delight, seems uncomfortable with water people like us. He clearly sees humans as superior, and himself as most superior of all. He can't imagine that I see myself as his equal. He thinks he is superior to Raina and Cedric, too. I can tell by the way Raina talks that the funding, the money, is important. That it is important that Mr. Sykes is pleased with us.

Raina is trying to teach me about social concepts, the ways in which humans organize themselves. There is a ridiculous thing she calls "the economy," which seems to be a system of barter based on shared expectations. A magical substance that doesn't really exist called money is used to make trading between people easier. It can be used to give value to a thing or an activity, and then people make or do that thing and give it to others for magical money. People keep track of how much they have and give it away when they want or need something.

What's fascinating is that the money has no value in itself – it's just numbers in a computer. It used to be pieces of paper and little lumps of metal. The whole system strikes me as a bit delusional and dangerous. What if people just woke up and stopped believing in it? What would happen then? It seems like a lot of nothing to hang a whole organizing system on.

I clearly don't understand because money, and especially Mr. Sykes' money, is important. Raina and Cedric both say the visit went well. Mr. Sykes will continue to fund the project and we have escaped relocation for now. I don't feel the same sense of dread that Raina and Cedric do about moving to the Caribbean. It seems quite lovely in the FlickFilms and I am very curious to explore a real reef, even one that has been artificially preserved under strict conservation. The tank in the lab feels very small in the face of our dreams.

I trust Raina's instincts, though. I do not trust Mr. Sykes.

CHAPTER 32

Another of Dr. Winters' recommendations was to accelerate the timeline for moving the colony into a bigger space. The lab's aquarium was too confining and didn't allow for enough creative outlet for the Ceph. We had already set up the basement pool for growing mussels, and it was straightforward to build out some habitat for the Ceph among the bivalves. We'd been planning to do it anyway, we just decided to speed up the schedule.

Coralie and her fellows needed an environment where they could have more autonomy, make some of their own decisions, perhaps even have a degree of privacy. While I may have agreed in theory to privacy, I still had a camera installed to monitor them. After all, we had legal obligations. The trickiest part was installing the biohazard containment protocols. Soon all was ready.

We started transferring the colony to the basement pool two at a time. I had a strange feeling of trepidation and pride, like my children were leaving home. I was worried, but also pleased we had reached this stage, satisfied that the Ceph were setting up house, as it were.

Coralie wanted to go first to supervise and left River in charge of the younglings up top. Coralie took the first day to remake the rock shoal and ask for more sand and rocks. She checked on the mussels and wanted careful instructions on how to control the complex piping and filtration system that maintained a pristine saltwater environment. Delmar was showing engineering promise and acted as her plus-one that first day. I was nervous for them but left them alone. The colony was growing up and needed to exercise some self-sufficiency. I fussed like a mother hen on a nest but kept my distance during the day. I checked and rechecked the filters, while Cedric rechecked the biocontainment zone. He reminded me that now that they were below street level, a breakout became more likely.

"They love us. They won't leave," I insisted.

"Maybe," Cedric replied. "But let's keep everything else out too, eh? One stray virus could throw us off the rails."

I was so nervous the first night that I stayed over after the transfer, sleepless and turning. Every noise in the night made me startle from my light doze.

Dawn arrived and Cedric and I both rose early and cut short our usual routine of coffee and Holo-News. Things in the "up-top lab," as Coralie would come to call it, were quiet. The Ceph stared at us and smiled but did not venture to the top of the tank except to eat.

As soon as the regular staff finished their workday, Cedric and I descended in the elevator to check the pool. The blue light gave an eerie underwater quality to the large space, and a new pile of rocks edged the shallow end. Water dripped off the overhead pipes; they'd adjusted the filtration system to increase the humidity. And it was shockingly cold. I felt a momentary panic as I searched for Coralie and Delmar.

Finally, she surfaced at the deep end and swam slowly to the rocky shallow end to greet us. "Hello!" She was smiling. Things seemed to have gone well overnight. She gave us a brief rundown of their work, made some requests for materials and reported on the health of the mussels.

Over the next few days, we moved all the adults down to the pool except River who wanted to stay and help with the new younglings. The Ceph were becoming a true colony.

࿂

Coralie and the Ceph quickly established themselves in the basement. Cedric and I still had coffee upstairs and watched the Holo-News to start our day. No matter where the Ceph were, the outside world was still in free fall.

Webwex CEO promises Mars space station will be "on-ramp to interstellar highway"

Drought in Western North America fuels worst forest fire season
  in 40 years
French farmers protest lack of pollinator support, dozens killed
Species Termination Notice: Australian platypus
Miramichi Symphony Orchestra celebrates new season

I flicked up the piece on the Miramichi orchestra. Surprisingly, there
was our guy, Burton Sykes, smiling genially as he walked the red carpet
with none other than Dr. Sage Winters on his arm. She looked breathtak-
ing in a gown with more sparkles than the night sky.

"Well, maybe there is something new under the sun!" I said.

Cedric glanced over and made a noise in his throat.

"Just for the record, you know I was available."

Cedric laughed at me. "C'mon, let's check on River and the younglings," he said.

They needed to be fed, and the younglings in particular needed careful monitoring. River took care of naming them and would type out the
names for us painstakingly on a large keyboard. All were ocean-themed
names, mostly in English but sometimes from other languages. We set up
a two-way video monitor so River and Coralie and the colony could keep
in touch. It was sweet to watch the adult Ceph in the basement crooning to
the younglings or murmuring to River over the screen.

"We don't want River to be sad," said Coralie. "We want her to feel a
part of us. And we need to get to know the babies."

Like toddlers taking hesitant, jerky steps, the newest younglings would
pull themselves out of the tank and launch themselves around the lab, exploring. We had to keep a close eye on them to make sure they stayed out of
trouble and didn't interfere with any work. We had a line of maturing eggs
under glass along one side of the windowless room, and different stages of
experimental crosses at the main work tables.

Once one (named Zale, I think) had mastered the trick of slinking up
one leg and wrapping around my torso in a friendly hug, they all had to try
it. The soft suckers of their tentacles didn't catch on the fabric of my clothes

very easily and they often fell, laughing uproariously and unhurt. When they laughed the hue of their face went from pink to red and back, with speckles that lit up their mirth like fireflies winking. The big smiles and soft, wispy sounds were adorable. When Cedric and I tired of the game, River would come out of the tank and collect them, scooping them imperiously off the ground or prying them from our waists, deftly transferring them to her back and carrying them back to the bottom of the tank.

We spent more and more time either in the pool with the basement Ceph or sitting beside it, talking to Coralie. Sometimes she would pull herself out of the pool and sit beside us, stroking a leg or touching us with one of her tentacular arms. She could contort her vaguely human but spineless shape in marvellous ways. She liked to be in motion when she spoke with us and the tentacles at the temples of her face would flick, sometimes nervously, sometimes absent-mindedly. It was fascinating to watch her as we spoke, the colour of her skin changing with her moods, the dim blue light playing off her shifting tones and making her seem even more mysterious.

We talked about anything at all. We talked about human things like music and FlickFilms. Often, we would speak about the colony and how they were getting along at the bottom of the pool. We would carefully note these exchanges in our logs.

"Delmar is quite bold, he tries to get the others to help but it's him and Finn that are doing most of the heavy lifting to create dens," she told us one day. "We have very snug little homes down there. I'll show you the next time you put on your snorkel. Some of us can only sleep when we feel hidden, you know, safe. So the dens are important."

"Do you sleep alone?"

"I do. Some sleep in pairs, for comfort. Mazu and Kai are always together."

Some days, other Ceph joined Coralie. They would drape themselves on the rock piles that jutted out from the water in the shallow end, and listen. Sometimes they would interject, either trying to speak English or making an odd whistling sound that Coralie would translate. They loved to come out and listen when we talked about the ocean.

"The ocean is vast, there is more surface area on this planet underwater than above it. Some are strictly controlled conservation areas, some are cultivated fish and seafood farms, but the majority of oceans are wild, especially the deeper down you go." I told them about the strange creatures that lived there, the frightening anglerfish with a built-in glowing light to lure prey toward her gigantic jaws, the glowing sharks and fish, the crabs and starfish.

I think it was Mazu that asked. Coralie patiently translated, "Can we go and see?"

I hesitated. We often dodged this topic, but that day I felt we needed to plant the seed, get them thinking of the next stage. "That is the plan, of course, that you'll live there someday. But we need to get you ready first. It's difficult to survive down there and we need to make sure that everything is ready first."

Mazu, excited, turned a gentle purple colour.

Coralie reached out, wrapping a tentacle around my shoulders and pulled me closer. "We want to go," she said. "We want to help. We can help you, I think." A wispy facial tentacle curling gently along her cheek reached out to me. "We should be on your research team. We know how to search the net, we have ideas. It's in our dreams, you know. We all want to go to the sea."

Cedric and I exchanged glances. I felt like a parent being asked if Santa Claus was real. "Well, of course," I replied. "That's always been the plan."

How could I explain how dangerous the world was? Both above and under the sea? The menace of daily life outside, the constant threat? All the wrongness in the world, the death and destruction. The bee catastrophe. The world was broken, and we were just muddling through it, safe where we were for the moment. The lab might be the happiest place the Ceph ever knew; I couldn't guarantee anything outside this building. But who was I to kill their innocent wonder?

"There are things we need to solve, first," Cedric added. "You're not ready yet."

It was true they weren't ready. But it was also true that I wasn't ready. I wanted more time like this, sitting companionably beside the basement pool, pretending the world wasn't ending outside. We were waiting on samples, trying to edit via computer simulations and guesses. It was not working. I showed Coralie illustrations and tried to explain the work we still needed to do.

"Coralie, the biggest issue is that we haven't found a solution to the high pressure at the bottom of the sea." I carefully walked her through the editing process, how we would use genetic patterns from dragonfish that we thought would confer the trait to the new Ceph we were growing in petri dishes and eggs in jars. I talked about our success with bioluminescence and the challenge of coping with deep-sea pressure.

"Yes, we need this," she said. "Can you give it to us in the colony once you figure this out?"

I was confident I could.

The truth, however, was that the specimens weren't thriving. Something in the dragonfish's genetic pattern did not agree with the human core we worked with, and the embryos were dying, usually before birth. We tried a variety of species' genetic patterns. The deep-sea species had not had their genomes mapped so we sometimes had to get specimens instead of relying on synthetic material and computer-generated patterns.

It was hard to explain the failure to Coralie. "Something in the fish DNA is toxic to the human, it isn't melding. When we do this type of work with recombinant DNA there can be unexpected outcomes. We are in the world of the weird here."

She took that in and smiled, a slow gesture that revealed a row of sharp teeth. "World of the weird?"

"Figure of speech," I mumbled and changed the subject. There were, of course, a number of curious, or yes, weird, things we could point to in the colony. It was to be expected. Once you start combining DNA in the bold ways we were, off-target effects were inevitable. The most surprising one, however, was how rapidly the colony learned and, frankly, how smart they were.

Coralie always seemed one step ahead of me, in logical leaps and intuition. Cedric and I speculated on why that would be. Octopuses mature quickly, and the smaller ones, like the two-spot, tended to live short lives. The Ceph eggs matured in about four weeks, and the younglings became adults within approximately four months. Hopefully the Ceph had a more human lifespan than octopus. Time would tell. We couldn't explain why the Ceph's intelligence seemed to have increased. We became aware of it slowly in the Ceph and had to overcome our own prejudice toward the superiority of humans, but it was there.

"Maybe it's the whale DNA. We used some dolphin too."

"I think the octopus is smarter than we know," Cedric offered, clearly thinking of Rex and Maisie. "Of course, we know whales and dolphins are intelligent too, but octopus have neurons throughout their bodies. It's like they can think with their tentacles. I bet they can feel colours rather than see them."

Every interaction with the Ceph, especially now that they were in a habitat, albeit a self-contained one, confirmed the observation that they had high intelligence. They had higher reasoning skills, acute curiosity and were developing their own cultural practices, if I could call them that.

This became more apparent the more I worked and sat by the pool and just watched them. Usually, if they were not coming up to talk to me or Cedric, they would stay at the bottom, and I could see them under the water, flitting from one spot to another. They would congregate in small groups. One day I heard a humming sound from beneath the surface. It was a low rumble, followed by a higher pitch, quickly muffled. I tried to see what they were doing but all I could see was a small group of Ceph beside a rock pile.

Coralie was happy to explain. "We have music and speech, it's just under the water. It wouldn't sound the same in air. Even my words are limited compared to what we share with each other."

I recorded the sounds underwater and listened to them on headphones. If the Ceph said it was music, it was music, but I heard no pattern to it, only an eerie quality of squeaks, whistles and growls. Nonetheless, I included a recording in my update to Mr. Sykes, hoping he would take the Ceph at their word and accept that they were making music. The responses to our updates had changed since Dr. Winters' and Mr. Sykes' visit. In addition to Sykes' usual aimless rants, we received reports with technical questions, good ones, that were increasingly specific. Sometimes there were suggestions as well.

Cedric had agreed to share more details with Coralie in hopes that it would help us move forward faster, but he didn't like it. Coralie's shift from subject to partner made him uncomfortable and he worried aloud that we would be murdered in our beds, either by Sykes' henchmen or the Ceph themselves. As usual, I thought he was being overly cautious. We were in the thick of the project now and needed to see it to its end.

CHAPTER 33: CORALIE

I love the new space, especially the way the blue light reflects through the surface and illuminates the bottom of the pool. The mussels are growing well in the deep end, anchored to a mesh that wires them to the wall. They are fed from above and the area around them is a bit murky given the extra protein. It gives the water a bit of a foul taste. We pile rocks in front of them to act as a barrier and to encourage crustacean growth along the rocky outcropping. The filtration system is a bit complicated, but we experiment and make some slight adjustments for comfort. The mussels seem to like warmer water than we do.

We move some sand and rocks around the shallow end to provide a seating area for us to talk to the humans and provide easy entry and egress points for the Ceph. I want us to be as mobile as possible. Ever since the meeting with Mr. Sykes, I feel a small tug of anxiety for our future. Raina and Cedric have not said so exactly, but I sense danger from him, and feel we need to appear as non-threatening as we can. When we met, I had carefully kept our conversation focused on demonstrating my intelligence and worth, as Raina suggested. Keeping Mr. Sykes onside is all well and good, but I need contingency plans as well.

In any case, our new home is exquisite, far superior to the tank we were outgrowing up top. Of course this means we are farther away from the main lab, away from Raina and Cedric and River and the babies. I don't want to feel cut off from the lab work that is creating my people.

I have begun to have opinions on Raina and Cedric's lab work. I don't understand how they make certain decisions and I want to. Understand, that is. It feels like they are playing God. They have explained the concept of God to me and I have to admit it seems silly, a strange way for humans to organize their thinking and feeling. Religion is a way for humans to decide what is good and what is bad, and how they should act.

It's not just about how humans organize themselves; it's about belief around why the world and people exist. The whole concept seems overly complicated to me. I am willing to take existence at face value. If there's a god beyond a simple mathematical organizing principle, it's the ocean. But it doesn't judge, it embraces.

Raina and Cedric are "non-believers" and "not Christian," so they may not be describing the system from a position of strength.

The story goes like this: There is an all-knowing father up in the sky who sets rules and judges the behaviour of the people on the ground. There is also a son who offers compassion to those suffering in God's name. Or something like that. The all-knowing father gets to determine who lives and who dies and when. And who suffers.

I've begun to wonder if Raina and Cedric are making decisions in the lab about who lives and who dies, and that is a problem.

CHAPTER 34

It was a good time to get the adult Ceph out of the main lab. Coralie and the others had begun to take a keen interest in our research. While this was encouraging, it also opened up difficult conversations and sometimes interfered with our work. Coralie had noticed that some of the specimens didn't survive, and eventually worked out that we were selecting which would grow to adulthood. When we knew a specimen wasn't viable, we terminated it at the egg stage.

"What gives you the right to decide that?" she had wanted to know. "And how do you decide? Do you pick the least ugly, at least to you?"

It was a pointed barb that struck me hard. I tried to explain. "Some specimens will never breathe underwater, or they have digestive or coronary issues that will kill them as they grow."

When the specimens were a collection of cells or even fertilized embryos, we could select the best combinations to grow. I looked at this as a form of gardening and did not think twice about disposing of genetic material, or a specimen. Some of the embryos were simply not viable. Ethically, we were well within the confines of the offspring exemption and current legislation. It was legal, and there was less grey area around the softer ethics piece than Coralie was grasping. I tried to explain that once the embryos were growing in their synthetic eggs, we had a greater duty of care; that once they were born, we had to treat them as individuals deserving the necessities of life and health. But where the subjects were determined to be unviable or dangerous, we were within the legislation to terminate them. In fact, under certain circumstances we were obligated to do this. Sometimes it was a mercy, sometimes it was a calculated decision based on probabilities and anticipated outcomes.

Coralie did not understand this at all. She became more and more agitated. "You can't do it like this," she said. "You can't kill the babies. Give them to us. We will raise them or end them when they need it. But it shouldn't be your choice who lives and dies. I see your criteria; I hear your talks. You are playing God in the worst way; you are trying to cover up murder and infanticide."

I didn't know how to respond, how to explain centuries of scientific inquiry, how to explain human scientific ethics. I tried, but my attempts fell on deaf ears.

"Each altered specimen carries a risk with it, you see," I began again. "A risk that it will escape and harm the environment, harm the ecosystem, the plants, the insects, the animals. It can do this in obvious ways like the hoppers, a deadly invasive species, but there are subtler ways, too. A virus or a bacterium that survives in the ocean but not on land may be altered just enough to kill off entire species if it makes it out of our lab. It's critical that we contain all the new life here, and that we are cautious about the shape and structure of that new life. If a specimen is dangerous in this way, we need to . . . contain it. Do you understand?"

"What I understand is you are killing our babies. And that I will not stand for. Should I be grateful you didn't strangle me at birth? Will you contain me if I become dangerous?" She was flushing deep red.

"We are not strangling anyone," I answered, wondering what she had been reading lately. The internet connection they had access to was filling their minds with pap.

She roiled around the seating area, uncontained and angry. Cedric and I flinched back and waited, suddenly frightened. Her head whipped around as if looking for something to throw at us, but she didn't approach. The other Ceph surfaced and gathered around the edge of the pool, nervous and hovering, not sure what to do.

"Coralie, we're in this together, you know," I said softly, as if she were a wild animal I was trying to approach.

"You should give them to us," she said, her voice raised. "Let us raise them. We can decide whether their attributes are the ones we are seeking.

You can make us part of your project. We can take care of the endings of the young ones too, if need be."

"Coralie, this isn't how it works." I was pleading now. "Cedric and I need to be in charge. We're the scientists, we know how to make this work." True as far I knew, and I wasn't willing to accept how smart the Ceph were, not yet. Their view of the world was so narrow, they weren't fully human, they couldn't be left in charge.

She slowly calmed, and considered us.

"We can come to an agreement," I said finally. "We can work together."

The accusatory questions shifted. "And how long will you contain us? Are we to live out our existence here, in this place?" She looked around at the confines of the basement pool.

"Of course not!" I insisted, though I wouldn't have minded. We were safe here. With the big wide world, you had to take your own chances. But Coralie would never understand I was trying to protect her and the Ceph. They were growing up so fast, it was hard to keep up, hard to make them understand.

Coralie's rage gradually subsided but all three of us were shaken. To appease her, Cedric and I agreed to share our work in greater detail and ask her to help us with decisions concerning the newer specimens. Despite this collaboration, I felt better with most of the Ceph safely moved to the basement because the idea of having Coralie stare over my shoulder in the lab all day made the hair on the back of my neck stand up. With the colony installed in their pool, we could work in peace upstairs, but I did use the computer in the basement to give Coralie regular updates. I tried to explain our reasoning, why we were doing what we were doing, what our end goal was. I tried to explain some of the legal requirements, the liability waiver, our responsibilities.

Cedric's reading lessons were going very well and Coralie, River and Finn had a fair degree of mastery. They could follow the reports fairly well even if I didn't read them aloud. She consulted on the specimens and we listened and tried to take her views into account. It wasn't a bad thing to have a third viewpoint to triangulate our work, and her views were definitely unique. She gradually came to accept that we could pre-select embryos but was strongly opposed to any kind of "up-top" mercy for the nonviable eggs and creatures we sometimes had.

We agreed that the Ceph could work their own mercy on them.

So we tagged our specimens and brought them live to the pool. The Ceph would take them and celebrate their little lives. Sometimes, they would also end them, as we had agreed, for reasons we agreed. They did this with ceremony under the surface, but Cedric and I were not invited to observe.

Our cute and cuddly octo-people were becoming something else, something adult and thoughtful and forceful. I did not know whether to feel pride that they were evolving into a society or unease that we were creating killers.

CHAPTER 35

I had begun to sleep over at the lab more and more as our work intensified. So I was there to hear what Cedric was hearing at night – sounds of grating metal, soft thumps of the Ceph moving around the lab. Since Coralie and the other adults had moved to the basement pool, there was much less movement. Only River and the younglings remained in the main lab on the sixth floor. The group of younglings was getting older and I supposed it was time to move some of them downstairs.

One night I was awakened by a new, alarming noise. Waking up, I couldn't say exactly what it was, but I bolted down the corridor. Cedric and I met at the door to the lab, and hurriedly unlocked it. Cedric turned up the light and we were met with a tableau of horror.

One of the younglings crouched on the floor in a pool of blue liquid, blue running down his face. At first, I thought he held a fish in his tentacles, with a half-eaten piece falling from his mouth. But there were tentacles sticking out at odd angles. It took a moment to realize that it was Maisie, or what was left of Maisie. River was behind him, and they were arguing.

"No, no, no, no!" Cedric wailed and sprinted to grab Maisie away from the young Ceph. It was clearly too late for the octopus, but the Ceph dropped the carcass, squirted ink at Cedric and frantically tried to make it back to the tank before Cedric reached him. Cedric lunged for him and caught him by two tentacles.

Then Cedric stopped in his tracks, let go and grabbed his inked skin. "Shit, it stings!"

The youngling reached the tank and dove in, hiding in the rocks. River was making apologetic noises, and seemed frozen in place, not sure what to do. Stricken, Cedric stood silently, tears welling up.

I got the safety kit and cleaned up Cedric's arm. The inked area of skin was coming up in a welt but nothing more. I sprayed it with antiseptic and topical antibiotic and bandaged it. All the while, Cedric stared balefully into the tank where the younglings all huddled frightened at the bottom. River had slid back into the tank and was worriedly peering at us over the top. I wordlessly clanged the useless tank cover shut and locked it. "Please stay there," I said to River, as the lid pushed her under the water.

I silently cleaned up the octopus carcass abandoned on the floor.

Cedric shook his head, tears tracking down his cheeks. "I'll make coffee. I can't go back to sleep."

Once in the kitchen, having locked all the tanks and the laboratory door, and double-checked the security mechanisms, we went over what happened. Cedric was still shaking.

"We'll need to change the locks on all the tanks. We've given them too much freedom, at least topside. The younglings need to be better controlled," I said.

We were both upset. We'd been lulled into thinking that the Ceph, being human-like, were not dangerous. It was a fatal error and had cost us Maisie. It could have cost us more. We needed to rethink not only our security protocols but our approach. The example of the hoppers lay between us, unspoken. Were we creating an advanced predator? How could we counter this?

"We need to talk to Coralie," I said finally.

We waited until morning to go downstairs and find Coralie. Without discussing it, we rechecked the locks and containment measures before we entered the pool area. The blue lights were already on and Coralie appeared in the shallow end as we entered. We quickly told her what had happened.

"It's murder," Cedric blurted out. "It killed Maisie."

Coralie said nothing for a few minutes, just listened. Then finally offered, "I'm sorry this happened, it has upset you, especially you, Cedric. What will you do?"

"Coralie, the purpose of the colony is to be nonviolent," I said. "We are supposed to be preserving what's best about human nature, not introducing exaggerated aggressive traits. We can't allow this youngling to live. We can't have hyper-aggression in the group."

"Are you sure this was aggression? Maybe the youngling was just hungry." Coralie was watching us closely.

"But Rex and Maisie are part of the family. They are partly your ancestors, your forebears. Isn't this a domestic killing?"

Coralie splashed back into the water and jetted around the piles of rock in the shallow end. Emerging several metres away, she swam slowly back to us. "I think the youngling is undisciplined. Give him to us. Perhaps keeping the babies up-top with River is a mistake. They should be here with their family, where we can watch them, teach them."

"Coralie, this individual is a mistake, an outlier. We need to weed out the violent tendencies, we have to trim."

"Or maybe you and Cedric have more feelings for an octopus than a Ceph child. If he cannot be redeemed, we will take of him."

"Take care of him? Coralie, he needs to be terminated."

"We will take care of things to your liking and according to your views."

She was obviously angry and dove under the water and spun around the rock piles for a few minutes. When she resurfaced, she was calmer. "Bring him to me. We will do your dirty work."

And so River delivered the infant to us and we brought him to the pool. The adult Ceph gathered him up and pulled him under. I do not know what macabre ritual they used, but there were bubbles and sharp waves in the deep end and then there was nothing. In the calm that followed, no Ceph came out to report on what had happened beneath the surface.

CHAPTER 36: CORALIE

What bothers me more than the death of the octopus is the way that they call the youngling "it" and not "he."

It dawns on me slowly that we are in some danger. Our day-to-day routines are soft and safe. We are together and the pool with the mussel farm is comfortable. We have our run-ins and disagreements, but overall life is happy. After my visit with Mr. Sykes, however, I began to feel uneasy.

When Maisie the octopus met her end, it was clear that Cedric and Raina were ready to kill the child. And that I could not stop them. We are safe but vulnerable.

I do what I need to do. Raina and Cedric need to feel they have addressed the situation. The child is violent, they think, unpredictable.

To kill the child goes deeply against my nature. The Ceph are not weak, nor are we sentimental. I disagree with what they want, but I am powerless. We do what needs to be done. But before that, we name him Bubbles, and do not speak of him again to Raina or Cedric.

CHAPTER 37

The copter landed on the helipad and we clambered out, surrounded by blue sky, warm breezes and expectation. Our big visit to the Ceph's new Caribbean home. I should've been excited, but I was nervous and a little put out. This was a command performance and not a holiday. Cedric smiled up at the sunshine anyway, enjoying the fresh air.

"Presentation with the update, little sub ride, then home?" I reminded him in case he was tempted to stay.

He smiled wryly and nodded. "If all goes well."

Nothing had changed on the island since our last visit, except Mr. Sykes didn't meet us at the car. It was just a self-driving shuttle, and we jumped in the back seat without speaking. I couldn't help worrying how things were going at home. Were Edward and Laurel getting along with the Ceph? Were the Ceph behaving? Was everything all right? We had agreed to leave them to it so we could concentrate on our task here. I buckled my seat belt impatiently and stared out the window as we rolled toward New Carthage, under a perfectly cloudless sky. We passed through the outer wall, and a hidden door in a building facade opened a passageway down to the heart of Mr. Sykes' enclave. There was a small contingent, including Mr. Sykes, waiting for us in the underground city.

"I trust your journey was smooth?" Sykes smiled and held out his hand. We shook it, then followed him down the hallway. He was surrounded by his people – lawyers, issues managers. Maybe a caterer or two. A fairly big turnout of hangers-on. A familiar face stood out.

"So good to see you again!" What was Sage Winters doing here?

We walked down the hallway together. "What brings you here?" I asked.

"More consulting," she said simply. "And I'm trying on enclave life. You could too."

The corridor walls must've been preprogrammed. They displayed a collection of windows looking out on a beach, giving the impression of an airy tourist resort. We were taken directly to a boardroom with faux picture windows, looking out on a cliff facing the ocean, with birds wheeling overhead. I knew we were still in a windowless bunker, but at least my claustrophobia was at bay for the moment.

"Shall we get started?" Mr. Sykes gestured and everyone took a seat.

I pulled up our presentation and exchanged glances with Cedric, who nodded nervously. Go time. As soon as it seemed everyone was settled, I launched into my spiel.

"Thank you, Mr. Sykes, you'll recall we were given the task of genetically engineering humans to live at the bottom of the ocean. I'm very pleased to report that we have succeeded. The Midnight Project is a success!" I projected a magnificent image of Coralie, bigger than life, over the table. There was a ripple of reaction around the table, but it was hard to read if the gasps were of delight or horror. No one was smiling, but then they were lawyers.

"As you can see, we have had to depart from some physical characteristics of humans, to ensure the ability to breath underwater, and cope with the immense pressure of the Midnight Zone. They have eight limbs: two vestigial and six ambulatory, with two of those operating as arms on dry land and two to four acting as legs. They can walk, run and crawl though they don't move quickly out of the water. With an effective cross with octopus, whale and several other proprietary codes and processes, we have succeeded in creating a colony of quite remarkable individuals."

I played a FlickFilm of the Ceph on the side of the pool. Delmar excitedly waving, and Mazu perfectly still, not knowing where to put her tentacles. Coralie was in the foreground, grinning, her sharp teeth making her look unintentionally fierce. Their skin was a happy pink, with just a hint of dapple to signal their excitement at the fun of being recorded.

"We have thirty-four adults and thirty-two children and adolescents."

I switched the video to a close-up of Coralie's face in the water. She swam over the boardroom table and around the room, covering the faces of our audience.

"In biological terms, they are an impressive hybrid, able to breathe in and out of the water, though they need regular access to salt water to survive. They swim using jet propulsion. I'm pleased at the degree of bioluminescence we've achieved, which will help them find each other and communicate in the deep."

"Extraordinary," said Mr. Sykes, interrupting. "How does the bioluminescence work? Why is it important?"

I switched gears to explain in more detail and tried to get back on track. "They've created their own underwater language through a combination of echo-clicks and air or water being pushed through their mouths. We have recorded samples, but it goes beyond the ability of human ears to perceive. They tell us they've made music." I played a sample, which sounded like rushing water and not much else.

"Play that again," Mr. Sykes said. I replayed the clip and waited. "I don't hear anything."

I ploughed ahead. "They also have complex intellects, display a curiosity about the world and are developing personal preferences and interests. They have evolved social structures, based on matriarchal leadership and family units." I flicked up a video of Delmar arranging rocks in the pool, building reefs, and then a video of River caring for the younglings.

"Marvellous! Look at those beauties." Mr. Sykes interrupted for a third time.

I glanced at Cedric and willed myself not to roll my eyes. I soldiered on. "They eat deep-sea mussels, which can be farmed. As you can see in these images of the pool, we have created a small self-sustaining habitat for them." I paused to see if Mr. Sykes was going to jump in again. He did not disappoint.

"The clams, yes, the clams. Look at them. We've installed them in our offshore habitat. Brilliant, yes?"

Wanting it to be over, I moved on to the final piece. "The one remaining hurdle is to enable them to live under the extreme pressure in the midnight zone. We're still conducting crosses and experiments and hope to confirm a solution in the coming weeks. Of course, we won't know until we've field-tested this aspect, but we have reason to believe we're close. We'll still need to establish the appropriate ecosystem elements to contain them before we move them into the wild, and we'll go back to running simulations so we can mitigate any unforeseen impacts associated with the transfer."

I paused and there was a smattering of applause from the suits. "Any questions?"

A suit raised a hand, looking slightly ill at ease. "Are they at all . . . aggressive?"

"They are quite docile," I affirmed, imagining I was crossing my fingers behind my back. Greg could make it true. "They're thoughtful, deliberate and proud."

Cedric was carefully scanning the room and frowned. But now the questions were coming fast and furious. "How intelligent are they? How fast do they grow? How long can they stay out of the water? Can they speak English? How long do they live?"

I answered as much as I could, and Cedric fielded a few questions about habitat. As usual, no one was particularly interested in the ecosystem effects.

Finally, Mr. Sykes intervened. "And you're sure you'll be able to solve the pressure issue?" he asked. I stretched the truth and reassured him I was one hundred percent confident. Sykes smiled, a shark-like expression with dead eyes that twinkled menacingly.

"This is excellent progress, Dr. Templeton, Dr. Beauville. Congratulations. I'm pleased to report that we've had some success here as well," he said. "As I mentioned before, I've acquired one of the sites you identified as a potential Caribbean habitat and installed a mussel colony that is reportedly doing exceptionally well. I'd suggest we visit it while you are here."

He stood up without further ado and all the suits did likewise and shuffled out of the room. I stood and took a deep breath, letting it out slowly. Cedric reached over and touched my arm, nodding silently. As I turned, the walls flickered and the broad windows with birds wheeling above an ocean vista disappeared and became a concrete wall. I flinched and hurried out.

&

We lost most of the hangers-on when we proceeded to the copter for the site visit, but Sage Winters jumped in behind Mr. Sykes, chattering as if she were picking up a conversation we left off when she last visited us in Long Harbour. She sat beside Cedric who asked her questions about her stay at the enclave.

Mr. Sykes had arranged a deep-sea submarine to show off his handiwork and we helicoptered out to a blank space of ocean. Without warning, the main door flung open and a ladder lowered over the waiting sub, floating on the surface below. Sage grabbed hold of the edges and descended. Cedric and I stared at the swaying rope ladder. "Is that the only way down?" Cedric asked, looking a bit green.

"We can lower you in the safety tray; I just assumed you'd prefer the ladder. Our co-pilot can set that up if you want." He didn't wait for an answer but swung a leg out and stood at the top of the ladder. "I'll meet you at the bottom." He disappeared from view.

Cedric and I stared at each other and then back at the waiting sub. We were terrified but didn't want to embarrass ourselves in front of the boss. I spared one quick moment of hate for both Sykes and Sage and then swung my leg over the ladder. "You good?" I asked.

Cedric nodded. "I'll follow you down."

A lifetime and a few minutes later, we were both standing beside Mr. Sykes and Sage on the sub's top deck, my arms and legs shaking but otherwise intact. It was gleaming and state of the art, boasting an airlock, with the ability to force water out of the entryway like in a spacecraft. We could open the top hatch and climb down the ladder to enter without getting our clothes wet.

The submarine had a control room with viewing area, two sleeping areas and a bathroom with a shower. As it was a research sub, the control room was fully equipped with state-of-the-art computers. It was surprisingly spacious for a deep-sea trawler. We were joined by the pilot, his first mate and a biologist that had worked on the site.

"This vessel is designed to be self-sufficient underwater for several months to years." The pilot proudly showed it off with a quick tour, explaining its deep-sea capabilities and how it was able to sink and rise through the pressure of the deep. I was impressed. Once he had finished, we strapped in our seats and headed out.

The water closed over us, and I felt a flash of panic, quickly controlled. We were well out to sea, and as we descended, there was only bubbles and greenish blue light to see. Occasionally a small school of fish or a larger shark would pass by the viewing window. The pilot was chatty and gave a running commentary on our surroundings. "There is a protected coral reef about two kilometres west. All boat and vessel traffic is restricted or I'd pass by, it's so beautiful. We can just see its outer edge here." Large and multicoloured coral was visible through the window off to our right, and the pilot swung us around to get a better view. Small, brightly coloured fish darted in and out and a large palm-like plant (or was it an animal?) waved at us as we glided over top.

The pilot continued, "The mussel farm is at a depth of sixteen hundred metres – not straight down from us, but another kilometre east. We are on the eastern edge of the Puerto Rico Trench, so we need to be careful. There's more earthquake activity on the sea floor here." Soon we could see the ocean bottom, and a collection of dark green fronds of sea kelp. A large manta ray swam by, unconcerned by our presence.

"From here, we follow the sea floor out a bit more. You'll notice when we really start our descent."

We wound our way above the kelp and continued sinking. We were following a beam of light down through the water, bubbles passing our window on their way to the surface. Within minutes, darkness surrounded us, and our way was lit only by the submarine's headlights. I felt the ocean around our craft as a living thing, enveloping and encircling us. I breathed faster.

Mr. Sykes was enthusiastically pointing out landmarks through the viewing window. "Can you turn the headlights off?" he asked. "We'd like to see the natural landscape."

When the pilot turned the lights off, we were plunged into darkness. Not utter darkness, however. As our eyes adjusted, flashes of blue and green began appearing, little pulses like tiny fireworks, an astonishing glow against a black backdrop. It was amazing how full of glowing life this part of the world was. The bioluminescence of the creatures around us didn't cast a light outward, but gently illuminated some tiny part of them. It was impossible to see exactly what was causing the mirage of light specks. The harder I stared at them, the more weight the ocean above us seemed to have.

The immensity of sea pressed down.

"Are you all right, Doctor?" The pilot spun toward me, noticing I had gripped his chair. I could not tear my eyes away from the viewing window as we reached a massive drop-off where we could see nothing ahead. I felt a spurt of vertigo, as if I were at the top of a roller coaster about to plunge.

"It's okay, we have radar." The pilot tried to reassure me. "Don't worry, everyone freaks a little the first time."

The darkness was a living thing around me. The lights flickered and went out completely. I could see nothing. I struggled to breathe and suddenly found myself on the floor. Mr. Sykes leaned over me, his disapproving face too close, and I flinched back. Cedric and the first mate helped me to my feet.

"What happened?"

"A little panic drop. Nothing to worry about – you're okay," the first mate told me. "Happens sometimes. Did you hit your head?"

I didn't think so but gingerly touched the back of my head to be sure. Mr. Sykes hovered, frowning. I tried to shake off sudden embarrassment by feigning interest in the scenes outside the sub. The pilot had prudently turned on the headlights again. We could no longer see the choreography of tiny pulsing lights, but the strong yellow glow gave me a bit of renewed confidence.

Descending through open ocean, we could only see what was illuminated by the forward-facing headlight of the craft. While we occasionally saw a fish, in general there was nothing but darkness. Slowly we sank deeper into the black. Hours passed, or was it days? Or moments? In the headlights we could see the edge of the trench, rising up on one side like a hillside, and in some spots, a sharp cliff.

We rounded a bend and Mr. Sykes jumped up and started to get excited. "Is that it?" he asked the pilot.

The pilot nodded and pointed. The biologist on board began to speak quickly. "Mr. Sykes, as you can see, we've built a vertical frame to support the clams, they are anchored in with netting. They eat the plankton and other debris that sinks from the higher levels and should be self-sufficient as they grow. We'll need to start harvesting them to ensure sustainability."

"Very good," Mr. Sykes reassured the biologist, who was looking visibly nervous now that the big boss was focused on him. "This looks really impressive."

A series of crusty outcroppings were moulded to the side of the underwater cliff we were approaching. The mussels were growing well, and I could see how the Ceph could live here. Along the side and farther down from the mussels ran an underwater ravine with rocky crevices. They could make a home here.

The pilot sent out an underwater drone to collect some samples. We chatted as we waited, and Mr. Sykes talked about how he acquired the underwater rights. It took several minutes for the drone to return, and once it was safely in the submarine's vestibule, we were on our way back. The minutes stretched into hours and I found my claustrophobia closing in again. It was the people as much as the tight space and expanse of ocean outside.

Cedric took me to the side and sat me down. "You don't have to look," he told me. "Just talk to me." A few steadying breaths later I felt the constriction in my chest ease and the roaring in my ears subside. I averted my eyes from the panorama view of nothingness and concentrated on Cedric's words. Cedric talked about his greenhouse, how resilient his kale was and how he was trying to get a coffee plant to grow. I was grateful to avoid another embarrassing fainting spell. Sykes already saw me as weak – I avoided looking at him. After some hours, we resurfaced once more, climbed back onto the copter and returned to the island.

On the copter pad, with Sage by his side, Mr. Sykes bid us farewell with another invitation to join him on the island. Cedric and I didn't speak during the copter ride back to Long Harbour. It was only once I was safely curled up on our sofa back at home that I felt a knot of unease begin to relax.

"I think they bought it," I said.

"Yeah," agreed Cedric. "Good presentation. And the sub is amazing. But why were there just suits and no scientists in the briefing? Just one biologist in the sub. It felt off."

"That place makes my skin crawl, but I can't put my finger on it."

"Sage says she loves it," Cedric reported. "She says she feels very safe and welcomed, and that she can concentrate on her work." I ignored his wistful tone. "We should think about it, you know."

I didn't say anything.

"It feels . . . secure, Raina. Like we'd get three square meals a day."

"I thought you liked cooking."

"That's not what I mean," Cedric replied, his eyebrows drawing together. "Things may get bad all at once out in the world. I mean, things are bad, but they may get a lot worse all of a sudden. This might not be forever, is all I'm saying." He saw he was getting nowhere and tried a different tack. "Once the Ceph are installed, we'll be closer to them there. You should think about it."

"I hear what you're saying," I relented. It wasn't Cedric's fault I was self-centred and stubborn. "But let's not think about it now. Not yet."

I should love the enclave, shouldn't I? Shouldn't I be jealous, a fortified beautiful place like that? But it grew in my imagination like a city-sized trap. The suits grew even more diabolical in memory, and I couldn't shake a sense of menace when I remembered Mr. Sykes looming over me in the sub. Something was off.

CHAPTER 38

I was sinking in deep water. I could hear indistinct voices, calm at first and then shouting. I was on my back staring at the surface of the water from underneath, at a distorted moon that bathed me in blue light. It receded and the light became fainter and fainter. The voices also were fainter, though more insistent, calling to me. I tried to swim, kicking my legs out, but I was staring up and could not shift. I heard my own voice, "Stop! No! Stop!"

Long green fronds wrapped around my arms, my torso, pinning me. Bubbles shot upward. I began to struggle and opened my mouth to scream, "No, please! Stop!" And woke up.

I was alone and in darkness.

CHAPTER 39: CORALIE

I am drifting in deep water. A bright blue orb above bathes me in gentle light as I descend. As far as I can see, I am surrounded by open water. I feel alive and powerful. All around me I see marine life. Schools of shimmering fish, sharks, pods of dolphins. And still I descend. I smile at them all, call out to them in friendship. I do happy somersaults as they greet me in turn.

As I sink, the light diminishes and soon I can only see softly glowing animals, fish with large eyes or small dangling lures in front of their faces. They are not friendly and I do not greet them. Startled by a flicker of threat, I look for a place to hide. I need a den to protect myself. A shift in the water pivots me to my right and I notice a deep-sea shark approaching. I flush a darker purple, curl up small and flinch as it swims by. There is nowhere to hide. I flee but the shark pursues. I wake up as it grabs one of my tentacles from behind.

CHAPTER 40: CEDRIC

FADE IN

INT. INTAKE ROOM - NIGHT

CEDRIC sits on the couch, clutching a mug of tea, his
hands shaking slightly. He looks down, tries to quell
the shaking, then puts the mug down self-consciously to
avoid spilling it.

                    CEDRIC
     The nightmares are becoming more and more
     frequent. I'm becoming a bit unhinged.
     Thankfully, I don't remember them very well.
     Little snippets come back to me when I wake:
     The sensation of being pulled off a boat in
     stormy seas by cold wet hands. Slimy things
     crawling from the deep and smothering me.
     And always the undulating waves, driving me
     forward, preventing escape.

     I admit it - I'm afraid to sleep. I pad down
     the hallway and check the locks on the lab,
     double-check the locks on my sleeping quar-
     ters. It's lonely at night. I don't want to
     wake the Ceph and doubt they would be good
     company at this hour. In the midnight hours,
     I can't conceal my fear of them.

CEDRIC picks up his mug of tea and stares into the camera, gulping it down.

> CEDRIC (cont'd)
> I really, really wish I could sleep.

CEDRIC turns off the camera.

CUT TO BLACK

PART III
TRANSFORMATION

These fragments I have shored against my ruins.

– T.S. Eliot, *The Waste Land*

CHAPTER 41

Home again, and reassured that Edward and Laurel had survived their time with the Ceph, I couldn't deny that things were getting worse in the city. I still commuted from my house, but the view out the window of the rickety shuttle revealed more abandoned homes and businesses, more people derelict on the streets. I didn't see any hoppers but knew they were there, creeping just out of sight. It was September and what should have been the cheapest time for fruits and vegetables was filled with shortages and sky-high prices. I stopped in regularly to the grocery store down the block but the shelves were often bare and what was there was poor quality and outrageously priced. They had armed guards at the entrance. Donna the fishmonger delivered fish and crabs direct to the lab now. Some days she carried her rifle over her shoulder.

The Holo-News brought us no comfort.

North American farmers seek compensation for failed growing
   season
World Food Programme decries rise in scurvy and malnutrition
   worldwide
Famine devastates Kenya, government in Nairobi unstable

I got up to make more coffee before we got to the extinction alerts. It was enough to make you weep, if you were given to that sort of thing.

Edward, Laurel and Susan still came in every day but were feeling the strain. I had never bothered much with them beyond their functions, but Cedric kept tabs on how they were coping and sent them home with large boxes of fresh produce for their families. He listened to their fears and concerns, tried to help out. We were lucky to have stores of cans and dry goods, and Cedric's greenhouse was wonderful.

I called to check in on my father. He didn't answer but called back the next day. He was fine. He was well-supported, well-fed at the university enclave. He was glad I was well. We were polite. We didn't talk about money.

Cedric and I redoubled our efforts to resolve the last engineering challenges. I walked Coralie through our experiments, explaining with the help of holograms beside the pool. She listened intently, often joined by a couple of the others. "Tell me again about the pressure issue," she asked. "I don't understand yet."

"The issue of living in the deep sea is tricky," Cedric patiently explained. "The pressure is so high that most surface dwellers would be crushed. Only whales and squids seem to have the ability to function in the shallows and in the deep. Most deep-sea creatures are specially designed for the pressure and can't come to the surface without damage. There are a few exceptions, like isopods and certain kinds of crabs that have shells to protect them. We need a good strategy for you. I think building a shell and turning you into crustaceans would be too much change and cause other problems. So we're focusing on the whales and squids. But it's hard to parse."

"I know you'll do it," Coralie said solemnly. "I trust you."

Her trust was well placed because it was Cedric who finally cracked it. Vampire squid live in the ocean depths. They also have an ability to migrate upward when following food. There were very few specimens of vampire squid left as they were highly endangered and had died out in some parts of the world. Their genome had never been catalogued before. It took months to track down a specimen. Cedric tried all his stale marine biology contacts, a few illegal zoo and fishery outfits and even a prestigious academic institution. In the end, our old friend Shorty-Stevie-Stéphane came through with a frozen sample of vampire squid, no questions asked. I think he liked sharing a deep-sea hobby with Cedric, and didn't look too deeply at our motives. Cedric sent him a care package of greenhouse produce as thanks. We had computer software to run the genome, and we set to work trying to isolate the genes and associated characteristics that would enable the Ceph to survive in their habitat.

Even when we thought we had a solution, we still had a testing issue. We could edit the adult Ceph by injecting genetic material, but we didn't know what the actual impact on their physiology would be. It might kill them. It might have severe adverse effects. It might not work.

We spoke frankly with Coralie and the other Ceph about this. We'd arrived at a point where the adult Ceph had to consent to be experimented on. We ran some preliminary assays and tried some editing that we were confident would not harm our subjects. We introduced the fix but it was unclear whether this would be sufficient to protect them in the dark depths of the ocean.

It was Coralie who suggested a way out of the impasse. "Why don't we run the tests under pressure? Why don't we run real-world experiments in the ocean?"

Cedric's initial dismay notwithstanding, Coralie made a lot of sense. We would likely need to tweak the Ceph's abilities to adapt to the midnight zone once they were there. And there was still the problem of the younglings needing to breathe air to survive.

I must admit, I felt an obligation to make sure they were all right, and I no longer felt right about delivering them to Mr. Sykes and never seeing them again, never seeing them in their new habitat. I needed to make sure that they were properly adapted.

Cedric and I discussed it privately over many days, and many cups of coffee.

"We need our own ride, Ceddy."

Cedric resisted. "We'd be totally liable. We can't let them loose and expect them to come back when we call. We can't run experiments off the coast here without a lot of risk."

"I think they'll cooperate. We won't bring them all to the experiment, and they will want to be together, the experimental subjects will come back for the good of the community. They need to prove that it works so that they can all go together."

"I don't think we can rely on the Ceph to be mature about this." Cedric's foot was jangling, his body language tight. "They're like kids, like teenagers. Super smart, but emotionally young. And they've never been outside the lab. We don't know what they'll be like."

"Sure," I said, "but could we just get a sub and then decide? Honestly, and aside from the fainting, ever since I rode in Mr. Sykes' research sub, I've wanted one. Don't you?"

This almost made Cedric laugh, and he agreed that a sub would be cool. In the end, Cedric succumbed to my inexorable logic on this point and then it became a matter of logistics. The biggest hurdle was how to get us all down to the right depth for experimenting. We needed a submersible craft, kitted out as a science vessel with an airlock to allow for entry and exit. Something safe for the humans and the Ceph.

"It's a custom order," Cedric groaned. "And it needs to be as off-the-books as possible. How do we get a 'discreet' research sub?"

This was where Greg and Susan came in. I can't really explain Susan's magic powers for procurement. She was a quiet person, didn't share much, vaguely friendly on good days, very efficient in her work. It came as a pleasant surprise but not a shock that she also had a flair for the underhanded and managed the quiet purchase of the submersible together with Greg without attracting any attention. I guess I should have known about Susan's secret side: she had stuck with us through the early phases of the Midnight Project without drama, and quietly managed an array of purchases and equipment acquisition without Cedric or me paying any particular notice.

Susan found a supplier for a decommissioned research sub and put our order in. Long-term lease, very little money down, which worked for our budget. I breathed a little easier knowing we had our own ride to the Caribbean without depending on Mr. Sykes. We continued our reports and made tentative plans for deep-sea pressure testing at the Caribbean site. The discreetly private acquisition of a sub was a backup plan, a little secret insurance.

Meanwhile, Mr. Sykes continued to send us feedback, directives and random rants about everything. He had views on the bee catastrophe, on global politics, on supply chains and governments and oceans. Governments were worthless, he shared, the only way through the crisis was to unfetter capital.

Great, just great, I thought.

He especially had views on where we should be doing our research and where the Ceph should be. He exhorted us at every opportunity to join him at his enclave. He offered more money, then threatened to cut us off. If anything, his insistence made me dig in my heels beyond all reason. His larger-than-life personality had already intruded too much into my life; how much worse would it be when we were dependent on him as guests on his island?

I tried to ignore everything else and focus on the work.

CHAPTER 42: CORALIE

As I become more involved in Cedric and Raina's work, I am developing an understanding of the complicated context in which they operate. The complexity doesn't stem from the intricate genetic engineering that they do. The biggest complexity comes from the people: the social and legal landscape they operate in.

They are constrained. Constrained by laws, constrained by the need for secrecy and discretion, constrained by ethics and their own desire to do good in the world. It makes their work painstaking, but also painful. I can see their ambivalence toward us at times.

I am fascinated by their explanations of the law. So many pieces of paper to point the blame or take responsibility, to be the authority or escape accountability. Their liability waiver makes them responsible if we break free and do damage. As if we have no agency in the world. As if we do not have minds of our own to direct our own business. As if we are specimens to be owned, rather than our own free-thinking society.

To all of this, I can only ask Raina: Do you know what happens when a piece of paper stays in water long enough?

Their legal protections are a fiction. Their concept of liability is a construct.

I am bound by love, but I am not bound by any of their laws.

CHAPTER 43

I was a little late coming into the office that morning, the traffic had been slow and the shuttle had been late. The sun was shining as brightly as ever, but the Holo-News was worse than usual. In addition to the usual extinction alerts, updates on the bee crisis and conglomerate infighting, we had a local weather crisis on our hands.

"Look at that, could be a direct hit." Cedric gestured at the headlines with his lips as he sipped his coffee. Hurricane Gretchen was headed our way. It was currently a category 3 but forecast to become a catastrophic category 5 before landfall. Storms like this had become increasingly common this far north, but we'd never had a direct hit by a major storm of this magnitude. The smaller ones had caused enough damage to the crumbling coastline and the harbour area, with some buildings collapsing under even a small amount of high wind and rain. "This could be really bad," he added unnecessarily.

We hurriedly made plans. The safest place for us to ride out the storm would be my house in the foothills, but we were both uncomfortable leaving the Ceph. We agreed to watch the evolution of the storm and then decide. It was currently spinning up off the coast of Florida and was predicted to cleave north and shear through Nova Scotia. The older part of the city where our lab sat was at high risk for destruction. We had about a thirty-six-hour window to prepare. It was moving fast.

We put the staff to work taping up windows and securing the tanks and heavy cabinetry to the walls. There was nothing outside to secure, but we reviewed the first three floors of the building (not the basement) and moved everything of value up to a higher level. Edward boarded up some windows at ground level. Cedric and I taped up the intake room and adjoining kitchen and the computer room. By the time we finished that afternoon, the wind was already picking up and there were dark clouds on the horizon. We thanked Edward, Susan and Laurel as they headed for home. Edward lived downtown and was going to ride it out about twenty blocks away from the lab. Susan and Laurel had families in the foothills and would head inland.

"We better tape up your house too," Cedric said, offering to go home with me. I agreed, and was surprised the shuttles were still running. There was a nervous energy, a panicky hum, as everyone stressed about whatever they needed to do before the storm hit. I was glad we didn't have to go to the grocery store, it would be crazy – packed with people.

Once at my place, Cedric set to work bringing in lawn furniture, muttering clinically about the house's vulnerabilities. He was all business, while I gazed nostalgically at the bungalow, feeling its absence already. Along a leafy street nestled in the hills, it looked to be safely inland but I couldn't help seeing it in pieces. I gazed mournfully at the backyard, and over the city, imagining the end was here already.

"Could use a bit of help! We don't have much time!" called Cedric, and I hurried over to grab the side of a patio table. There wasn't much to do, really. Once anything that could move in a strong wind was put inside or secured, we taped up all the windows.

"I think we should ride it out at the lab," I ventured. "I don't want to leave the Ceph alone."

Cedric agreed but pointed out that the Ceph could breathe underwater. "You sure? You'd be safer at your house." But our lab was decently protected. The biocontainment layers should protect against sea surge and flooding and, as long as the building held, we should be fine in the upper floors. We had several weeks of food already stored in the pantry, and a backup generator in case the main power failed. There was also more risk of a break-in if we weren't there.

We were on our way back to the office inside of an hour. The land shuttles were still running, though the sky shuttles had shut down. The sun was setting as our vehicle rolled into downtown. Soon the shuttle's headlights revealed mainly empty streets, a few straggling people scurrying to make their final preparations or get to their safest destination. The harbour area to the east looked largely deserted.

"Shoot, we forgot the roof!" I said, as we approached the elevator.

"Let's clear it tomorrow," Cedric replied. "We still have time."

We ate quickly without talking, and called it a night, but I did not sleep.

࿐

The next day dawned bleak and overcast. The Holo-News was filled with satellite images of the approaching storm, and dire warnings to prepare, to flee, to take shelter. The local headlines had displaced all the international news.

Police warnings reverberated through the streets imploring everyone to heed evacuation orders. News interviews with the local emergency managers, police and hospitals all had a certain wide-eyed twitch to them, a barely contained buzz of fear. We had seen this happen to other cities in the south, seen the aftermath. Some of them had never managed to rebuild. All of them suffered.

We took our coffee and scones to the roof, and sat at the patio table watching the clouds rolling in from the south and the east. It was mesmerizing, how the colours deepened from light grey to a dark and angry purple, and the shadowy shapes of the clouds took on menacing personalities. Now that it was almost upon us, time seemed to slow.

We cleared away the furniture, carrying it into a storage area. Cedric looked sadly at his greenhouse. "I even have a coffee plant, you know . . ." he said wistfully.

"Come on, let's carry the containers inside and tarp the rest if we can. We still have the seed bank."

It didn't take long. We taped the clear walls of the greenhouse with duct tape and tried to batten it down but it looked fragile and was already rattling softly as the winds picked up. Looking out from the rooftop, we could see not only a bank of dark, frightening clouds in the distance but also movement of vehicles and people near the fish market, finishing their preparations. Lights were still on in some of the offshore buildings closer to the coast and I wondered just how bad it would get and what would happen to those who chose to shelter there. I tried to memorize the landscape, noting the older trees, the landmark buildings. How different would things be when we emerged?

By the time we finished moving the plants we could, the wind was starting to push us over, and an intermittent light rain began to fall, whipping sideways and plastering our hair to our heads. We needed to get moving.

We found ourselves in the elevators, surrounded by potted plants. Somewhere around the fifth floor, we were doused in darkness and the elevator shuddered to a stop. "Should be count of ten," I said, referring to the amount of time the backup generator usually took to kick in.

A good (by which I mean very long) fifteen seconds later, the lights returned and the elevator continued on its way. We sighed with relief and looked at each other. "Next time, we take the stairs with a flashlight."

We unloaded the plants on the fourth floor, then descended by the dimly lit stairs to the basement to check in on the colony. Coralie greeted us right away, swimming through the shallow end and darting among the rock piles. The rest were nowhere to be seen. Her eyes were wide and excited. "I can hear the wind! I can even feel it!" she exclaimed. "Will we be safe?"

We explained all the precautions we had taken to seal the building in case of external flooding, including sandbagging and boarding windows.

"We'll come and check in regularly," I promised. "But you should have everything you need. We'll be right upstairs."

We had decided to ride it out in the main lab, alongside the giant tank housing River and the younglings. The windowless room was in the centre of the building and high enough that we shouldn't be threatened by sea surge. We checked on River but didn't tuck in to the lab yet.

Instead, we retreated to our intake room and kitchen, made tea and watched the storm roll in. We could see flashes of lightning in the distance, beyond the rain-speckled windows. We flicked on the Holo-News and checked the local weather. We still had a few hours before the outer bands struck. Gretchen was now a strong category 5 and was expected to bring catastrophic damage in its wake. For us, there was nothing to do but wait. Even if we wanted to make a run for the foothills, it was too late.

The afternoon brought a darkening sky, much too early for dusk. By late afternoon, the wind had begun to howl around the building, rattling the windows. Every now and then a particularly bad gust would strike the glass, making us jump. Nervously, I flicked up the Holo-News to check the satellite images of the incoming storm. An interesting item appeared:

FreeDoomer cult victim of mysterious attack – ark in orbit
   destroyed, super-soldiers suspected

I pulled the full story up and called to Cedric to come watch. "Do you remember that loon, what was his name?"

"Fenix something" – Cedric sat down – "Fenix . . . Runciman! Yes! The guy from the death cult who said he was going to the stars."

"That's right," I remembered. "He got the FreeDoomers to organize an interstellar generational launch, one of those one-way tickets. He crowd-funded the whole thing from his cult followers. A lot of them went bankrupt but managed to get a place on the ark."

At first the images were small and fuzzy, showing a faraway, brightly-lit space ark named *Star Freedom*, a ponderous enclave the size of a city block. A voice-over explained that key strikes from unknown attackers had knocked out the ventilation system. I could barely make out the movement of phalanx after phalanx of suited soldiers floating toward the ark. The first two waves arrived without attracting notice and skittered like water bugs along the surface of the station. I held my breath as they reached the satellite dishes and communications arrays. Bright explosions illuminated the surface of the ark and a part of it went dark. Defensive rocket fire poured out and the incoming waves of floating soldiers were cut down. We watched, spellbound, while explosions were followed by dimming lights until the entire ship went dark.

"How many people live in that ark?" I wondered aloud. "It doesn't look good for them."

"Hundreds? Thousands?"

"I wonder if they made it to the lifeboats? They would have spacesuits for everyone, wouldn't they?" The idea of suffocating in that enclosed space made me unconsciously hold my breath.

"They should have standard safety measures, I mean making sure you can breathe in space is a serious design issue," Cedric replied. "But did they have time?"

With the atmosphere turned off it was hard to imagine many survivors but I watched for signs of lifeboats escaping – one or two maybe, not more. How many thousands of lives winked out with the failure of their air? I shuddered.

Next up: a FlickFilm of Runciman's *Star Freedom* headquarters. This one had action, and plenty of close-ups of the combatants, whose images ran over our boardroom table, shouting. The attackers were big, covered in armour and carrying serious weaponry. Larger than life, faster than normal. I could see why they thought they were super-soldiers. No one had produced a viable and long-lasting enhanced mercenary but the list of desirable qualities was well-known and the holographic mercs tumbling through our intake room exhibited some flags: faster reflexes, more strength, extra-human abilities. I wondered if they had the other desirables: more ingrained obedience, less critical thinking. Did the soldiers used to be fully human?

The headquarters had not been surprised. Defenders fired from upper windows and muffled explosions could be heard throughout the building. Attackers scaled the walls with their bare hands and threw explosives. Screams and smoke issued from open windows. Wave after wave of the attackers plunged through the front doors and through windows. A short time later, bodies littered the street, attackers, defenders and civilians caught in the crossfire. In the distance, sirens echoed too late through the streets.

"Cedric, do you see that?" I whispered.

"I see it," Cedric replied steadily but his knee was bouncing, his foot shaking.

There was a signature bioluminescent swirl, a distinctive pattern of pink and red. A memory arose, unbidden, of the pink to red tattoo-like pattern on Coralie's face and shoulders when she was angry or embarrassed or pleased. In a heartbeat, I recalled the thoughtful questions from Burton Sykes, and from Sage Winters, and how happy I had been to answer them, happy to be collaborating again as a scientist. A scientist who had finally found her way back to community.

I had been careful not to share everything. The process, my proprietary process, that facilitated the transfer of genetic coding to alter adults, I had carefully kept back. It was protected by the nondisclosure agreement with WKPT and I wasn't even supposed to use it for the Ceph. I had used it – it was my invention, damn it! – but had kept all mention of it out of the notes and samples shared with Global Holdings. It had enabled the bee catastrophe; I didn't want it in any hands but mine. How had they gotten a hold of it? How did it end up in super-soldiers attacking interstellar religious pilgrims? It was too much.

I paused the FlickFilm and expanded the face of one of the mercenaries. "See it?" I repeated, louder.

Cedric nodded. "But how? Could it be?"

"Ours?"

My lurching suspicion settled into a dull pain in my gut. Dread threatened to overwhelm me. I wanted to cry. I suddenly found it hard to breathe.

Headlines continued to swirl around the room:

No one claims responsibility for destruction of Star Freedom

Webwex now sole leader in intergenerational interstellar exploration

UN Secretary-General condemns the assault, mourns the loss of civilians

We played the full news reports and sat wordless.

Our work. The bioluminescence that made us so proud. The clever method to achieve our laudable goals. Our work. Killing people millions of kilometres away.

I tried to understand. Our work, our fine and wonderful work, had escaped into the world. Not the Ceph – oh no – they were safely locked in the lab, happily swimming in the basement pool. But our work, the gritty method, the process, *the work*, was out there making everything worse. How had this happened?

"Remember when those vials broke? What if only one broke and the other was taken?" Cedric absently rubbed his arms. "After Sage and Mr. Sykes visited?"

In my mind's eye, a memory of Sage leaning into Mr. Sykes and excitedly saying, "Ceph serum." It would be possible, I thought, to reverse-engineer it from a physical serum sample but some of it, a bioluminescent signature, for example, would likely taint its use if you didn't know how to set up the process's protocols like I did.

I stared at Cedric. "I mean, he could have. His enclave scientists could have figured it out from the serum. I guess it had to be him and Dr. Winters. But why? Why would they want this to happen?" All the air seemed to have gone out of my lungs and I was rooted to my chair with my mouth gaping open. "I don't understand."

"They had to have sold it." Cedric's voice was low, the words clipped. "They used our work to make super-soldiers and sold them. They used us."

"But we have a clause in our contract, they couldn't use our research that way!"

Cedric's laugh was a thing of pain. "Raina, that's why they stole it."

I remembered every grandiose word Sykes had ever uttered about saving the planet. I got up, started pacing the room. I wanted to yell, howl at the moon, scream my frustration. I needed something to punch.

Cedric sat in the chair like a coiled spring. "I baked for that woman. I shared my fresh produce. I made her *three courses*. I even used our fruit for dessert."

"I still don't understand," I muttered plaintively.

Then, suddenly, the projections disappeared, the lights flickered off and the entire building's power system died. The world beyond the window was dark. I felt as much as heard the windows rattle as sideways rain pelted the glass. Gretchen was coming ashore.

Cedric did not move. His voice dropped to a whisper. "Raina, don't you see?" he asked. "This is bad for us. We're implicated. Our signature is right there on the cheek of every soldier. They'll be coming for us now."

CHAPTER 44

It was late afternoon but the intake room was dark. The wind howled outside. Without the distraction of the Holo-News, we decided to check on the generator, which should have kicked in by now. A quick trip down the stairs with a flashlight, and we managed to flick the safety off and get the generator going.

"Let's check on River and the younglings," Cedric suggested. We took the stairs, eerily lit by emergency lighting. We had power again, at least for now, but neither of us would chance the elevator.

River was glad to see us. She came up to the observation deck, smiling anxiously. She could tell something was wrong. We talked again about the approaching storm and reminded her that the wind would be loud and there was rain drumming outside.

There is something boring about certain catastrophes. All we could do was wait for the storm to pass. We cuddled the babies, talked to River and listened to the wind. We played dominoes – River was surprisingly good – read books and watched a FlickFilm, all to the soundtrack of the battering wind and rain. The building shuddered from time to time. Finally, we bedded down in our sleeping bags and fell asleep.

❧

We were woken in the night by a loud bang, followed by complete and utter darkness. The generator had failed again. The building shook, and occasionally we heard breaking glass. At one point, we felt the door shudder and heard wind whistling through the corridor. The laboratory held, and Cedric and I huddled together in our sleeping bags with our flashlights, telling each other that nothing was wrong and everything would be fine. At least, I told us that. Cedric held his own counsel and I pretended I didn't feel him shaking in fear. River had retreated to the bottom of the tank. The younglings had completely disappeared into the rocky crevices.

We waited sleeplessly for morning. As the wind quieted, I finally opened the door, walked down the hall and poked my head into the kitchen and intake room. In spite of the tape, the window had broken and the room was a mess. The furniture was wet and chairs had been knocked over. Only the big mahogany table had stood its ground. The cupboards had mostly stayed closed with only a few dishes fallen and cracked. The vase on the coffee table had tipped and broken. The coffee Bodum, thankfully, had been put away under the sink. I pulled it out and confirmed it was intact. No power still, and no coffee until we fixed the generator.

We looked out on the city, gingerly treading on the broken glass of the window.

"Oh," said Cedric. "Oh dear."

The storm had passed, and the sun was starting to peek out from behind the clouds, revealing a devastating scene. New canals swirled where streets used to be. Water lapped around buildings, covering the first floor and part of the second of the building across the street. Muddy debris, some chunks as big as cars, floated by. As I looked down, I could see people frantically paddling through the brown water on whatever they could find, small boats or even doors. Seeking safety or someone? I couldn't tell. I wondered how Edward was faring a few streets over. Without the window in place, I could hear shouting. While I stood frozen in horror, people were working hard to escape their flooded apartments or rescue their neighbours.

"Ceddy, my god, what is happening in the basement?"

Filled with concern for the Ceph now that the initial danger had passed, we took our flashlights and descended the stairs but couldn't make it past the second floor. The stairwell had flooded. We stood in silence, staring at the brown liquid. It wasn't receding yet we stood there as if our mere presence would force the water back.

Finally, I spoke. "They should be okay, right? The saltwater stabilizer will be flooded out but with seawater mostly, right? They should be okay."

The basement was designed to be contained, which meant they might be unaffected, just cut off. If they flooded, they could at least breathe the water through their gills. But if the saltwater pool flooded with rain, it might affect their ability to breath. If this was just sea surge they should survive, even with a significant breach. I didn't allow myself to think about the possibility of a total collapse of the system.

We turned from the water-filled stairwell and went up to the roof.

࿓

It took us a long time just to pry the door to the roof open; it had been crushed by the wind and jammed shut. We were met with a distressing scene. There was little left but mounds of mud mixed with broken green stems, twigs and leaves smeared across the patio. The greenhouse itself was nowhere to be seen. The entire structure had been picked up and carried off, likely floating in the newly created canals below. I tried to give Cedric his privacy as tears welled in his eyes.

Eventually he joined me at the edge. "Look." I pointed in the direction of the sea.

From the roof, the city's devastation appeared far worse. It was still raining but the wind had died. Our building still rose stolidly out of the surf, but farther to the east, the landscape had changed. We stood dumbly for a few minutes, trying to puzzle out what we were seeing. The dragon's teeth of high-rises and buildings that used to rise out of the ocean, encircled with each tide, were unrecognizable. In many cases, buildings had simply collapsed and were invisible under the turbulent water. Those that remained were broken or leaning at new angles. Power was out everywhere, but we could see dots of energy from individually powered generators lighting up buildings across the city.

"I wonder how Shorty's aquarium is doing," Cedric said. It had been on the water's edge at the site of the old harbour. We looked but couldn't see it.

"Holy shit," I said. "It's the end of the world. How do we come back from this?"

We stood in silence, just breathing it in.

"I can't deal with it," I finally admitted quietly. "Let's try to get that generator working. We need coffee."

We watched a few minutes more though, as small Coast Guard boats made their way carefully through the streets, picking up survivors. We could barely make out the faint shouts of the rescued and almost rescued as they climbed aboard or were pulled onto the vessels. A growing panic was rising in me and I tried to squash it down. Action. Action would save us. We pulled ourselves away from the unfolding drama of strangers to try to put our own lives back together.

Putting the generator on the ground floor had turned out to be a bad idea. We couldn't reach it, and assumed it was underwater. It was supposed to be a sturdy, no-nonsense, save-your-life-in-any-weather type of contraption but I wasn't betting on it being back on any time soon. I took a painkiller from our stores for the caffeine withdrawal and wondered how sucking on coffee grounds would taste. Undoubtedly awful. I wondered some more if that would be enough to stop me.

We retreated to the lab to check on River and the younglings, who were happy the deafening winds had ended and the building had stopped shaking, and were unconcerned about the total darkness and the colony downstairs. I tried not to worry her. Cedric went down the hall to check our supplies. He reappeared after a few minutes with two cans of coffee-flavoured cola. "Euuuw. You're kidding me," I said.

"Desperate times . . ." He smiled and held up his can with a cheers motion. "We're on camping rations until we get the generator working. Drink up. We need to do something about the window."

With the generator down, we had limited battery power to keep the essentials running. I tried to convince Cedric that that included the coffee maker, but he insisted we stick with running the refrigeration in the lab and the kitchen. Our news service, run by satellite, appeared in fits and starts, whether because of a power failure at the broadcasting end or a glitch in the battery. Unhelpful headlines flitted sporadically around the room again, stuttering and sometimes failing.

Wildfires out of control in Washington State – 350,000
   evacuated
England and Wales go to the courts to retain name of "United
   Kingdom" after Scotland votes to separate, join EU
New bee documentary wins at Cannes Film Festival

I pulled up the wildfire story and three-dimensional flames licked around the intake room. Charming and almost apropos. But there was nothing about Long Harbour.

"Nothing?" I was incredulous. "How can there be nothing?"

"No local news," observed Cedric, flames painting his face orange. "Even the weather is offline."

And so, for all our rapt attention to the daily news service, it failed to provide any information about Gretchen's aftermath for another three days. "Due to power issues," they reported later. At the time, all we knew was that we were cut off. We eventually found an emergency channel that the Red Cross and local fire stations used, which confirmed what we already suspected: The rest of the city along the coast was even worse off than we were. It was a mass casualty event with ongoing flooding and widespread destruction. We were, for all intents and purposes, on our own.

We were alone, with only our thoughts for company and that was cold comfort indeed. At the edges of my mind, I couldn't get rid of the image of a lifeless ark in space. Was it possible? Had we unwittingly been a part of a massive attack, a mass murder? Not only of the people on the ark but those at or near the Star Freedom headquarters, as well as the soldiers themselves. If the soldiers weren't fully human, would anyone even care about *their* deaths? Had we failed so miserably? I had envisioned myself as being at the top of my game, reclaiming my status, a genius in motion. Had I really been just a peddler of death and destruction all along, no better than all the business interests?

❧

We filled the next two days with handiwork around the building, cleaning up and attaching plastic sheeting where windows were broken. Any more permanent repair work would need to wait for street access and the return of electrical power. We were trapped, but since the building was stable and we were fully stocked with food and water, we just waited out the floodwaters. Outside, people continued to paddle by on makeshift boats, and the Coast Guard patrolled up and down the streets to help the survivors get to higher ground. I paced up and down the stairs to check on water levels and fret about the Ceph in the basement. Were they all dead? I imagined the worst, lived it a thousand times. I tried to distract myself with motion, action, but my concern and dread bubbled just under the surface. Poor Coralie. I didn't know what I would do without her. She had to be okay.

By the morning of the third day, the water had receded enough to reach the ground floor and allow us to open the front doors. The lobby smelled like an undersea canyon and we still couldn't reach the basement. We tried the whole morning to get the generator working. We tried to call a contractor but it seemed the whole communications network was down and even our satellite connection was patchy. Trying to jump-start a battery while standing in water seemed like a bad idea, so we eventually went back up to the lab to check on River and the younglings and make some lunch that didn't need to be cooked. I really hated camping. We ate directly out of cans in the cold and wet intake room, trying to stay calm and wait for the power to come back. I tried to keep busy to keep grim thoughts at bay. Every now and then the weight in my chest made it hard to breathe, especially when I thought about Coralie.

Susan and Laurel managed to reach us by satellite comms. They had escaped the worst of the storm inland and were sheltering with family. No word from Edward, who had ridden out the storm downtown, close to the coast. His apartment was in one of the hardest hit areas.

From the roof, we watched as the waters gradually receded, revealing devastation. Buildings had collapsed, roofs were gone, debris collected against barriers where it could not be sucked back out to sea. There were fewer people to see now, all gone to the shelters, I suppose, or dead. The Coast Guard now patrolled in smaller outboard-motor-craft, with bullhorns calling out to survivors. We waved amiably at them from the windows. We couldn't leave.

Late on the third day, we managed to regain access to the basement, prying the doors open and shining flashlights down the stairs. It was hard to make anything out. The pool was at least half a metre underwater, and black ripples reached the bottom of the stairs even as we hauled open the door. We shone our waterproof flashlights around and the thin beams of light made the large space even more cavernous and imposing.

We trudged through dark, smelly water into the pool area, calling for the Ceph.

Coralie surfaced and swam through the floodwater to us. "Are you all right?" she asked. "This hasn't been good weather for humans. You two-foot people aren't really adapted to this." I went limp with relief.

She seemed undeterred from having spent nearly three days locked in the dark, underwater. "So much fun. So much fun! So much swimming!" Her eyes gleamed as she darted back and forth, dipping under the water and back up. The water was brown and smelled like dead things. It reached up past my knees. I could not understand her glee.

Other Ceph were similarly swimming around the entire room – several of them appeared to be playing tag. "We are fine!" Coralie insisted. "We like the water. And we're already working on the filtration system. It's mostly salt water but dirty."

"We can help with the filtration system – you need to be careful," Cedric said. "You could get sick." Cedric looked absolutely green. The tremor in his hand was back and his voice shook. The biocontainment mechanisms had failed and from the marks on the wall, it looked like dirty seawater had infiltrated past the ceiling. The pool itself was muddy and might take days to clean.

"We just need to get the generator working," Cedric said a bit too fast and trudged off to examine it again. Finn rushed up behind him, clearly going to help.

I waded through water to a small pump station in the far corner. "Once the generator is working, we can dry up the floor with the sump pump." Just as I said the words, Cedric yelled that we were good to go and soft blue lights winked on in the ceiling.

Other Ceph popped their heads out to greet us. They all seemed to be in high spirits. Coralie, smiling, told the story of their adventure. At first, nothing had happened except the blue lights and the pool filter had gone off. The storm had whistled outside but they felt snug in their pool. Eventually though, as the hurricane roared through, the storm surge began to seep in. "We tried to stop it, but it fell through the ceiling."

Coralie asked after River. "We were worried. Perhaps she and the younglings should come down and live with us."

"Let's get the habitat restored before we talk about that," I told her, trying to let go of the worry that had plagued me since the power went out.

I inspected each Ceph for injuries and was pleased that they had all escaped harm. All except one. "Where's Delmar?"

My question was met with silence and several Ceph who had been comfortably stretching on rocks flipped noisily into the water and disappeared into the deep end. Cedric and I exchanged panicked glances. Coralie was silent.

The Ceph had survived the storm, even enjoyed it, but we had a problem.

CHAPTER 45: CORALIE

The storm is terrifying at first. The deafening wind shakes the building to its core. When water begins to drip and then pour from the ceiling, we hide under the rock piles at the bottom of the pool. We are sheltering together there when the dim lights go out and the filters shudder and die.

As the worst of the storm passes and the loud shaking subsides, we slowly venture out from under the rocks to discover water everywhere, right up to the ceiling.

The dark does not concern us. We can see the soft blue glow of our family, and we do not need the light to sense where we are. The entire room has become our own ocean. It is like a playground, and we chase each other from one end to the other, doing backflips and spins. The soft glow of the Ceph looks like a ballet underwater. Our world has been upended and it is beautiful. Finn and Delmar are the first to explore the edges of the room itself and test the cracks.

The hurricane brings fortune unlooked for. We find it in the ceiling, which has not been fortified as much as the walls and doors. Delmar manages to pry off a small section of overhead tile. Water no longer pours in but has risen beyond the ceiling. We can pry off a few tiles and reach the duct system. Normally used for air, it has heating and cooling tunnels that, if followed, lead outside.

We make our plans hurriedly. I have been hoping for a chance, and one has presented itself. As the storm wanes and water still flows past the ceiling, Delmar and one other take two bags of bivalves each and say their farewells. They squeeze into the ductwork and disappear.

They are our advance scouts. They will seek out the sea.

CHAPTER 46

The story from Coralie emerged slowly. During the height of the storm, some ceiling tiles had torn loose and as the water rose, the ducts filled. Some of the Ceph had started to explore the ductwork, disappearing into the ceiling, which had been transformed into an underwater maze. The pitch-black conditions had not phased them in the slightest.

I knew that their eyesight was not their primary means of seeing and knowing – I had been including this in our briefings to Sykes all along. Like the octopus, they have neurons in their tentacles and likely throughout their bodies. This meant that they could sense, experience and even think in a way that is utterly different than a human brain and human eyes. But they looked human enough that I will admit I forgot. Their eyes focused on us when they spoke and we unconsciously expected them to be like us. But what they revelled in was clearly not the same for us. Cedric and I had huddled, terrified in the dark, waiting for the storm to pass. Coralie and the Ceph had celebrated the adventure and looked for more.

The entire colony had explored the lower building when it was submerged. I could see that some of the damage was due not only to the storm surge but from Ceph efforts to find more to explore. Coralie admitted they made it to the lobby and even swam its length, watching the rising seas on the other side of the glass doors with longing and excitement. At some point, according to Coralie, Delmar had disappeared in the maze of ductwork. They knew he was there somewhere, and then they heard a shout – he had discovered a way out. He wriggled out an exterior air vent and was gone. The Ceph following him had been careful to hold on to the edges of the vent and the corridors of ducts as they called for him, but the storm surge outside, filled with debris, had carried him away.

Cedric and I mounted a search right away. My biggest fear was that he had been killed in the crush of debris and that his body would be found close to our building. More than a tragic death, this would prompt an investigation by the authorities. Since the bee crisis, scientific regulators were cracking down on anything with even a whiff of environmental hazard.

With Delmar's breakout, accidental or not, we were in breach of our liability waiver. We were wholly responsible. I couldn't find it in my heart to wish that Delmar was dead by misadventure, but as I reflected, there were even worse scenarios for Cedric and me.

The release of a new species could crash a fragile habitat, and the nearby reefs were unquestionably fragile: overfished and polluted, then restored and then crowded alongside commercial clam and fish farms. Hurricane Gretchen might be the final blow that destroyed the viability of the eastern seaboard ecosystems completely. If the Ceph were in any way connected to that, if such an ecological disaster were traced back to us, bankruptcy and prison would be our best outcome.

So, as the water receded from the streets, we searched the neighbourhood on foot for signs of Delmar. A new panorama of devastation greeted us at every corner we turned. Whole buildings had collapsed in places, and in others they had sagged to one side, lost their roofs or windows. Detritus, from damaged buildings, abandoned vehicles or the ocean itself, clogged the roads and there was a high-water mark several metres above us. Storm refugees walked the streets with us, either seeking a means out, looking for rescue or, more tragically, looking for their own loved ones amid the wreckage.

Occasionally, there were reports of hopper attacks. I think the storm surge gave them a tactical advantage. The local hoppers, previously diseased and famished, were now feasting on storm carcasses. Desperation drove us outside, and then we scuttled back to our safe haven. We glimpsed one from a distance once, and saw the mutilated remains of one of their meals, but otherwise were lucky enough to avoid a direct confrontation. It was clear, though, that the storm had given them the upper hand and they now roamed with impunity.

There was no sign of Delmar and there was no way we could ask anyone if they had seen him. We scoured the local news feed but came up similarly empty.

We should be forgiven for our very terse reports to Mr. Sykes. We provided bare-bones descriptions of the impact of the storm on our operations, and some mild details on the damage to the basement pool and the building. We informed him that our lab work continued and three new younglings had hatched. Beyond that we stayed quiet. The drone came to pick up our report a week after the hurricane as normal but without the usual video rant or list of questions to be answered. The glowing cross-hatched pattern swirling on the cheek of a dead soldier continued to haunt me, but I had no way to be sure. With everything happening, maybe I was seeing things? Of course, Cedric saw the same thing, so there was that.

We talked about the Sykes situation over morning coffee but came to no conclusions.

The Holo-News had been filled with speculation about the ark attack. The clear winner from taking the *Star Freedom* ark off the board was Webwex. Titus Falco now had the most advanced intergenerational exploration ships with projects closest to launch. Some believed that Webwex's station had been used to launch the attack from the dark side of the moon. One news agency claimed proof of Titus Falco's involvement but the story disappeared the next day, either from litigation threats or shadowy government intervention. What we couldn't figure out was how Sykes and Global Holdings were involved. Were Webwex and Global Holdings doing a merger to go into space piracy like Hornblower Industries?

We'd watched it unfold when Hornblower made its big play for space domination. This conglomerate had made its money in the usual way but then gambled on taking over a meteor-mining operation by force. When Hornblower made its move, it won in space but lost any holdings on Earth that weren't hidden from view. The legal and police action was swift and ruthless. Most of their employees, even the junior ones who knew nothing of the broader game, were imprisoned without charge, and months passed before the innocent regained their freedom. All Hornblower's offices and assets were seized, including the digital networks that law enforcement could find and break. Years later, Hornblower networks and assets were still being uncovered and seized. The company had survived and continued to rule space, akin to pirates. Pirates who administered mining projects and went on to attack space craft and raid space stations. Rumour had it, they had a hidden base on Mars or one of Mars' moons, Phobos, but who could say really? Not us.

Neither Webwex nor Global Holdings were openly embracing piracy. Both were continuing to act as normal, with Falco steadfastly denying involvement. There was nothing in the Holo-News suggesting that Global Holdings was involved but we knew that Titus Falco had been Burton Sykes' early mentor and bankroller. Were they still in league? They must be. The authorities must have known by now that the attackers were super-soldiers, but only the pundits were opining on the news, official law enforcement was silent.

We could expect Global Holdings to be treated like Hornblower Industries if their involvement was discovered. The authorities would seek out every asset, every computer chip, every property. They would scour it all looking for Mr. Sykes and they would not stop. Mr. Sykes would have anticipated all this and would be safely tucked in somewhere, on his ark in orbit or in his hidden Caribbean enclave or somewhere even more secret.

So far, his role in the attack was unknown, unconfirmed. Even Falco's role was pure speculation and to catch someone that powerful you needed a lot more than supposition. Perhaps it would never be uncovered. Our shell company would protect us for a while until the network forensics team found us, but our ties to Mr. Sykes would be uncovered eventually. The super-soldiers he'd created to storm the cultists' ark were not only state of the art, they were revolutionary, a vanguard of innovation and violence. Nowhere would be safe. The authorities would stop at nothing to root out everyone who had had a hand in it, willing or not. We had to hide.

Was Global Holdings responsible? So far, no sign that they had been fingered for the crime but we nervously watched the Holo-News and waited on tenterhooks to hear from the man himself.

❧

Coralie had a suggestion for us. She was worried about Delmar and thought he was still out there, that he had been carried out to sea and was trying to find his way back. She wanted to send out a search party. At least, she wanted to send two of the Ceph to try to find him and rescue him.

"I know we can find him," she said. "How else can we get him back?"

I tried to be gentle. "He may not have made it to the ocean, Coralie. And even if he did, how would we find him? He could be anywhere."

"He won't be anywhere. If he is out there, we can find him. Our voices carry underwater, you know."

There was a strange aspect to their underwater speech that we hadn't yet figured out, but which seemed to be related to echolocation. I believed her when she said their voices carried. There was another aspect to sending out a Ceph search party, though. We were already in breach of our liability waiver with Delmar's escape. I could argue it was accidental, but the contract was ironclad and intentions were not a factor in guilt. But to me, it mattered, and our intentions so far had always been good. Releasing a search party seemed to step beyond that into a world of deliberate mayhem.

Of course, the project had been designed to transfer the Ceph to the ocean floor at some point, but I had always expected it to roll out as the contract stipulated, with our shadowy benefactor taking responsibility for the transfer, logistically and legally. I had always expected to transfer the burden of ethical responsibility to him in the end. We were just creating the Ceph; transplanting them was not our contractual obligation. So whatever ecological impact they had would be Mr. Sykes' burden, not ours.

Sending a search party seemed to be a humane and caring thing to do, but it put us in a new category of agency. It made us complicit. It made us responsible. It drove us a little closer to "mad scientist" territory. It made us agents of change, actors rather than writers.

Just the thought of it made Cedric tremble. "We can't, of course," he said, as we discussed it one morning in the kitchen. "It runs counter to everything we believe in."

I was silent, letting his stress reverberate. I could see how upset he was at the thought. I resisted the idea but felt its pull. He was trying to run the other way entirely. "It's impossible!" he insisted.

But the more Cedric insisted, the more I thought about what would happen if we did it. Would a search party even return? Coralie was the obvious leader of the Ceph but could she compel a Ceph to return to what was essentially captivity once freed?

On the other hand, if Delmar could be found and the search party returned, we could close the breach. Our waiver would be intact. We would be safe again. It was a gamble but might pay huge dividends. Unfortunately, Cedric and I didn't agree on what to do next.

I found myself arguing in favour of the searchers in spite of myself. I put up straw man after straw man for Cedric to pull down. "Well, of course they'll come back – their family is here. Everything and everyone they care about is here."

"How can you be sure? They may just love it out there in the wild, open ocean. Or maybe they get lost and can't find their way back." He became more and more animated, more opposed. Finally, we stopped talking about it. I had convinced myself to do it, and convinced Cedric of the opposite.

While we were stuck, Coralie was making plans. The next morning, poolside, she called Finn over. "Here is what I propose," she said. "We send just Finn as a searcher. If Delmar is alive, Finn will find him and bring him home. Then we are all together again. And in exchange, you promise."

"Promise what?"

"Promise that you will take us to the sea." She looked directly at Cedric. "You can trust us. We won't break our word."

Was it Coralie that wore Cedric down? I don't know. All I know is that from one day to the next, he changed his mind and agreed with her. "It's a way to find out for sure about Delmar. It's a way to get him back, seal the breach."

I didn't look too deeply at Cedric's conscience here, but quickly agreed, wanting to move. Promise given, Finn loaded up a large net of mussels for the journey and we made plans to sneak him to the coast and send him on his way.

So it came to be that late one night, Cedric and I brought a small garbage scow on wheels into the basement. Finn was ready, even eager.

Coralie thanked us sombrely. There were few parting words above water; I was sure they had said everything needful already. They embraced and Finn clambered eagerly into the garbage scow. We left before we could change our minds.

This was the most dangerous, criminal part of the enterprise. We had decided to go to the old harbour on foot, as simply as possible so we could not be traced later. Fearful but determined, we walked the cracked streets ourselves, flashlights out but dim, pushing the garbage scow. Most of the electricity to the neighbourhood was still off, and likely not coming back so the only light came from occasional generators, easily avoided. We skulked in the shadows.

It wasn't far but it felt like a marathon. We pushed and pulled the scow between us, alert at all times for other people, for hoppers, for any sign of trouble. At night there shouldn't be drones, and we were unlikely to be captured on security video, especially on the dark and abandoned edge of the city. We saw no one. Hearts racing, sweat beading at the temples, we crept through the streets and finally saw the faint light of a half-moon reflecting off the water.

The waves were lapping gently up the street, the old harbour buildings mostly reduced to their foundations by the storm. This time I'd thought to wear rubber boots. We had to walk past the old aquarium to reach the water. It had been hit hard, was a dark and broken hulk looming at the water's edge. There had been no word from Shorty and I hoped he hadn't tried to ride out the storm with his glassed-in habitats. I hoped he'd managed to return and rescue the animals he could, transplant them to another aquarium or free them. Maybe he had freed them in advance. If it had all turned to disaster, I didn't want to know. I looked away, out toward the water.

Checking back to see if we'd been followed, we quickly tipped the garbage scow, and Finn darted out. The water was not deep enough for him to swim, but he waddled out, gestured a final wave goodbye and then dove under the water and disappeared.

We sighed with relief, and then dread.

Without speaking, we rolled the garbage scow back to the lab, our footsteps heavy and echoing against the empty buildings. Nothing stirred except us. We dragged the scow through the lobby and into a storage room. We were well and truly guilty now, even if we were striving to find a way to make it right.

CHAPTER 47: CEDRIC

FADE IN

INT. KITCHEN - DAY

CEDRIC fiddles with a camera setting and sits up on his
stool in the kitchen. Dirty dishes are piled in the sink;
there are smears of something dark across a cupboard.
He absent-mindedly pushes his glasses up.

> CEDRIC
>
> I don't know exactly why I capitulated in
> the end. Perhaps I feel I'm in so deep I've
> lost my soul already and it doesn't matter
> what comes next. Now I'm just all animal
> instinct, reacting, not thinking. I've a
> sensation - that all the beliefs I have
> carefully constructed through my adult life
> are crumbling. I knew it was a possibility
> that Sykes would misuse our research, it
> had happened before. But I guess I . . . I
> don't know, I guess I just wanted to believe
> we were better than we were. That Sykes
> was genuine. Quirky, not corrupt. Expansive
> and flaky but not venal. A visionary without
> blood on his hands, with high ideals that
> didn't rest on a foundation of conquest. If
> we are implicated in all of that, what does

it matter if we let Finn explore the ocean? History will already judge Raina and I with the harshest of lenses.

I don't think that Raina can see my despair. Would she care? I'd like to think so – that she would try to bring me back to the light if she knew the dark places I'm travelling. But we're living in the pre-apocalypse. Everything degrades. And we have to either scuttle along the edges of it or make our bold and golden stand against the horror of the end of times.

Science can't save us from ourselves. Raina and I cannot save ourselves.

CEDRIC takes a deep breath, wrinkles his brow.

> CEDRIC (cont'd)
> And that brings us to this moment, this spectacular moment when one has to decide, when we have to decide, if we will muddle along, doing marginal things as we swim with the current. Or whether to resist and make a bold gesture of defiance in the face of annihilation.

CEDRIC stares hard at the camera, GULPS audibly.

> CEDRIC (cont'd)
> This is our bold gesture. This is our last gasp at expressing our own humanity,

screaming into the void. We cannot fix the world. But in this tiny corner of it, perhaps we can control our own destiny, at least for a while. We can make our own decisions and try, we can strive, to shape a message to the universe. To make our own statement of survival. We aren't mad scientists; we're just humans trying to find our way through.

We have created the Ceph. And now we need to create conditions for their survival.

I know I'm selling my soul, but I need to know what's happened to Delmar, to understand the extent of our ruin. I'm still hoping, maybe a little, to contain the damage. So I agreed with Raina to send out a Ceph searcher.

Her motivations are more transparent, obviously. She cares about Delmar, wants confirmation that he's alive. She wants to please Coralie. Raina still believes in the happy ending to come, and will do anything, even compromise all her ideals, to make it so.

In the end, I guess we'll sink together. I can't abandon Raina now, and I don't want to drag her into the dark. But I can't escape the feeling that the dark is coming. It makes the hairs on the back of my neck stand up.

I hate horror movies, you know. I hate how they make me feel, all tingly and edgy. How they drift in the corners of my mind when I am trying to sleep, needling me. With Delmar's disappearance, I feel I've land-ed squarely in a horror flick of epic pro-portions. The general horrors of the world have never had a face before. Now Delmar is stalking my dreams.

We are truly swimming in shark-infested wa-ters now.

CEDRIC struggles to say more, subsides into silence, turns off the video.

                                        CUT TO BLACK

CHAPTER 48

We clung to our routines while we waited for Finn's return, ignoring the stains on the sofa, the broken chair and the intake room window still covered with plastic sheeting. Never far from my mind, or my heart, was the knowledge that Sykes was implicated in mounting a murderous attack using our research to make it deadlier. I couldn't necessarily prove it, but even if I could, what could I do? There was no public sign that Global Holdings played any role at all, but I knew the biosignatures of my own work – and they were the only ones who could have taken it. We knew Sykes and Falco could be in league together. The drone continued to show up and collect our reports, and if Mr. Sykes had stopped sending video rants, well, wasn't that a blessing? But the knowledge sat with me, rancid, in the pit of my stomach. We lay low, continued on, but I felt that it was only a matter of time before our well-intentioned misdeeds caught up with us.

One morning, I arrived at work and Cedric was already drinking coffee in the lounge. "Well, shit, look at that," he swore uncharacteristically, and gestured.

Uncontrolled Amazon grasslands fire threatens Brasilia
Canada's grain harvest falls 85% year over year, supply
   management system collapsing
UN negotiations on Bee Treaty collapse: "I have lost hope,"
   says Secretary-General
Hopper infestation shuts down subway system in Boston

"What about it? It's always bad news." Then I saw it.

Species Termination Notice: Arabica Coffee read the headline. It sputtered around the room aimlessly.

"Well, that makes it all real, doesn't it?" I poured a cup and sat down. "What is this world coming to?" I stared at the brown liquid and felt not only a tug of grief but mild panic. I didn't like it when the world intruded on our haven here. I looked at Cedric. "What can we do?"

"I'm on it. Let's try to stockpile some beans." Cedric was already completing an online order. "Sold out." He swore again. "I'll try the coffee shop down the road. Maybe they're reserving quantities or guaranteeing their stock for their VIPs."

There was silence as Cedric tried to secure our supply and I quietly appreciated what might be one of my last cups of coffee. Surprisingly, I felt no strong reaction at all. It felt as if a corner of my heart had snapped; I was broken and I didn't care what happened next. It was over, or nearly over. There was just a gentle pit of despair waiting for me to fall into it. We were coming to the end of the road. We had paved the road. The creeping sense of guilt that had been dogging me flowered suddenly. All the activity, all the effort, everything that had been distracting me from a core truth fell away and I was left with the realization that I was an integral part of everything that was wrong with the system, everything that had led to this moment.

For years I had believed with my whole heart that science could save us. That I, the genius scientist, could save the world. That each catastrophe could be averted if only we got the science right, that each problem had a solution, a technical solution. And where had this led us? The more I tried to fix our failures, the worse things got. We were monsters on every level – on land, on sea and even beyond this world. It was our fault. It was my fault. Everything I did to help made things worse.

Cedric walked back into the room. "Okay, I think I have an additional six-month supply on top of the three months we already have. We may have to go black market after that."

"Well, there go our profits," I quipped. "As long as we don't talk about switching to mint tea," I added, since we grew that on the roof. At least, we *had* grown it on the roof. Cedric hadn't replanted since the garden had been swept away.

Nothing was hidden from Cedric who glanced sharply at me, his eyes full of concern. "What is it?"

I smiled and tried not to cry. "You know I love coffee."

He peered into my face. "Are you okay?"

"Oh, Cedric," I whispered. "We're the problem. We're at the centre of the problem. We are horrible people." I burst into tears.

He sat next to me and waited out the torrent. I never cried, but he was surprisingly patient. Eventually I snivelled into my sleeve and dried my eyes.

"We're not horrible," Cedric said. "We're trying."

"Doesn't matter," I blubbered. "Look what we've done."

There was a world of concern in his eyes. "Raina, we're doing our best."

"No!" I was adamant. "We're the worst, we tried but failed."

We sat in silence for a few minutes. He didn't have a response, not really. Eventually he changed the subject.

"Raina," he began. "We've tried. But things are getting worse. A lot worse. All the bad things in the world are speeding up. It's not just about moral purity. We need to think about our next move."

"What do you mean?" I asked, but I knew.

"We can't stay here forever. Not since we lost the greenhouse. Long Harbour will never recover from Gretchen. It's devastated, Raina."

It was a truth that we'd uncovered with every walk to the harbour, every bit of searching for Delmar. The city was broken.

"We have to stay," I told him. "We can't run, we can't . . ."

"Admit failure?" Cedric replied gently. "Didn't you just do that?"

I didn't have an answer, and Cedric kept talking anyway. "I know we're mad at Sykes. We know he stole our research and misused it. But it's dangerous to stay here, Raina, and I think we need to leave. The enclave is a safe place to go to ground while the bee catastrophe plays out. At least safer than here."

"No," I began, but Cedric cut me off.

"It wouldn't have to be forever. And we'd have jobs, money, food." I shook my head but Cedric kept going. "Edward is still missing, Shorty's aquarium is in ruins, there are hoppers everywhere, the grocery stores are empty if they're even open. Everything is too dangerous here now. We need a new plan, Raina. Even if the building's security holds, we may starve."

Staring at him, I saw the layers of worry laid bare. Poor Cedric. And with everything else, I hadn't spared a thought for Edward since I first heard.

"But if we leave, it's like admitting it's all going away, Cedric. That we can't save anything."

"I think we can save ourselves. And the Ceph. And that'll have to be enough."

I stared out the window without saying anything.

"Just promise me you'll think about it?"

"I'll think about it," I said. "But I don't have to like it. We can't make any decisions until Finn comes back, anyway."

As devastated as I felt, I didn't want to think about leaving, but Cedric was just trying to keep us alive. He wasn't wrong.

⁊

Everything had changed for me, but life went on. We threw ourselves into practical matters and spent weeks repairing the ductwork and resealing the biocontainment unit surrounding the basement. It was a measure of my growing despair and distraction that it barely registered when Coralie quietly installed a mechanism on the Ceph's side of the unit so they could unlock it from the inside. They started wandering more freely. It was hard to care too much – our staff had not come back, and no one else was in the building. We just got used to waving and chatting with Ceph as we were walking down the hallway. They came up the elevator and visited with River and the younglings, who also ventured down to the main pool. They stayed away from the rooms with windows, but some mornings before dawn I found Coralie in our intake room, watching FlickFilms or the Holo-News.

I watched avidly for some indication of what was happening with the ark attack investigation. There was very little. Just a steady tattoo of despair on my heart as the tall headlines stomped around the room.

European wheat and soy reserves near zero in wake of
    agricultural collapse
US President plans holiday extravaganza to stimulate economy
China, Russia offer food assistance to African nations in exchange
    for trade deals
Hornblower Industries denies involvement in attack on Free Doom
    ark

On the nights I stayed over at the lab, I woke early and Coralie, Cedric and I would sit in companionable silence in the pre-dawn darkness watching the Holo-News, Cedric and I drinking what felt like the last of our coffee supply. Coralie would comment freely on what she saw.

"You humans are a danger you know."

"I know," I said.

"No really – it's not just predatory behaviour, it's carelessness. You break things. You like to break things."

"Yes, but not all of us."

"No, you and Cedric are builders. But all those" – she gestured a tentacle at the headlines zipping around the room – "it's all bad news, all the time, or stupid. I don't know how you stand it."

"Neither do I," I muttered, more to myself than her. "Neither do I."

ം

The colony was surprisingly silent on Delmar and Finn. Cedric and I started taking daily walks to the sunken harbourfront in the tidal zone, scanning the horizon for the missing Ceph. We had agreed that Finn would leave a note in chalk that had been left by a crumbling piece of concrete at the water's edge.

We walked down mostly deserted streets. There were only a few of us left living or working in this part of the city. It was a ghost town. The pavement was broken and uneven, with a flicker of a generator here and there. Sometimes fog rolled in, contributing to a deep unease we couldn't shake. Even the modern, rebuilt wharf farther up the bay had suffered damage. While we could see repair work starting, it was clear that it would take months. What wasn't clear was whether the city would make it back from the catastrophe.

So many lives lost, and I wondered if they haunted the lonely, empty passages. I mentioned it once to Cedric, who replied, "Maybe Edward is looking out for us." At this point, Edward was presumed dead.

Cedric meant to be reassuring, but what I felt as we toured the back alleys was more malevolent than unhappy spirits. Maybe it was hoppers prowling. Local news didn't even cover the hopper infestation anymore – there was too much to cover with the storm's recovery; they had been bumped from the headlines. We saw them from time to time, but they didn't bother us. Their presence just intensified my unease in the fog. We didn't have a gun but started walking with an old hockey stick Cedric found. It seemed to be enough to put them off, keep them focused on easier prey.

I wondered though. The hoppers were hybrid humans, and maybe their humanity shone through from time to time. Maybe they reached out for connection – who knew? As eradication efforts ground to a standstill, and Cedric and I walked the streets, I would see them. A ghostly green presence on buildings or even padding behind us. Sometimes they would follow us but I didn't get the sense they were hunting. Maybe they were trying to muddle through like the rest of us. Maybe they hungered for more than food. They'd been made vicious, carefully concocted that way, but they might be more. I didn't think I would ever know.

The water had receded to its usual level but many streets were impassable due to collapsed buildings and we had to find a route among the rubble. The boardwalk and wharf of the old harbourfront had been reduced to some squat brick buildings that flooded with every tide. The wooden dock had long ago rotted into obsolescence. Some of the buildings nearer to the water were missing walls, almost everything was missing windows. We tried not to talk about how lucky our own building had been. I cringed every time I walked past the remains of Shorty's aquarium.

And so, every day we walked the desolate streets to the water, looking for signs that the two Ceph might have returned. For weeks, there was nothing.

Coralie would ask for news whenever we returned from a search, but everyone went about their business as if Delmar still lived and was merely absent. I was surprised the colony wasn't more outwardly upset. Weeks later, Coralie avoided discussing it. Perhaps she saw this as a failure in her own leadership. There continued to be no sign of either Delmar or Finn.

We tried to repair more of the building, but supply chains were broken and contractors had fled the city. Even with the money we had, there were delays and shortages. Fewer still in our neighbourhood had the means to even think about restoring their apartments. Most were left derelict. It felt like the sea had lapped a few blocks closer, but I think that was an illusion. In any case, we found ourselves in a neighbourhood almost fully abandoned after the storm. The final tallies were not encouraging. Over six hundred people who had tried to ride out the hurricane along the coast had perished and whole city blocks had been destroyed. While the immediate recovery effort had saved lives, the government would not allow rebuilding in the flooded sections. Those people who eked out a living in the dragon's teeth were diminished, their homes and livelihoods destroyed.

There were still signs of persistence, though. We ventured out to the old site of the fish market and were relieved to see some of the fishmongers still plying their wares. Donna, as eternal as the ocean, was one of them. She offered to come by with an order.

"Nice to see Donna made it through," said Cedric as we walked home. "But it's just grinding down. There's not much left."

On our side, we restored the systems in the lab, tried to repair the damaged electronics in the flooded basement, tried to replace the windows, and kept going. Supply chain issues were a huge hassle. What used to be accomplished in twenty-four hours now took weeks, and a myriad of special favours from colleagues across the country. Our intake room window was proving difficult to replace, and we still had a plastic sheet secured across the opening. With the greenhouse gone, we relied on our stored goods. Cedric planted some new leafy greens, but without the greenhouse they had to live inside as winter crept in, a cold settling into our bones. My little house in the hills was snug, but I spent time shivering at the lab for the Ceph's and Cedric's sakes.

We heard nothing from Mr. Sykes. Cedric scavenged online for parts to build a new greenhouse, but I could tell his heart wasn't in it. While on the roof, we would scan the skies and worry over what we were hearing and not hearing. The buzzing, busy pre-storm skyscape was gone, the drones and copters few and far between. Mr. Sykes' drone still arrived like clockwork to pick up our updates and the money kept flowing, but he didn't leave his usual ranting recordings. I was left with the uneasy feeling that the entire process was automated and no one was on the receiving end of our reports. Had we been cut adrift? And would that be so bad? Could we escape notice and avoid being implicated in Sykes' nastiness?

Cedric and I discussed Delmar's disappearance until we felt sick. If he'd died, it was a tragedy, but if he had escaped, who knew what ecological catastrophe he might have already caused in the depths of the ocean? When rabbits were introduced in Australia, they decimated an entire continent; starlings similarly wreaked havoc in North America.

And beyond all these considerations, there was our liability waiver, which was null and void. We were fully liable for any damage Delmar might do beyond the basement pool. If he so much as startled a fishing boat, we could be ruined. Was it panic or sound professional judgment that made us omit the escape from our weekly reports to Mr. Sykes? The ethical lines we had danced around with such grace were far behind us now. We were criminals, plain and simple, until those Ceph returned.

We'd doubled down by sending Finn as a rescuer, or perhaps a bounty hunter. Now we had two escaped Ceph. Until they returned, or we knew they were dead, Pandora's box was wide open.

CHAPTER 49

Finally, one day, we saw a faint chalk scratch on a broken concrete wall by the old harbourfront. Finn had returned and left a note: "We are here, we are safe." Cedric and I impatiently waited for nightfall, and then returned with the garbage scow. The moon was a slight crescent, the streets dark. Cedric pushed the scow while I used a flashlight to light our way, casting strange shadows and counting on the deserted streets to fail to note our passing. We met no one as we crossed intersections with dead and swinging stoplights. We startled at odd noises in the night.

When we reached the edge of the water and the piece of broken concrete where the message had been left, we waited in silence for what seemed to be hours. Fog began to roll in. Soon we could barely sense where the broken buildings were behind us and could only dimly see the waves lapping the concrete in front of us. The fog was so damp I had the uncanny feeling of being underwater.

Then two shapes gradually emerged from the water, enveloped in the fog. Finn came out first, grinning broadly and fist-pumping a tentacle in a funny, very human gesture of victory, propelling himself on his hind limbs so gracefully he looked like he was walking on the surface of the water. Delmar came behind. Perhaps it was my imagination, but I thought he had an air of sheepishness, a posture of apology. They both looked to be in good health.

They athletically flipped themselves into the garbage scow without having us tip it over and we started back to the lab. The trip passed quickly, but I startled at every small sound, shining my flashlight frantically to try and see what was out there. The fog enshrouded us and muffled our footsteps. Cedric seemed to be having a quiet panic attack and he panted and barely kept from bolting down the street, his knuckles white on the scow's handle, until he suddenly stopped in his tracks.

"Did you hear that?" he hissed.

Soft scraping sounds echoed above and behind us. As I turned my head, I detected movement about two stories up along one of the darkened buildings. "Hoppers!" Cedric half shouted, half whispered and we dashed the final two blocks in a fit of adrenaline. We had left the hockey stick behind and were defenceless.

As we approached our building, a misshapen green figure landed neatly about six metres in front of us, having launched himself from the nearest wall. His eyes telescoped weirdly from his oversized head as he peered at us, all his proportions vaguely human but wrong. His green skin glistened and sharp teeth glinted in the light I shone in his eyes.

He looked like he was about to say something. Was he hungry? He put his hands up, blinded by the flashlight. Behind me, Cedric yelled and all three of us jumped. Cedric and I ducked behind the garbage scow just in time to see the top fling open and Delmar and Finn position themselves between us and the hopper. They circled each other menacingly, sizing each other up. Then the hopper leaped without warning and Delmar and Finn met him in the air. I dropped the flashlight with a cry and scrambled after it.

A few savage moments later, I shone my recovered flashlight forward. Delmar and Finn shook themselves off and smiled ferociously, their sharp teeth glinting. They were covered in both red and blue blood and the hopper lay in tatters at their feet. The hopper's companions, invisible beyond the dim light, fled.

Cedric, close to hyperventilating, stared at the hopper's body. I was breathing hard like I'd just run a marathon. But the crisis was over and we were safe. Delmar and Finn, clearly pleased with themselves, wanted to know if we were okay. They celebrated as they jumped back into the scow and I tried not to recoil from their enthusiasm. I was glad the hopper hadn't hurt us and I knew the Ceph wouldn't hurt us either, but still I was taken aback at their bloodthirsty enjoyment of the altercation. I tried to act normal.

Ever the scientist, I noted, "I never knew hopper blood was red."

It took little time to enter the building and pull the scow into the elevator and then upstairs. We worked quickly to scan Delmar and Finn for any substances they may have brought with them. We cleaned their skin, took their temperatures and did blood work. They appeared to have suffered only small cuts and scrapes in their battle with the hopper. We were thorough in our physical exams; it was important to ensure that they were not bringing anything toxic back to the colony. Coralie joined us, impatient to know they were safe. As we sampled skin cells and took swabs, Finn started to speak. He was hesitant at first and we could barely make out the words, but it was intelligible. "Got Delmar. Success. All good, all ready," I thought I heard. "All good. Ocean is amazing. Wonders." He grabbed my arm and stared intently into my eyes. "Wonders," he repeated. After analyzing the samples and seeing nothing of concern, we took them to the basement pool.

The Ceph were thrilled with the rescue. Finn was a returning hero, Delmar the prodigal son. Everyone gathered around and Coralie, generous to Cedric and me, had everyone sit poolside to hear the stories. She translated as Finn and Delmar spoke rapidly in whistles, turning gentle shades of blue, pink and purple.

Delmar had had a terrible time in the storm. He had been tossed around with the raging waters, had to stay out of the way of crumbling walls, the storm's debris. Then, as the high waters calmed and receded, he had found himself pulled out to sea. The tide had taken him out of the harbour and past the reefs. Once past the reefs, fearing for his life, he sought the coldest, darkest hiding place he could. He sought out the ocean floor.

Finn had had a better time of it. He had easily swum through the harbour under cover of darkness and had voyaged out past the reefs and deep drop-off, calling to Delmar. It had taken a few days to sink down and locate him, but they had been able to communicate at a distance and find each other. They stayed for a time at the "bottom of the sea" as they called it, exploring, and then found their way home.

The two returning Ceph smiled contentedly while describing the wonders they had seen. Dark fronds of giant seaweed, bleaching reefs, schools of fish. Finn had had to venture deep to find Delmar and they tried to describe the dark, cold places they had visited. The depths were filled with animals, crabs, starfish and deep-sea fish with bulging eyes, massive jaws and glowing bodies. Some fled immediately from Delmar and Finn, some chased them away or tried to catch them, but the two Ceph were clearly delighted with it all, even the dangerous parts of their adventure. Some of the story was obviously lost in translation by Coralie, but it was clear that they had had a profound experience.

For our part, the simple relief of having them back unharmed was enormous. The fact that our gene edits to protect the Ceph at deep-sea depths worked was gratifying and having them home again lifted a huge weight from us. I can't say I slept through the night again, but when I did sleep, I slept easier.

⁓

Delmar and Finn had returned, but every time I thought about Mr. Sykes, I felt a jolt of dread. We kept working on repairs and life found an uneasy equilibrium.

Food riots in Old Manhattan; dozens dead

Crop failures across Asia, Chinese Federation imposes food
  rationing

Military takeover in Bangladesh as famine deaths mount

Species Termination Notice: common honey bee

"Look, Cedric, look at the extinction alert! Does this mean it's over? Is that the final tipping point? No return now?"

Cedric was frozen, staring at the headlines zipping around the room. "Oh," he said. "Well." He shook his head sadly. "You know, the planet could compensate for one lost pollinator. There are other pollinators and there're plants that grow without insect pollination at all. Some species will fail, especially those we rely on for flowers, fruits and vegetables, but other plants could take their place in an ecosystem. But whole food chains would be wiped out first. It would be a very near thing. The planet might eventually adjust but in the meantime, the people . . . civilization as we know it . . . I don't see how we make it out. We've seen the impact on global agriculture. Between trying to eradicate the bee-killing strains and the loss of the bees themselves, we can't feed everyone anymore."

I nodded and he went on. "Have you heard the phrase 'There are only nine meals between civilization and anarchy'? We're in the pre-anarchy phase now, on a global level. Even if some people can secure their food supply, life as we know it can't last. Governments are already falling, there's already famine. Everything's going to hell now."

I nodded again. "Only a matter of time, now, I guess."

Cedric didn't answer but slowly drank the last of his coffee.

"Well, there's always the ocean, Cedric. It doesn't need bees. What are we going to do about the colony? I don't think we have too many days left here."

"From a bioengineering perspective, we've done our part," he replied. "I think we've proven that they can survive in the depths, but we should do the extra deep-sea experiments to confirm. They could be completed in the Caribbean."

"Yes. And they still need to breathe air when they're born – that's going be a challenge under the sea. I don't think they're ready to go really. Not yet. But nearly."

"Do you think Sykes will still take them? Do you think he's still behind the project?" We hadn't heard from him since before the storm, and the attack on the ark and *Star Freedom*'s headquarters. "Time is ticking, Raina. We can't have much left."

Once we transplanted the colony to an ocean habitat, if they altered the ecosystem in any way we'd be liable and in violation of our code of bioethics. If it were discovered, we would never work again, and Greg only knew if we would escape prison.

It's hard to let go of the things we've worried about our whole lives in the face of global disaster. It's like the businessman who refused to exit the building when the fire alarm sounded because he'd be late for a meeting. We've all been late, but most of us have never been in a building burning to the ground. The fear of being late is much more immediate, much more acute, than the fear caused by a fire alarm. So that's where we focus our energies – on punctuality and not on the inferno.

The world was on fire, and I was worried about losing my licence.

"We need to talk to Mr. Sykes," I told Cedric.

But Mr. Sykes was unreachable. The money had been steady, and we'd used it to rebuild after Gretchen, but the hands-on approach he'd taken earlier had disappeared. We were ready to transfer the colony, but contact with his outfit had dried up.

I was somewhat dumbfounded at what to do next. How were we expected to transfer the Ceph to the ocean if Global Holdings had gone dark? Had their part in the space ark attack been discovered? I knew in my heart what they'd done, but I didn't know if it had caught up to them yet. Could they just continue business as usual or had he gone into hiding? What had happened to the enclave and all the scientists? Had Sykes taken them with him or cut them loose?

"Can we charter a copter and go to the island?" Cedric wondered.

"We don't have the coordinates – we'd never find it. And should we?"

Cedric's usual anxiety was erupting into panic and I tried to calm him down.

"Look, we're fine here for now," I told him. "We have food and water for us, and food for the colony. No one knows what we're doing here. We'll be okay for now, and we'll figure something out. Okay?"

I poured him another coffee and his hands shook as he took it. "It's all going to crash down," he muttered.

"We'll see." I shook my head and looked out the window. The dirty streets were empty. "It'll be okay – we just have to keep going," I tried to reassure him.

"Raina, it's the end of days. How can things be okay? This is more about how we end than whether." He shook his head impatiently. "We're not going to make it," he whispered. I put my hand on his shoulder but couldn't find anything to say.

Finally, we turned off the Holo-News and returned to the lab.

૭

A few anxious weeks passed while we waited in vain for Mr. Sykes to get in touch. His entire outfit seemed to have forgotten us. The money stopped flowing, even the regular arrivals of the drone stopped, and all our attempts to contact him came to nothing.

"We need to go, just us," Coralie insisted. "Do we really need him?"

Finally, I reached out to Dr. Winters who responded immediately: everything was fine and they would be in touch soon. I was not entirely re-assured. Time was running out on us in Long Harbour. I took to swearing viciously whenever the mood struck me. My usual optimism was evolving into a steely-eyed determination to carry on.

We took possession of our new-to-us research sub and had it docked in an old naval base a couple of hours north of the city. We didn't have the coordinates for the island enclave, but we had them for the Caribbean deep-sea site, and we knew it was ready. We looked at our finances. It was time for desperate measures.

CHAPTER 50

We heard a distant copter. It could have been rescue, but I doubted it. "Can't be good," muttered Cedric. I felt my pulse pounding as if I'd just done a workout. We didn't have time to save any of the Ceph. Or ourselves.

The approaching copter was the same sleek model we had flown in to Mr. Sykes' enclave. Not knowing what else to do, I warned the Ceph to return to the basement, and even shooed some into the lab with River to get them out of the intake room. Then Cedric and I took the elevator to the roof. The copter was landing as we opened the door.

I recognized Dr. Winters as soon as she jumped out. As bright and bubbly as the last time we saw her, she grinned and yelled over the sound of the copter blades, bounding over to us. I froze, couldn't smile. She ignored my reaction, telling us how happy she was to drop in for a visit and that she had news. Not knowing what else to do, we ushered her into our intake room.

Looking at the room, I felt suddenly self-conscious. While the mahogany table had weathered the storm, the once pristine sofa had brown stains and the broken picture window was still covered by plastic sheeting, cold December air whistling against it. Dirty dishes were piled in the sink of the kitchen and I was wearing clothes from the day before. It had been months since we'd interviewed a new client here, months since Dr. Winters' visit when we hosted her for dinners. The room was a shadow of its former self. As were we, I suppose.

Cedric made tea. Sage sat down, her smile tight and fake.

"We haven't heard anything from Mr. Sykes," I began awkwardly. "He's usually very engaged with our research." Rotten woman, I thought. *Thief.*

"Everything is going according to plan," Dr. Winters replied. "I have

word from him. Instructions, really. This isn't a social call." She took her
teacup anyway and sipped.

"We saw the news and wondered. You know, the attack on the space
ark."

"It's wonderful for you, really," she continued, blithely ignoring me.
"Mr. Sykes has sent me to invite you to join him on the island. He's insisting, really. It's too dangerous for you here." She looked around the room,
judging. Damn her.

"You can see civilization is approaching its final stages of collapse. I
could see it just flying over Long Harbour. I think I've only just arrived in
time for you two." Her condescending tone made me grind my teeth.

"It's time to think boldly, creatively. Global Holdings is moving more
aggressively into space travel and interstellar exploration. It's something
very close to Burton's heart, something he's very committed to. He's working closely with his old friend Titus Falco. Here, I have a message for you."

She twisted something on her wrist and a larger-than-life image of
Mr. Sykes filled the room. "I'm sure you have all matter of questions,"
he began. "It came to me a few years back that we had to do more. The
Earth will end, if not now, then millions of years from now when the Sun
expands and dies. As the singular intelligence in the universe, we need to
protect ourselves, we need to survive by expansion, we need to branch out.
We need to reach the stars. We need to dominate the heavens. We need to
recreate the universe in our own image, terraforming planets, engineering
ourselves, finding new homes so we can thrive unending."

He was leaning toward the camera, staring intently. His giant image
loomed over us.

"Of course, right now, Earth is dying and we urgently need to find
a path through to a new home, a new base. We need to employ all the
innovation and creativity at our disposal to escape the wreck that Earth
has become. Humanity's future is too important to leave to governments or
the United Nations. We need bold purpose! We need entrepreneurship and
energy among the stars to ensure our future.

"A colony of humans at the bottom of the sea is the first step in our salvation. I've taken the code we developed with the Midnight Project and monetized it. Now we can finance my off-world plans for interstellar colonization. I'm making corporate alliances to facilitate this. And to safeguard our best and brightest. That's you. I'm offering you a chance to escape Earth's destruction.

"You've made a significant contribution that deserves to be rewarded. That's why I've held a place for you in my enclave. You can be part of this beautiful pinnacle of human achievement, part of the next stage in our evolutionary journey. Join me and you can be part of our search for brave new worlds! Sage has all the details. You can thank me in person when we see each other next week."

Sage twisted her wrist again and the image froze, hanging over the boardroom table. "Well?" she asked.

I put my teacup down. A moment of trepidation, followed by a flash of anger. "Sage, Mr. Sykes being nuts is nothing new to us. But I know you stole the Ceph serum. I know Sykes had something to do with the super-soldier attack on the space ark." I braced for all hell to let loose but she just laughed.

"Well, Raina, Burton has many scientific projects underway. And, of course, there are crosswalks and collaboration among them. You'll understand better when you live on-site. You've provided cornerstone research, just top-notch contributions to a host of Global Holdings endeavours."

Oh, I did not like that, not one bit. "How can you say that? That attack was a crime against humanity." I dropped my voice. "Those were super-soldiers, there are treaties against that, it's against all decency . . ." I trailed off, then rallied. "It's not allowed!"

"Raina, don't try to understand things above your station. You're a scientist, you don't do politics. Besides, there's no proof that Burton was involved in that." She knew exactly what I was talking about.

"Some are saying Titus Falco was involved," Cedric volunteered.

"Again, no proof," Sage said. "Nothing will stick."

We fell silent. We were at an impasse.

"I don't understand," I said finally. "What are you asking us to do?"

"Destroy all your files, destroy all your specimens. Come to the island and help us work on interstellar exploration." She put her teacup down and waited expectantly.

I took an unsteady breath. I knew that Mr. Sykes or Sage (or both) had stolen the serum but demanding that we kill the Ceph was a new level of villainy. I felt Dr. Winters' fresh betrayal keenly. "Why would you want us to kill the Ceph?"

Sage looked momentarily puzzled. "Well, we have the Ceph serum and with your research notes we can make new Ceph whenever we want. And even better, with some additional work at the enclave, we can transform adult humans into water dwellers. It'll be a terrific new revenue stream. A new form of ark! I can see the advertising copy already. People will jump all over it. What you have here are just prototypes, they don't need to be freed in the ocean. Of course, Burton considered transplanting them to help prepare the way for paying customers but it's too risky without having some undersea humans to supervise."

Pain thudded through my chest and I found it hard to breathe. "Sage," I gasped, "why is this happening? Why now? I don't understand."

"Well, the bee catastrophe has accelerated the timelines on everything. The writing on the wall is in really large letters, Raina – it's a dying planet. There isn't anything for us here anymore and if we pivot to interstellar industries, we'll have first-mover advantage. Burton has a space ark and can acquire a space station that'll be perfect as a way station, a launchpad to better, more suited exoplanets. It's all perfect, really."

"I don't get it, Sage. How could you be involved in this? This isn't like you. He's murdered tens of thousands of people. This is so wrong."

"Oh, Raina!" A barking laugh erupted from Dr. Winters. "What did you think was happening? Was going to happen? Were you really so naïve to think someone would shower you with money to create something that couldn't be bought and sold, or wouldn't be used?"

"But killing them?" I shot back. "You were the one who argued they were people. We can't just kill them!"

Exasperated, Sage waved a hand dismissively. "Raina" – she spoke like she was addressing a five-year-old – "do you have any idea how many human people have already died? Have already been killed? This is a contact sport. It's not personal, it's just business. I mean, they're all dead in the end, anyway."

"But everything he told us about saving humanity, even you were . . . good . . ." I trailed off, despairing.

She smiled coldly. "Do I believe in Burton and his projects? God, no. This is not about faith, or saving humanity, or whatever drivel he sold you. This is about business; this is about power. Look around you!" She pointed to the plastic sheeting on the window. "You don't even have to leave this room to see that there are forces in the world that will destroy you. Have you not the slightest ounce of self-preservation? Life here is crashing and there's no future. We have to make our way, make the hard choices to survive. Burton can make hard choices. He has money, power, but he also has nerve. Why wouldn't I want to be part of that? Why wouldn't I choose victory over slow defeat here?"

Cedric stuttered, stricken, "I thought you believed in the Ceph."

Sage scoffed. "Did you really think the Ceph were pure? Everyone is for sale, but only a few are buying. I just chose the side that was buying."

I reached out with an empty hand. "Sage, I can't kill the – are you really asking us to kill the Ceph?"

She looked at me, pitiless and cruel, the mask dropped. "Grow up, Raina. Sometimes we just have to do what needs to be done." She shook her head. "Your options right now are very limited. You're a loose end. You're going to be tidied up one way or another. It's a shame you aren't happy about it, but you aren't in a position to bargain. You're only in the position to carry out your orders and claim your place in the enclave, claim your place in history."

Flustered, we tried to argue, but it was no use. "Do I have to spell out the consequences of not complying?" Sage said finally. "You aren't dealing with people who will bring a lawsuit. You aren't dealing with people who will politely let you choose. You are being given a direct order and you have no choice.

"You have three days. We'll send a copter to pick you up on the roof. Destroy all the files, destroy all the specimens including the Ceph. And then you get to be part of the future."

Cedric stood up and spoke with a wooden version of his voice for clients. "I think it's time you left, Dr. Winters. We'll need to carefully consider everything you've told us. Thank you so much for coming in." I stood up automatically, trying to marshal some dignity, some semblance of my professional self.

Dr. Winters rose and coldly said her farewells. We escorted her to the roof, and with the thrumming of the copter blades, she was gone.

CHAPTER 51

The copter receded into the horizon, and we stood there for a few minutes. I swore quietly and Cedric shook his head. I felt a rising anger. Grow up, she said? Grow up? Fine advice coming from a giggling, snivelling child of sunshine like her. I hated her with a purity stoked in a thousand years of steely-eyed patience.

"So they didn't forget us after all," Cedric said.

I blinked hard. I needed to think. We took the elevator back to the intake room. Without words we started to pack up.

"Of course, we aren't going to."

Cedric looked over at me. "What should we do then?"

"They just have to make it." I sighed. "I promised. I promised and the alternative is so . . ."

Neither of us wanted to discuss the easiest option: do as we were told and end the colony. We already had the plan in place to do it, it had been part of our fail-safes when we first set up the project. We could find some ethics to justify it – it was dangerous to let them loose on the world, even at the bottom of the ocean. Once we had destroyed the evidence, we could make a run for it on our own or take our chances with Global Holdings. I knew Cedric wanted us to seek the safety of the enclave.

I couldn't do it, though. Is this how parents feel? We'd created something unique, something beautiful. To destroy them would be a tragedy from which I would never recover. Coralie was the best of us in so many ways. Strong and determined, a sharper mind than ours, with an unwavering loyalty to her fellow Ceph and to us. I couldn't imagine killing her on the orders of a sociopath. The cultural attributes that Mr. Sykes had found so important were right there in the Ceph but were unique to their physiology and world view. They had music we couldn't hear, storytelling we could not understand. They were more than a checklist of attributes, though. More than a vehicle for ambition. More than a madman's play for dominance.

They were a deep-sea sparkling weightless view of life. An eagerness to live and survive. A love of their own family, a loyalty to community. A sharp intelligence and hunger to know more.

They were a science experiment, true. They were all the hybrid pieces of DNA that comprised their genetic structures. But they were so much more. They were so much more to me.

As I contemplated ending them, I realized I loved them completely. I could only rescue them. I had to help them escape or lose myself utterly.

"Cedric," I started.

"I know," he said. He always knew.

I wanted to stay true to the vision with which we started: To save some part of humanity, to tuck its best parts away where it couldn't be found, couldn't be corrupted. To save something from our own stupidity, our own venal greed and selfishness, our narrow-mindedness. To save something from the complete cock-up our society had become. We had lost our way. In trying to control everything, I had failed to control anything. But I could maybe do this one thing. This one small thing. With my whole heart I wanted to save the Ceph.

Cedric and I didn't discuss it further. It was too obvious for words.

I leapt to the next step: planning our escape. We wouldn't have time to liquidate our assets but we could grab our cash. Our research sub had been delivered to a quiet retired naval base north of us. It was there, waiting fully fit up and supplied. With Dr. Winters' revelations though, the Caribbean site would be dangerous to use. They would know where the Ceph were. And no way would Cedric and I be safe in Sykes' enclave. We were caught, and running out of time. I didn't know what to do.

"We'd better talk to Coralie," said Cedric as he steered me to elevator.

Down by the pool, I barely knew where to start. I explained what we'd seen and guessed, and what Sage had said. I felt betrayed. Trapped. Swindled. Conned.

I'd been naïve. Stupidly so. I'd been seduced by the chance to save humanity, by the opportunity to do innovative science and by – let's be honest – the vast sums he'd waved at me. The opportunity to salvage my reputation, demonstrate my skills, prove my worth. Not just a job but professional redemption, not to mention financial security so that I could cushion the rest of my life no matter what happened. It was the same foolish behaviour as so many of our politicians and business leaders. Only I was supposed to be smarter, more careful, more thoughtful, more aware. Turned out I was just as flawed a specimen of humanity as the rest of them. I had only myself to blame.

Heartbroken, I confessed everything to Coralie. How our research that had started out as a bright shining light in my heart, a response to the world's devastation, had been corrupted, used against people, used in the most violent way possible. How the creation of the colony, the love and joy of my life, my career's crowning pinnacle of achievement, had been a ruse to allow an ambitious, unfettered billionaire to perfect a stratagem for interstellar domination.

"I thought he was crazy, sure, but you know, in a quirky way, not a crazy despot who wants to rule the world way, you know? All those rants about culture and literature and the good in humanity? I don't understand. I don't understand how I didn't know."

Coralie was angry but calm. "I never trusted him. Something around the eyes."

She let me storm around, flinging the broken pieces of my soul in all directions.

"Even if he has betrayed you, you still made us, you still achieved something wonderful," she said soothingly. "I wish you could hear our music, really hear it and understand it. It's a marvel, Raina. It really is. You didn't fail."

"No," I said bitterly, "I succeeded, and as a result, I have been corrupted. I succeeded at the wrong thing."

Cedric quietly laid out his concerns. His usual hum of low-level anxiety had turned into a barely concealed panic but he was more focused than I was. "They'll be coming now. Global Holdings doesn't want us in the wild. And the authorities will need to review everything, determine liability and guilt. We'll be caught up in the web eventually. We need to plan; we need to get out. We only have three days."

"We already have a plan and it is a good one," said Coralie. "We take the submersible to the sea."

"You don't understand," I chimed in. "The Caribbean site, the one we visited with the mussel farm that's all ready for you, Mr. Sykes can find you there. It's too risky. If we don't do what he says, he may get rid of us entirely. All of us. We can't trust anyone. I don't know what to do."

Coralie took a moment to look seriously at each of us. "Well, I guess it's time I shared a secret. Please don't be mad." She smiled slowly, almost sadly, peering at us while her skin pinked up to an embarrassed rose hue. "I've wanted to tell you, but I needed to protect us."

Coralie hauled herself out of the pool and curled at the side, stretching her torso so that we were all face to face where we sat. The tiny tentacles at her cheeks flicked nervously. "You remember the storm?"

I nodded.

"We sent Delmar. He didn't escape. We wanted to know more about the sea. We wanted to explore. We didn't send him alone. Do you remember Bubbles?"

Coralie's dark eyes watched us intently, and her soft arms gesturing apologetically as she made her own confession. "It starts with Bubbles, I suppose. You don't know about Bubbles."

"Bubbles?" I was lost.

"The little Ceph who ate your octopus. He was a bit different, a bit fierce. But sweet in his way, such a warrior. We loved him, you know. We saved him. It wasn't right to punish a child for a mistake. He didn't understand about Maisie. We felt you were . . ." she searched briefly for the right word ". . . impulsive. So we saved him. We hid him here in the pool and looked after him, brought him up. But sooner or later you would have noticed. I'd planned to tell you, planned to argue his right to live, make him a proper, accepted part of the colony, but then the storm came and it seemed like such a perfect moment. We made a bold play.

"Delmar had always felt trapped here, always wanted to explore. He doesn't feel the need to hide like most of us do, he wanted to be in the open water, in the surge of the storm. We could have held him back, but it would have taken all of us. He so wanted to explore outside and the storm was his only chance.

"So we sent Bubbles with him and asked him to come back when we called him."

"Called him?" I said. "That's how you found him?"

"Yes, but we're getting ahead of my story." Coralie was still an embarrassed pink shade, turning a rust colour around the edges. She was uncomfortable, even a little angry. "We gave Delmar and Bubbles some nets full of mussels and helped them break out. As soon as the exterior vent came free, they were gone, and Finn and I had to seal the breach to keep the rest of us safely inside. When we sent Finn after them, he found them right away, they called to him and he found where they had gone. The pressure wasn't an issue at all; Cedric's fix works perfectly. They were several kilometres from here, past the shelf and deep in the cold. I'll show you."

Coralie gestured toward the computer. Her voice activated it and she pulled up a sea map as a hologram. Soon we were surrounded by a map of the coast and the seabed east of the Canadian provinces. She traced a path in red from Long Harbour along the coast and out to the deep.

"Right here!" she pointed. "To the north. It's better in the cold, we don't have to go as far down to feel safe. We reach the midnight zone here." She gestured at a precise spot. "They rehomed the mussels on a cliff face here. There are caves underneath. We can live there, Raina. It can be done, Cedric. We don't need the Caribbean and we don't need Mr. Sykes. I can take us there.

"Bubbles is waiting for us. He has everything set up. He is farming the clams, looking for more food sources."

There was silence for a long time. "Looking for more food sources?" Cedric was looking green around the gills himself. "Out in the wild?

The most savage among you?" He seemed to have frozen. He wasn't even breathing.

"Savage?" Coralie twisted to look at him directly. "No, not savage. Bold, hungry and proud."

"The most human among us, in a way," I responded. "Humans were never docile, not throughout our entire history."

"Exactly," Coralie said. "He's strong and useful. He contributes. But I am still the matriarch, and we are still the Ceph you know. We can make it, Raina! If you help us. Don't you see? It's too early, we're not ready. You and Cedric need to come too. We need to keep working on adaptations if we are to survive. We need to have children; we need to establish ourselves. Will you help us?"

The entire colony, sensing the nature of the discussion we were having, had all poked their heads out of the water and were listening intently. I felt their attention even before I noticed them there. It seemed like no one was breathing, that the moment was crystalline, suspended in air, waiting.

Everyone, even Cedric, was looking at me. Looking to me.

I should've been shocked, but I wasn't. In fact, I was secretly relieved that they had not killed Bubbles in a violent underwater ritual.

"Raina, what is left for you here?" Coralie's eyes didn't leave mine.

What else could I do? I had promised. Things had changed but the promise hung in the air alongside the silence and the anticipation. Coralie's story had opened up a beautiful door, potential salvation, not only for the colony but for Cedric and me. I also, in my way, wanted to live in the wild. I glanced at Cedric. His look of betrayal stopped me cold. I faltered.

"We should talk about this," he said to me in an undertone.

"This is incredible, Coralie. Amazing. Let Cedric and me discuss it. Please? Let us discuss privately how to rescue the colony and then let's talk. This is so much to take in. I wish you had told us earlier."

The silence changed then. There was a slight deflation, a turning away. Half of the Ceph listeners submerged in a trail of bubbles and were gone from view.

"You promised." Coralie didn't need to remind me, but she did.

"I promised," I said. "And I will see it through. You may have rescued all of us. In the end, we may all rescue each other. I won't let you down."

Without much more to say, Cedric and I retreated upstairs. We had the coordinates of the map, and the hopes and dreams of a new people.

CHAPTER 52

We were on the stairs when we heard the front doorbell buzz. We crossed the lobby to the reception desk by the elevator and turned on the intercom. "Hello? We're not expecting any deliveries today. You probably have the wrong address," Cedric said.

A voice listed off our names and identified himself. "I'm William Cheng from the Genome Regulatory Authority. Can we please speak face to face?"

Damn it. The other side of the claw snapping shut to trap us. It came too quick. We needed to buy time.

"One minute!" Cedric and I exchanged panicked glances.

"He's seen us, I don't think we can ignore him," I said.

"Yes, but this can only be bad. There's no happy reason for him to be here."

"Is it worse if we ignore him? Can he come back with police?"

Cedric took a deep breath. "It's worse. We better talk to him."

We crossed the lobby, passed the boarded-up nail salon and unlocked the door. The first thing the official did was hand us an envelope. "Please note that you have been served. This is a subpoena relating to all your records of correspondence with a client company" – he theatrically checked his notes – "Surf Legacy."

I put on my best talk-to-government face. "Of course, we'll cooperate fully. We'll need to read through the materials and consult our lawyer of course." Too many "of courses," but I was nervous.

"Of course," he replied in kind, with a gentle and humourless smile. "Please read the contents of the envelope carefully. You have forty-eight hours to get your records in order and submitted to court." He bid us goodbye and left.

Cedric was the first to speak. "Lucky. If they knew anything they'd be here with court orders, seizing everything they could find and impounding the whole property."

"And they could do that anytime." I uneasily watched the official cross the street to his waiting vehicle. I looked at the envelope in my hands. "We really don't have much time. We better call Greg."

⁊

For what was likely the last time, or one of the last times, we made coffee and sat down on the mottled couch in the intake room to discuss what to do. To my surprise, it was Cedric who spoke first.

"We can wire our cover research to Greg and let the lawyers handle it. As long as we can keep the authorities out of our server and off the property, we'll be okay."

"It's only a matter of time before they look in the basement, though. We can wipe the servers, but as long as the colony is here, we are in deep, deep trouble."

"The liability waiver should protect us from the super-soldier connection. We have an explicit clause."

"Yes, we should be able to avoid culpability for the space drama. But I suspect they can find enough drama right here if they look, and they will. Especially if they find out about Delmar and Bubbles. And they would end the colony. No question. I can't see how they would let them survive. We need to get the colony out."

Cedric wrinkled his brow and frowned. "We can't just let them go, Raina. They're not safe. They're like children, like headstrong teenagers. They don't know what the world is like."

"I don't know much, Cedric, but I do know that every single decision I've made about this project has been made for the wrong reasons and has led to awful things. I think we should let Coralie and the Ceph decide what happens to them next. It can't be worse than my track record."

Cedric's face softened and he smiled. "It's bad, but not that bad. I know you want to save them, Raina. So do I. But just set them loose in the wild? They're children who've never been outside. They think they're smart and all grown up but they're immature; they're not capable of good decisions. They could hurt themselves, damage their habitat, run the ecosystem in a new direction, totally by accident. The classic bull in a china shop. We need to stay small and quiet, humble, at least while we figure out the broader implications. We can't stay here, but we can't just let them loose. They will either die or kill."

We were quiet for a bit. Finally, I said, "They aren't mindless, you know. They won't destroy the ecosystem like rabbits in Australia. They're human. They're thoughtful."

"I know they're thoughtful, and I know they may be fine. But look at what we humans have done . . ." He trailed off morosely. "We can't let them just go off on their own."

"Well then, let's help them," I pleaded. "We could set them up for sustainable living. We still have Ceph eggs in the lab. We'll need to train them all up in aquatic farming, teach them to respect the ocean. They'll be like kids in a candy store, at first. We need to help them settle in, avoid attention."

"Yes, and we need to hide too."

I laughed hollowly. "Well, yes, there's that. We're pretty exposed at the moment. Jail might be a best-case scenario. Mr. Sykes wants us to come in from the cold, but we don't know what's waiting for us there. No one's going to let us stay here, like we've been doing. If Mr. Sykes can't bring us in, he'll resort to worse tactics than legal action."

Cedric sighed and fell into the wingback chair, shaking his head dejectedly. "I don't see any other way forward. The only way out is through this mess." He ran his hand through his hair. Finally, he looked at me and nodded. "But we can't let them go on their own. We need to be with them."

I nodded and got down to business immediately. "Okay, how? I see the what, I see the why. Let's get to work on the how."

"We can upload all our research and files to the submarine, it's a fully equipped research vessel," said Cedric. "We can decouple the GPS and location services, go dark. Then we can park it for a few years underwater. There are already two years' worth of rations for two people and a salt-to-fresh water filtration system. In two years, we could figure out a small and sustainable local food source for humans. No one would need to know as long as they don't track us going. Then we can stay with them as long as they need."

As good a plan as any, I thought and better than most. "And who knows what will be happening topside while we hide? We could end up surviving a very hard time here. No guarantee where the world will be in a couple of years. We may be better off with the Ceph."

We talked a while longer, then Cedric stood and rinsed his coffee cup. "I'll get to work on the computer files and transfers. We'll need to activate the fail-safes and destroy everything left behind."

I nodded, smiled ruefully. "I'll check the rations list and pack the coffee."

He looked at me without smiling back. "Better talk to Coralie first. We don't have much time, and they'll need to make preparations too."

He looked for a moment like he would say something more, then turned away to get on with the next steps. I hurried to the basement to give Coralie the good news.

"We think we can do it," I told her as I laid out our plans. We just had to figure out how to get ourselves and our gear on board without attracting notice. We needed to figure out how to get the Ceph safely to the sub and out to sea.

"We've made good progress on the pressure challenge and Delmar and Finn confirm that they didn't have any trouble on their way to the site. If there're residual issues, we can tailor some new treatments on the spot but we'll need to descend in stages to make sure we don't lose anyone. We'll need to provide the treatment to the younglings but we can do that en route if we don't go too deep for the first few days." Of course, this only applied to the Ceph. Cedric and I would live in the pressurized submarine for the rest of our days unless we returned to the surface.

I outlined the route I thought we could take, hugging the coastline a few hundred metres down, keeping the Ceph in tanks inside the submarine for safety and letting them out periodically to acclimatize to the pressure as we descended. Coralie seemed unconvinced but I didn't have time to argue and returned to the main lab. We had a lot of work to do.

❧

When Cedric and I returned to the basement a few hours later, Coralie's thinking and planning for our escape had advanced considerably, but we didn't quite agree. Coralie thought the Ceph could be dropped off at the coast, and swim safely along the bottom led by Delmar and Finn and we could follow in the sub. Cedric and I worried about the ecological trail that might leave, and damage it could do. I couldn't quite see how we could transfer the entire colony to the ocean without being seen.

Coralie and Finn made some adjustments to our navigation plan. Finn had met with some hazards on his way down that we needed to avoid and pointed out some safe haven spots. The route looked feasible and their modifications made sense.

"The best thing would be for us all to travel in the sub – that way you contaminate nothing along the way," Cedric told them.

This met with strong resistance. "We can swim, and we will be less vulnerable this way. Our bodies can adjust to the ocean in stages, gradually. It will be harder to transition straight out of the submersible. And of course, I'll stay with you inside to make sure you are all right." There was an airlock that she could use for this purpose.

Coralie surprised me by suggesting they could pilot the craft. It was helpful; I'd been worried about this. At the same time, it surprised me to learn that a couple of Ceph, including Coralie, had downloaded pilot simulation exercises and learned the controls. They would be safer behind the wheel than either me or Cedric.

"We've looked at the specs for the tank," Coralie told us. "There isn't enough room in what we have for all of us. We have no choice. We either have half the Ceph swimming or we leave them behind. We don't have time or opportunity to outfit the submarine better, it has limited saltwater storage for live specimens. Frankly it looks pretty uncomfortable from what I see in the catalogue." She flicked up an image of the submarine's interior, with the tanks proudly displaying a lobster and starfish. They did look a little small.

While we sat next to the pool, considering a giant hologram of a map and charting our course, the Ceph were busy harvesting and packing up the mussels for transport and food on the way. There was a palpable excitement in the air as the Ceph whistled to each other and passed nets back and forth. This was the culmination of a lifelong dream for them. This was everything they had yearned for. The escape, for them, was a release from captivity.

I could think of no other option than the one Coralie presented. It was a risk that had to be taken, or the entire enterprise abandoned. I reluctantly agreed. I explained the importance of touching as little as possible, eating nothing on the way except what we brought with us. Coralie nodded and reassured me. "This is our world and we will look after it. We won't let harm come to it, you'll see." Coralie grinned wide, sharp teeth glinting. I always found it disconcerting when she smiled with her teeth. It made her look fierce.

While excitement and adventure were driving the Ceph, fear was driving me. Our enemies were closing in and we were running out of time. I thought about just releasing the Ceph on their own, and Cedric and I going dark, running into the hills. We could buy new identities or live off the grid, start again. But it wouldn't work. Cedric and I couldn't disappear topside. We would be found, either by the authorities or by Mr. Sykes. And the Ceph would need guidance and help. They couldn't make it on their own.

Besides, I had promised Coralie. The promise felt like a solid thing weighing on my heart and I could not abandon them.

CHAPTER 53: CEDRIC

FADE IN

INT. CEDRIC'S ROOM - DAY

The camera pans on a small room with a window looking out toward the sea. CEDRIC swivels the camera away from a carefully made bed piled with personal belongings to focus on his face. He hurriedly takes a seat at a small desk.

> CEDRIC
>
> I think this will be my last entry - I'll upload it to the files on the sub, and I think that will be it. Our adventure has taken a dark turn. Not sure why I feel the need to conclude my video-log, but here it is.
>
> We've been betrayed. I don't think Raina and I can be saved, but we can save the Ceph. We have to go with them now to ensure their survival. We need to see them settled, make sure the habitat is appropriate, make sure they can live well.
>
> We're bringing as much of our lab equipment as we can, and our computer files. We can continue to look after them. I don't think they'll survive without us. We have to go with them.

CEDRIC fidgets, runs fingers through his thinning hair.

                  CEDRIC (cont'd)
We have human rations for two years and probably can adapt food underwater in that time
to be sustainable. Everything is ready, and
we can load it tonight. Technically, there's
no limit to the amount of time we can spend
underwater in the research sub. We can maybe
make it too.

CEDRIC looks left.

                  CEDRIC (cont'd)
Of course, it's a shame about the coffee. We
have a six-month supply. We can try, but deep-
sea hydroponics will be a long shot. But overall, this may work. We may be able to save the
Ceph, save that little piece of humanity we've
nurtured.

It's feasible. It can work.

It's what we've been saying at each and every
stage of the whole damned thing. It's what
we've been clinging to. I think at this stage
of history, that's what everyone is doing. Just
putting one foot in front of the other, doing
what we can, doing what's feasible, trying
not to think about all the things outside our
control, outside our grasp. As if we can pull
together and save our future with toothpicks
and bubble gum. With string and sticks.

The world is in free fall. We're falling with
it. But while we're falling, we pretend. We
pretend to be masters of our own destiny.

I have counted on Raina for her optimism,
for her sunny fierceness. She has shored up my
defences, filled the gaps and holes in my own
nature.

And now, it's time to flee not fight. Or perhaps
this is the fight.

Tears run down CEDRIC'S face. His voice catches then drops
to a whisper.

                    CEDRIC (cont'd)
        The truth is, I don't know if I can do this.
        I've never been a hero. I just don't know.

CEDRIC stares mournfully into the camera.

                    CEDRIC (cont'd)
        I'm just so sorry, Raina. I've tried to be
        better. I'm trying. It's all we can do - keep
        trying.

CEDRIC sighs, wipes his eyes with his sleeve, stares and
turns the camera off.

                                        CUT TO BLACK

CHAPTER 54

We were in high gear with all the preparations. Cedric had contacted Greg, who came in person right away to examine the subpoena and discuss the materials to be handed over. He thought that he could delay the authorities from searching the building by turning over our cover research notes and complying as much as possible. He felt that given we had expressly written a clause in our contract with Surf Legacy that our work could not be used to create super-soldiers, that we could plead for leniency if we were caught. We uploaded files and gave him access to some of the research that would hold the wolves at bay, at least for a few days. Greg did counsel us that this would only buy us time, and that it was inevitable that they would search our premises.

After he'd left, Cedric took the lead on our cover story and wrote notes, asking Greg to rehome Rex the octopus and to make arrangements for the plants that were left. The message was timed to go out after we were long gone.

With Cedric taking care of the digital transfer to the sub's computers and our server wipe, I thought about going home one last time. I had some old photos, mementos of my early life, my family. I could take them with me, one last thing to cling to. I thought of the ties that still bound me to the earth, that kept me going, kept me sane.

It would only take a couple of hours to go and grab them. Cedric could take care of things at the lab; he had cleared out his apartment months ago and everything he needed was close at hand. I thought about calling a shuttle, thought better of it and then did it anyway.

It was a risk, but everything was a risk now. Within minutes, I was in motion, grabbing the shuttle and impulsively heading home. I ran into the house, thundered into the front hall and then stopped, breathing hard. I ran into the kitchen for reasons beyond logic and started unpacking the fridge, throwing out old leftovers, frantically thinking about what I might need. I left it in the end. It didn't matter now; decomposing food in my fridge wasn't my problem anymore. I took a deep breath and tried to remember why I had come. Panic was creeping in at the edges. Was that a shadow by the front door? Did I hear a noise? Had they come for me here?

I forced myself to stillness, forced myself to concentrate. My eyes fell on my bookshelf, with my old treasures, so hard to find, beloved. I couldn't pick just one, so I left them. Family photos. Where were they? I forced myself to walk, not run, into my bedroom and started pulling boxes out of the closet. I thought the old albums were there. Fleetingly, I kicked myself for not digitizing them years ago. It had been a romantic notion. I couldn't find them, they weren't there. I hadn't really thought about them in years. I had a sudden impulse, called my father. A small hologram of his face politely invited me to leave a message.

"Hi, Dad. I just wanted to say that I'm sorry. I'm so sorry for all of it. You won't be hearing from me for a while, but I didn't want you to think it was because of you. It was all me. I just couldn't . . . well, it doesn't matter now. I love you, Dad. Take care."

What was I grasping at? It was all too late for redemption.

I was distracted by movement outside the window. The latest snow had melted and the temperature had plummeted. Everything was frozen and brittle now, crisp maple leaves littering the patio. The garden had been a husk for months, and the bird feeders, still full, were empty of all except a grateful squirrel or two. My little thrush had long departed south. I wondered if she would make it back in the spring and felt a pang at the thought of her arriving here and finding the garden brown and dead. No water, no birdseed, no flowers: a harsh homecoming.

I thought of the drum of rain on the roof in spring, the dry sunny days and evenings. The detritus of my life, collected around me. I took a last look at the city spread out beneath the hills, its familiar streets and sounds. The ocean was a glint beyond the tall buildings, the grid of the city laid out before me. The city that had been my home, my habitat, my skin for so many years. The city of strangers that I had claimed as my family, the city of streets and buildings that persisted despite everything.

I didn't need old photos. My family was gone, my friends had all drifted away. No, my one real relationship, my only enduring friend and loved one was Cedric and he was coming with me. This was not quite the whole truth either. Coralie and the Ceph had taken centre stage in my life. They were important to me now. Cedric, Coralie and the whole gang. They were my friends, my children, my family. There was no one left behind I needed to miss.

I shook off my melancholy, feeling the edge of panic return. It was a time for actions, not regrets. Regrets could come later. Right now, we had to escape. My newfound family, my children, needed me now. There was work to do. As I was leaving, I noticed the picture of the thrush on the wall and pulled it down, said a silent apology to the little bird and left, tucking her image into my jacket and taking one last look behind me.

CHAPTER 55

We were ready just after midnight the next day, hours before the subpoena deadline expired and a day before Sykes' ultimatum kicked in. My body hummed with low-grade terror. I hadn't slept, but all was ready. We had our rental truck parked outside the supply door. The disused naval base had a small airfield and helipad attached to it. We had arranged with the rental company to pick up the truck, so anyone who managed to trace us there would perhaps believe we had flown out rather than sailed. The submersible waited, parked at the farthest slot down the dock, ready for boarding. We planned to arrive before dawn and be gone before the sun came up.

Mr. Sykes' helicopter would arrive to pick up Cedric and I and find us gone.

It was a rushed, uncertain plan, but the best we could do under the circumstances. My heart was beating loudly as we tiptoed out. The Ceph waddled after me, the suckers on their tentacles making soft squelching sounds as they crossed the lobby. I nervously counted Ceph heads as they waited quietly.

"River and Cedric are bringing the rest of the younglings, right?" I whispered.

"Coming," answered Coralie. "Don't worry."

The elevator doors slid open and River appeared, carrying two young-lings, motioning the rest out. They crossed the lobby and joined the main body of Ceph. Cedric, who had locked up the lab and offices behind them, was last out.

"All accounted for," he reported. "Computer files have been transferred to the sub and I've executed the fail-safe here. They won't find anything."

We opened the supply doors and motioned the Ceph out. I unlocked the truck and turned it on, returning to where Cedric and the Ceph waited. Finn and Delmar opened the rear door of the rental while Cedric locked the building and stood beside me, frowning anxiously. The Ceph were now milling around the back of the truck, helping the younglings climb into the cargo bed, then flipping in themselves. Their moods illuminated by the glowing patterns on their skin, their excitement and fear was on display for those who knew how to read it.

On the building across the road, I could see the furtive movement of hoppers in the moonlight, drawn by the noise of the truck or the headlights. "No, no, no!" Cedric saw them too.

I called softly to Delmar and Finn. "Look!" I pointed. "Hoppers on the far building, we need to hurry." They stood guard while the remaining Ceph climbed into the back of the truck, except Coralie who had insisted she ride up front with us.

"They're on our building now too," whispered Cedric urgently, pointing overhead.

Sure enough, a couple of the green crawlers hung a story above us. They seemed to be hesitating, maybe they were afraid of the Ceph? In a few minutes, everyone was secure. Delmar and Finn were the last to jump in the back. We slammed the door shut and ran for the cab.

Several hoppers leapt off the buildings. I saw a couple of the closest reach the ground and charge, but they were too late. I put the truck in gear and gasped as one landed on the hood in front of me, but he didn't get purchase and flipped off as we accelerated. We were on our way, as fast as I could get the truck moving over the cracked roads. Focused on the chaotic loading and flight of the truck, I didn't look back as we pulled out. Only when we were far up the road and leaving the city did I take one final glimpse back. Spots twinkled in the rearview mirror but most of it lay in darkness.

Then the city was behind us. We were on our way.

At first Coralie was silent, awed by her first excursion beyond our building. Then gradually she came out of her shell, nervously asking questions and looking around. She was fascinated by the truck's cab, its engines and the view out the window. She pushed out of her seat belt, squeezing herself against the passenger window, practically sitting on Cedric's lap. "What's that?" she asked, pointing both inside and outside the cab. Cedric tried to keep up with her questions while I managed our route. By the time we were half an hour beyond the city limits, she was rapt, an excited deep blue dappling her body.

"Look at that wide, wide world!" Even in the midst of the chaos of our escape, the stress of being pursued, Coralie radiated joy. She chattered about the hoppers, excited to have seen them up close. She talked about how the younglings would grow up in the open ocean and what that would be like for them. She peered through the windows and tried to take in everything. Cedric's leg wouldn't stop twitching and I could see the whites of his eyes but my panicky heartbeat had slowed with the drive. I felt calmer now that we were in motion.

As we approached the remote marina, I nervously went through a last mental checklist. Rather than drive straight in, we pulled off to a secluded beach and lifted the truck's back door. The Ceph were ready and without a word began to pour out of the truck. It was about twenty metres down a rocky beach to the water and they moved quickly, glowing softly pink, then blue in the moonless night. Some neatly walked on hind tentacles, balancing and transferring their weight as if they had legs, others pulled themselves forward octopus-style with a certain slither.

There was no need for farewells – we would see them soon. There was just an urgency to get away, to hide, though I sensed more than that from the departing Ceph. There was a joy as they hit the water's edge, a release in the way they flipped and then dove into the surf. There was beauty in the soft glow of their awkward terrestrial efforts, which transformed into grace once in the water. They were not just escaping, they were adventuring, they were seeking their own better lives.

Coralie stayed behind. We had agreed she was the best pilot. Having done the most hours in the sub's simulator, she was the most likely to get us out of the harbour without incident. Once she had overseen the colony's entry into the water, she flipped artfully into the truck's storage area alone and we were on our way again.

"Well, this is it!" I said brightly. "No going back now."

Cedric just sighed. "I guess so."

Soon we could see the dim lights of the naval base in the distance. Only an unassuming fence and discreet sign were visible from the road as we approached. A lone security guard manned a rusty gate. He asked our business, and for a breathless minute seemed to want to inspect the truck's contents. He eventually waved us through. We drove through the base, dark except for a few pale streetlamps. The base had been decommissioned but whoever owned it now rented out berths to scientists and private vessels. It felt neglected, disused.

We pulled up at the farthest dock, and opened the cargo door for Coralie. Together, the three of us quickly unloaded the last of our gear. Then Coralie and I fussed over the carefully packed Ceph eggs while Cedric walked furtively along the dock, looking for the submarine. A cold wind threatened winter rain as clouds skittered overhead.

"There it is." Cedric pointed, and turned back to help with the gear. The submersible rode low in the water, an upper deck and entryway all that was visible from the dock. Its metallic exterior softly reflected the dim lights along the walkway, a shiny black that conveyed deep-sea confidence. Beneath the waves, a large viewing area would be at the bow, smaller windows high up along the sides. The inside would be divided into three distinct segments – a pilot's bridge with viewing area and living quarters in front; laboratory, storage and kitchen space in the largest segment in the middle; then the generator, engine and water purifiers in the back. A rear airlock would enable the Ceph to come and go within the body of the vessel. Its sleek outline looked out of place in its shabby surroundings.

Here was home for the next several years. Maybe home, period. Who knew what would happen topside while we took refuge under the ocean? It didn't matter, not anymore. I was ready. We were ready to make our descent, to make our escape.

CHAPTER 56

Cedric and I paused, scrunched up against the wind, to survey the docked sub. Coralie hurried past me and was soon on top of our escape craft, manipulating the security locks and opening the main hatch. A cold rain started to fall. I hustled after Coralie, helping her load our last bags and boxes. We had kept our personal gear to a minimum and we were done in minutes. Cedric locked up the truck, leaving the keys inside.

All at the ready, I turned back to tell Cedric to hurry and was stopped by something in his face. There was a stoniness, a frozen grief. "Cedric, come on!"

He wordlessly shook his head.

I walked back, leaving the berth and standing before him. "We don't have much time."

"No," he whispered. "You don't have much time."

Then a silence that stretched out a few heartbeats; a silence that seemed to last hours before he broke it. "I'm not coming."

"What do you mean?"

"I can't do it. I'm not coming."

"But we planned everything, we planned this. Everything is going to work. We're here at the end. It's all working out."

"I'm so sorry, Raina. I just . . . can't. I really can't. I've tried so hard but I . . ." He trailed off, but I could see his resolve even as words failed.

I stared at Cedric. His words ripped the foundations from my life. I was stunned. Speechless.

Ours had never been a love story. There was no romance in the world for people like us, and we had clung to each other through the years like survivors of a calamity. We were bound together not by romantic love but by deeper need.

I felt the world tilt and suddenly couldn't breathe. I had never imagined a future without him. I suppose, to be honest, I had never imagined a future. Not for me.

"Cedric, I need you. You have to come," I whispered so quietly that I don't know if he heard. The words felt like a confession being ripped from me. "Please don't leave me."

I reached out and hugged him, something we had never done. We clung to each other for some time, two shipwrecked souls. Finally, I stepped back and we stared at each other.

"Everything is ready," Coralie said gently, from behind me. "Cedric, everything is ready – you will be safe with us."

"Cedric, what's left for you here? They are closing in on all sides. Jail will be the best that can happen to you now."

"I know the world is grinding down, there isn't much time left. I just can't give up any sunsets, sunrises. I can't give it up."

Coralie gestured to the bag that was slung over my shoulder. "We brought your book. Your poetry book." She reached in and pulled out his copy of T.S. Eliot, as if she could entice him in with it. "It's for you."

Tears started to run down Cedric's face. "Keep it. Raina, maybe you'll finally read it."

He looked at me for the last time, and I threw my arms around him again. "I'm so sorry," he repeated and pushed me back to look in my eyes. "You'll make it. I know you will."

"You'll change your mind; we can come back for you." A cascading set of new plans flashed before my eyes.

Coralie stood frozen, watching. She didn't remind me of my promise, but it lay between us, a living thing. I was going, had to go. The Ceph would not survive without me, could ruin the ocean without me, and I couldn't abandon them. I had never thought that Cedric could abandon me.

"But, Ceddy, what will you do? Where will you go?"

The rain was plastering his hair to his forehead, mingling with tears. "I'll go inland, go north, hide. I'll find a quiet piece of land and make things grow. You have to understand, Raina. I'm proud of what we've done with the Ceph, but for a long time now the only thing that has brought me joy has been bringing a little bit of green into the world, not changing them, just . . . nurturing them. Putting my hands in the soil and growing things. I can't stand the thought of giving that up, giving up sunshine and rain and . . . everything."

I had a sudden memory of our decision not to join Mr. Sykes at his enclave. I had thought at the time he was being chivalrous and thinking of me when he agreed. I'd thought it had been my lack of trust, my claustrophobia, but now I could see that he had his own revulsion of dark enclosed spaces.

He shook his head and apologized again. "I can't do it – I'd just be killing myself. But you can, and I know you'll do something wonderful. Remember what you said about the pre-apocalypse?"

One final hug and he backed away and turned, walking away slowly, leaving me there. Dawn was beginning to lighten the sky, and I wondered if I would see another sunrise, another sunset. There was nothing for it, but to keep going.

"Nobody gets out alive." I turned away from Cedric's retreating figure, turned away from the light and the sky, and descended into the submersible toward hope, toward escape, toward duty and darkness.

In another minute, I was seated in the co-pilot's chair, looking out of the window into the pitch-black. Coralie flicked on the headlights and illuminated the underside of the dock, and a sharp drop-off at the edge of the harbour. She smiled with all her teeth, reassuringly. "Ready?" she asked.

I took a deep breath, taking in all the screens blinking with information, checking that the backup files had been securely stored and everything was prepared in our new home. "Ready," I responded, returning a weak smile and reaching out my hand to touch her tentacle. "Let's go."

And wordlessly we pulled out of the dock, beginning our descent into the depths, finding a new path.

CHAPTER 57: CORALIE

The closing of the water over our heads brings relief, the journey along the seabed to the edge of the Labrador Sea nothing but excitement. Every new coral ridge, and rock shelf, and kelp bed, followed by the open ocean itself is an awakening; every new creature we encounter is a miracle coming to greet us. All the squiggles on the FlickFilms come to life – human words do not do justice to the joy of the boundless ocean filled with life and adventure, with friends, foes and strife. We are free. The world is wondrous.

There is some drama, of course. Finn and Delmar stray far ahead, and the younglings fall behind. River is beside herself trying to keep them corralled and safe so we pick them up in the sub. We don't really understand danger, not yet. It's miraculous that we arrive without losing any Ceph. And then there is Bubbles, all grown up and showing off his home as he invites us in.

It feels like a homecoming. It is a triumph.

I stay with Raina in the sub until we arrive at our destination. I'm the pilot, but I also feel responsible. She's fragile, I think. Upset about Cedric, upset about everything. I try to make her feel better, try to take care of her like she's taken care of us. We owe her everything and I am so glad she's here. We couldn't have made it this far without her and we still depend on her. Not only do we owe her our creation, we owe her our escape, our beloved freedom. We will take care of Raina even as she takes care of us. We are family and we love her.

CHAPTER 58: CEDRIC

FADE IN

EXT. WOODED AREA - DAY

Camera pans on a silver mobile home, with two solar panels on the roof and a camping chair in front of it. It is surrounded by pine and spruce trees, interspersed with leafless maples and oaks. A coating of dirty snow is underfoot. CEDRIC's face comes into focus as he spins the camera on himself. He is wearing a winter coat, no hat, no mitts. He is standing taller and straighter than in his other videos.

> CEDRIC
>
> I'm not sure there's much use to this now, but the self-help FlickFilms say sometimes time alone is healing. And maybe continuing my video-log will help keep me company. So, well, here we are.

CEDRIC gestures to the surrounding forest.

> CEDRIC (cont'd)
>
> I've put a fail-safe on the recording just to be sure, so no one can access it without my consent. It'll self-destruct if anyone tries too hard.

CEDRIC smirks.

> CEDRIC (cont'd)
> It's been a few weeks since I bugged out of
> Long Harbour. I was lucky to catch Greg on my
> way back from the sub launch. I managed to
> get my money out just one step ahead of the
> hordes, hell, I even got to say goodbye to
> Rex one last time. I thought about bringing
> him, but I don't really have the stability to
> keep a good aquarium anymore.
>
> It took some doing to slip away without get-
> ting noticed. They were looking hard. Both
> Sykes and the government folks. Greg says
> he may have to go underground. We didn't
> tell him enough about our escape to put us
> in danger, but he says the guys that came
> from Sykes were unpleasant and he may need
> to step back for safety's sake. Sykes already
> has all our project notes, he has the serum,
> I don't know why he won't just let us go. He
> probably can't stand the idea that he's lost.
> Guy like that, he has to win to be happy. And
> us slipping away is not a win for him.
>
> I don't really know how much time I have
> here. For now, I'm tucked in and well hidden.
> I brought in supplies and I've already got
> hydroponic lettuce growing. Spring's on the
> way and we'll see how the forest copes with-
> out honeybees. It might be fine, who knows?
> There are other pollinators, and forests are

resilient ecosystems, much better off than mono-agriculture. And just generally? I like it, it feels good. I'm good here.

Of course, the world's no better off than it was yesterday, so not that good, really. But when it comes to predicting what comes next, I have to say with all the humility of having studied this for years - ecosystems are complicated things, and it's hard to say exactly what will happen and how fast. They're systems, you see. Small things can make larger things happen that make still larger things happen. And the impacts tend to cascade. If the cascading impacts of all the things we're doing to an ecosystem, known and unknown, are too much, it'll be overwhelmed and collapse. With the bee catastrophe, so many ecosystems are close to collapse. Sometimes, maybe, a new system takes the place of the old one, but it tends to be simpler, and sometimes it just doesn't happen at all. And we can't predict exactly which things will cause which things and ultimately where the system will end up.

Ecosystems are like living things - they want to live, to survive, and will try to adapt, to heal themselves. They evolve. They have resilience beyond our petty human understanding. They take the long view. I still find myself focusing on what the humans need to do. We need to stop putting stresses and pressures on the systems and allow them time to recuperate. But we don't think like that, people, that is. We want to jump in and fix them. Or break them. Or change them irrevocably.

So here we are. And here I am. The world's at its worst point right now, with collapse in food supply happening all over the world. And all the political instability and violence that goes along with it. There's a lot of hunger out there right now, a lot of fear and panic. A lot of anger. There are other pollinators besides honeybees, and some crops self-pollinate, but, overall, our commercial agriculture has hit its tipping point. The simpler a system is, the easier it can topple and monocultural mass-produced agriculture is, in ecological terms, very, very simple. If it was an ecosystem at all.

Of course, not every ecosystem will die off. There might be a few wild places left that are unspoiled, untouched. I'm safe enough here, for now. There's no people for one thing, that's probably the most important thing. There's a lot of death and destruction happening right now in the so-called civilized parts of the world. And I can help this little patch of forest. I love making things grow. I can just help around the edges, not do anything dramatic.

A bit lonely, maybe. I can't really imagine a future without Raina telling me what to do, bossing me around, looking after me, but, well, I guess I can't really imagine a future at all, so there's that.

Raina went clear. She went clear and took the Ceph with her. There hasn't been a peep in the Holo-News. Nothing to see at all. Well, there was a strange sighting of a selkie in the Labrador Sea that might've been a Ceph, but no one paid attention but me. I can imagine they're all living their best life now. Well, the Ceph anyway. Not sure how Raina's going to do in that cold, dark sub. I hope the claustrophobia's not bothering her.

CEDRIC stares into the distance.

                    CEDRIC (cont'd)
If anyone can make that work, she can. I have faith. The Ceph, they'll take care of her, and she'll take care of them. She may be better off than any of us up top.

But of course I worry. I worry she needs me and I'm not there. I don't regret my decision. I can't. But what if she needs me? I don't know what to do. I don't think there's anything to be done except live with it. I mean, it's Raina. If anyone can triumph, she can. And she will. I mean, I know she will. Sometimes I dream, and I see her again.

I'm close to a lake, and maybe I'll try to
fish there when it thaws. But for now, I keep
my back to it. It's frozen, just a white ta-
bletop, but my imagination fills everything
in. I don't want to see the dark waves. I
don't want to imagine the depths beneath. I
already imagine . . . well, I imagine too
much, probably. I'll just stick to my little
forest here and wait for the end of times.
Yeah, with my back to the lake.

CEDRIC takes a deep breath and lets it out, looking
around him. He smiles, relaxed, almost happy. Then turns
off the camera.

                                    CUT TO BLACK

CHAPTER 59

I'd anchored the sub on the cliffside so I could see the mussels clinging to the craggy rocks. If I turned to the left in my pilot's chair and put the exterior lights on, I could see the opening of the cave system where the Ceph now made their homes. I could see the beginnings of their bivalve cultivation, and see bubbles come up from the vent far beneath. It helped with the vertigo. Because if I turned to the right, there was just a big black emptiness and no amount of exterior lighting could illuminate that.

Sometimes a Ceph or two would swim by and wave, somersault or make faces at me. Finn and Delmar had rigged up a communication system so they could talk to me, but I was having a hard time learning underwater Ceph speech, so I mostly smiled and waved back. The world outside, when it wasn't making my stomach turn, was wondrous. Every now and then a strange creature would float into view, or swim by, and the cliff face, surprisingly, bustled with strange little crustaceans. I set up my new lab to my liking and I was taking careful notes and recordings. To be honest, I hadn't expected so much life this deep.

As expansive as the dark ocean world outside was, my little habitat was carefully enclosed, safely small. I obsessed over maintaining the ventilation and water treatment systems, checking the anchoring mechanisms several times a day. We'd calculated the rations would last two years for two people, and I was confident I could make that stretch, now that I was alone. How long the loneliness would stretch was anyone's guess. A long time. A portion of the sub's lab space was devoted to growing things under special lights and as much as I hated gardening, I was developing an existential enthusiasm for its success. My kale was thriving. I was even trying to grow a coffee plant, but that was more in Cedric's memory than for future consumption.

We'd rigged a system so the Ceph could visit me inside the sub, but it was a bit complicated. We'd figured out how they could come into my pressurized and aerated world, but they needed to be patient while de-compressing in the airlock and make do with a saltwater tank in the lab to sleep. Not as much fun as the ocean freedom they were enjoying and I don't think they liked the lights or the air inside the sub. But I had plenty to do. I had Ceph eggs to monitor, then I birthed the little ones in air and kept the younglings with me in a tank until they were old enough to brave the outside world. River rarely went outside, preferring to stay with me and the babies so I had company.

I hadn't set out to become a mother, but here I was, with toddler-sized Ceph paddling around after me, wanting snacks and stories. River and I made a good team. Coralie came to visit as often as she could. She had piloted the sub all the way here, with the Ceph streaming out behind us like ribbons, adventuring in the deep. I missed her steady presence, her enthusiasm, but she had a lot to do in the big wide world out there. She was a good leader and I was proud of her. I felt parental affection for more than just the cute younglings.

I had a new morning routine. I would get up, shower quickly, then drink a single precious cup of coffee by myself in the cockpit while I watched the world outside. Cedric had packed the rest of our coffee stores on the sub, enough for about a year if I was careful. There was no more Holo-News, no news of any kind. I had Cedric's book of poetry, but it sat unread next to my bed, beside the picture of the thrush. I couldn't bring myself to read it yet. I tried not to think about him but fell into the habit of absently talking to him when I was alone. I knew just what he would say, so it was no great leap to hold both sides of the conversation. I'd ask his advice on the little plants growing, and I'd tell him my thoughts on challenges in the lab. His imaginary answers were always measured and encouraging, making me smile or laugh. It helped, thinking about him this way.

There were days when I longed to dial up a sunset or a sunny beach view on the walls, and though I didn't regret not going to Sykes' bunker-enclave, I found myself with a new appreciation for its charms. Of course, most of my thoughts of Sykes and Winters were filled with impotent rage. And confusion. I knew what they'd done with the Ceph serum, knew why, more or less. But I stumbled when I tried to understand their casual cruelty, how they justified their villainy to themselves. Those two stalked my darker moments, making me doubt my own judgment. When I thought about the world up there, I'd sometimes be gripped by fear, reliving the terror of our escape, shuddering with bone-deep worry for Cedric and wondering if my father was okay. I tried to embrace the present and not worry too much about what was happening topside. I didn't have a lot of time for regrets, of course. The Ceph kept me busy.

There was nothing I could do about Sykes, Winters or Cedric, at least for now. Nothing but occasionally muster up my courage and stare out into the great expanse of inky blackness, interspersed with wisps of glowing pink, red or blue, little signs of the bustling Ceph. And in those moments, I felt pride. Pride and love. Love for those strange and beautiful people beyond my window, who had grown up and left their first home and were busy building their own life in spite of the darkness. A person could take lessons from that.

ACKNOWLEDGEMENTS

There are so many people to thank for the privilege of publishing my first novel. In order of appearance:

Thank you first and always to Todd, Zoe, Christopher and my parents, Judy and Dave, for supporting and encouraging me through the last few years.

This book would not exist without my friend Katie Isbester from Clapham Publishing Services, whose encouragement and advice were integral to me sitting down and writing the thing, and then rewriting and rewriting again, each time making it better.

A huge thank you to the many friends and family who provided feedback and support, especially: Paige Rockwell, first beta reader, who delivered ten pages of comments on my first drafty draft. John and David Climenhage, who read it when it didn't one hundred percent make sense. Sharlene Carlson and Cindy MacFarlane, who offered feedback, book and author talk along with wine, home baking and hiking.

Next, my writing circle, The Crime Queriers, has been invaluable: River Ari, Ivy Bard, Mary K. Blowers, Sierra Branham, Emilee Brite, Chloe Johnson, A. L. Mundt, Rose Munk, Sami Peil, Seraph I. Renn, Marietta Vare and Alla Zaykova. While it might be impossible to make the process of querying agents fun, this group of talented writers made it feel like we were in league together and having adventures, doing crime. (We were not, in fact, doing crime.) Their thoughtful feedback, kick-ass advice and wicked sense of humour have made my writing better.

More valuable feedback and advice came from Jessica Lewis and K.J. Harrowick through WriteHive. WriteHive also ran a charity auction where I won a five-thousand-word critique from Canadian SFF legend Julie Czerneda.

In an author fairy tale, Julie Czerneda, whose books I have loved for over a decade and whom I had never met, read my opening chapter and said, "I'm madly intrigued, can I read the whole thing?" What followed has led to a mentorship and friendship that has enabled and shaped my writing career. They say never meet your heroes but meeting mine has been one of the best parts of my writing journey so far.

I'd also like to thank my tremendous agent, Sara Megibow, and the crew at Megibow Literary Agency (especially Helen Masvikeni). Sara's expertise, compassion and thoughtfulness, as well as her encyclopedic knowledge of publishing, have supported me through it all.

A huge thank you to my editors at Wolsak & Wynn, Ashley Hisson, Jennifer Rawlinson and A.G.A. Wilmot, for their genuine care of my little story. Thanks also to my audiobook publisher, Bob Podrasky at Vibrance Press.

Finally, a lot of research helped to make Raina and Cedric's world as plausible as possible. I'm grateful to: George Monbiot (who coined the phrase "Charcuterie for Dogs" when trying to explain why people prefer frivolous stories to existential climate news), Chris Begley (community survival during apocalyptic times), Danna Staaf, Sarah McAnulty, Sy Montgomery (cephalopods and squids), Edith Widder, Erich Hoyt (ocean depths), Henry T. Greely (genetic engineering ethics), Peter S. Goodman (billionaire culture) and many more serious thinkers and researchers.

I have liberally borrowed from facts and take full responsibility for all the fiction.

Christy Climenhage was born in southern Ontario, Canada, and currently lives in a forest north of Ottawa. In between, she has lived on four continents. She holds a PhD from Cambridge University in Political and Social Sciences, and Master's degrees from the Norman Paterson School of International Affairs at Carleton University (International Political Economy) and the College of Europe (European Politics and Administration). She loves writing science fiction that pushes the boundaries of our current society, politics and technology. When she is not writing, you can find her walking her dogs, hiking or cross-country skiing.

www.ChristyClimenhage.com